RELIABLE IN MANILA
An Asian Thriller

by
Valerie Goldsilk
& Julian Stagg

The Reliable Man Series

Reliable in Bangkok
Reliable in Jakarta
Reliable in Hong Kong
Reliable in Danang
Reliable in New York
Reliable in London
Reliable in Lapland (Short Story)

The Inspector Scrimple Series

Classified As Crime
Dragon Breath
Perfect Killer
Fatal Action
Random Outcome
Yellow Hammer

Other Books by Valerie Goldsilk

The Oldest Sins
Negative Buoyancy
Sins of Our Sisters
Sins of Our Elders
White Bishop

About the Authors

Valerie Goldsilk is English and lived in Hong Kong for over thirty years. She is now retired but used to run her own business, travelling frequently around Asia working with factories. Her better half is a former Hong Kong police inspector.

Julian Stagg is a British investment banker who, after a thirty-year career as an adviser, entrepreneur and investor, can still be found plying his trade in the City of London.

This book is a work of fiction and except in the case of historical fact, any resemblance to actual persons, living or dead, is purely coincidental.

First published by Thaumasios Publishing Ltd in 2020.

Copyright © Valerie Goldsilk & Julian Stagg 2020

Cover design: Mark Hevingham

Valerie Goldsilk and Julian Stagg have asserted their right under the Copyright, Design and Patents Act 1988 to be identified as the authors of this work.

This book is sold subject to the condition that it shall not, by way of trade or otherwise be lent, resold, hired out or otherwise circulated without the publisher's prior consent in any form of binding or cover other than that in which it is published and without a similar condition, including this condition, being imposed on the subsequent purchaser.

Authors' Note

The events of this novel take place in 2007 and describe a fictional coup loosely based on actual events in the Philippines in 2003 and 2007. Inserting fictional characters into real historical settings is an established literary device. It is not the authors' intention to imply that any of the events related in this novel actually took place or that the public figures with whom their characters fleetingly interact are anything other than fictional simulacra of their real-life counterparts, for which the authors ask forgiveness.

"The only way to get rid of temptation is to yield to it... I can resist everything but temptation."

"When I was young I thought that money was the most important thing in life; now that I am old I know that it is."

"There are only two tragedies in life: one is not getting what one wants, and the other is getting it."

"The good ended happily, and the bad unhappily. That is what fiction means."

O.W.

To Rannie, who knows how much of this is true and which bits I made up.

To Trevor, my old company commander who showed much patience.

To Danny, for some technical input.

To Roscoe, in memory of fine days diving.

To Goran, for the Aquavit.

To William, Paul, Matthias and Tony - you know who you are.

To Dickie Goodyear, larger than life in real life.

To Roger, we never did go to that party.

To Babelyn, you win some and you lose some.

To Nadine, who dated the President's son.

To the two Michelles.

To all the Carlas.

To James Horsfield - RIP.

To Josef Wandeler - RIP.

To John Bennett – RIP in 2004.

To Tim, who really knows his weapons, in grateful thanks for good times at Bisley.

1

I was lying on a thin foam mattress in a room no more than three metres square. It stank of urine, male sweat and police stations. I knew those smells. I had been a police inspector in Hong Kong for eight years. Since then, I'd been avoiding jails.

Many people wanted to put me behind bars. I had been at the top of my game for nearly twenty years now. I was The Reliable Man and I killed for money. I had started life as an equal opportunity killer: men or women, providing the money – and I asked for a lot of money – was right. Now I was a bit more selective, and my rates were even higher. I had killed more people than there had been Spartans at the Hot Gates of Thermopylae.

I didn't deserve to be in this jail. A man was dead, but it was not my handiwork. I was just in the wrong place at an awkward time. I had been set up.

But as luck would have it I was in a country where connections mattered. I had a phone call to make in the morning that I was pretty certain would solve my problem. The man owed me a favour. Funnily enough, that story had begun in jail as well.

That had been about nine years earlier.

I had been drinking that time, otherwise they wouldn't have caught me. When I wasn't working, I moved around the Far East spending time in Hong Kong, Singapore, Thailand and the Philippines chasing pleasure. I took my recreation seriously, but sometimes trouble found me when I wasn't looking for it. Some people are just like that.

I'd been diving the wrecks in Subic Bay and spent the morning on the USS New York. The next day I was planning to move South so I was letting my hair down around the bars of Olongopo.

The girl was stunning and dancing by herself in Cheap Charlies and I was on my eighteenth San Miguel. If I had been sober, I might have realised that she belonged to the man who called the shots in that part of town.

It was a sultry night: she liked the look of me and I liked the look of her. Her minder should have simply moved in and warned me off. Then it might have ended differently. I had been diving Subic for years and I knew Veracruz was not to be trifled with. But the minder called his boss. The first I knew was when Veracruz's hand was on my shoulder and the girl sprang back in horror at the sight of her lover. Which was a problem as I had one of my hands inside her blouse. A button pinged from it as she wrenched herself free.

Veracruz was a stout man with a short Filipino fuse. He was heavy, but muscular, with curly dark hair and a pencil-thin moustache that made him look like one of the men who was running for President. There was blood on the cuff of his shirt from his previous meeting. His temper was up and I was next. I didn't have a choice, because drunk as I was, I knew that attack was my only option. This was his *barangay*, and here life was cheap even for a Westerner like me.

I drove my fingers into his throat and swept his legs from under him. Then as we tumbled to the floor I wrapped my arm around his neck and snapped it by tugging left and right.

There was a tiny revolver in a holster on his belt. I crouched behind his body and shot the minder in the fleshy part of his shoulder. He took off in a hurry.

When I'd calmed down and sobered up I realised that I'd over-reacted. A dead gangster could be embarrassing. The security guard from the ground floor arrived quickly with his shotgun and I put my hands up high in the air until the police arrived. They gave me strange stares but still took me back to the station and locked me up as much as I declared that it had been self-defence. What it had been would be decided by the Superintendent of Police.

"I should thank you, not keep you in jail," he said the next morning, when he had me marched into his office. It was a Sunday and he seemed happy that there was a reason to avoid church with the family.

"Was Veracruz starting to become difficult?" I asked.

"Yes, he was getting above his station. Senator Guzman was hoping something like this might happen."

"Who is Senator Guzman?" I said.

The Superintendent, a thin man wearing an Arsenal football shirt for some unaccountable reason, smiled. "He is running for President and wants the area cleaned up. He is a good man."

Being good and being honest were not entirely the same thing in my experience of Asian politicians. Only Lee Kuan Yew, the founding father of Singapore, had managed to pull that one off in my estimation.

"I would like you to come with me," the Superintendent said. "The Senator thinks you might be able to help him."

"I'm a helpful fellow," I said. "If he is serious about cleaning up the area, I'd like to meet him, even if I were given a choice."

The Superintendent drove. It was an American muscle car, a Chevy V8, and it powered along the bumpy road out of town, taking the potholes in its stride. I realised we must be getting near the Senator's ranch when the suspension stopped having to work so hard and we were on smooth hardtop.

I was ushered into a large airy room, decorated in the Spanish colonial style which the rich here still aspired to. The man who came forward to shake my hand was about ten years older than me, with piercing brown eyes and a firm grip. He smiled and let his charisma wash over me. He had a teenager with him. The child resembled his father but lacked his father's vital spark.

"I am Eduardo Guzman," the Senator said. "Welcome to my home. This is my son, Bonifacio. We call him Sonny." Sonny proffered me a limp palm. He was sallow and distracted. At the first sign of an opening he made his excuses and left, followed shortly afterwards by the Superintendent.

"Thank you for taking care of Veracruz. Charlie Santos told me about you and that you are very capable."

"It got a bit out of hand," I admitted. "I was just going to slap him around but he jumped me." I shrugged ruefully. "All the witnesses agreed that it was self-defence."

He regarded me with a patrician smile. The one reserved for your best gladiator or your fastest horse. "Yes, when the Superintendent mentioned your name to me last night I called around and made some enquiries. The Vice President spoke highly of you."

"That was very kind of him. He saved my life once."

"How much do you know about the history of my country?" Guzman asked, as we sat drinking whisky and soda on the veranda.

"Enough to suspect that you named your son Bonifacio after the leader of the *Katipunan*, the secret society formed to free your country from Spanish rule, and the godfather of the First Republic."

"So you know the story of my country's attempts to gain independence?" he asked, his eyes glowing with pleasure.

"I have been coming here for many years to dive, on and off," I said. "I know that you traded one imperial power, Spain, for another, the United States, and then exchanged colonialism for 'constitutional authoritarianism'."

Guzman looked unhappy and nodded.

"What do you think of our current President?" he asked.

"He has been capable," I said noncommittally.

"It is time for change," Guzman said. "Things have not improved since the deposition of President Marcos. He is just the last in a long line of people enriching themselves at our country's expense."

"I've never met him, and I have no interest in politics, so I can't comment on that," I said carefully.

"The problem with us Filipinos is that once we have power, we can't help ourselves. We must take advantage of it to barter influence for money."

"That is a common human trait," I said. "If a man has the opportunity to make himself and his family rich, it's hard to resist it."

"Politicians should not be corrupt," the senator said. "Politicians should use their power to improve the condition of the people."

I admired his alliteration. It must have come from a speech he had given many times.

"In my experience," I said, "democracy is a very poor form of government. It's highly inefficient and prone to manipulation. It barely works in Europe and that is only because the people are too stupid to realise that they are being manipulated by the press and the powerful."

There was a sharp intake of breath showing interest from the Senator. "What is the best form of political system, in your opinion? Communism?"

I shook my head. "Of course not. As a former policeman I respect order and authority. I've always been a great believer in the Platonic notion of the benevolent dictator. The philosopher king. The educated Emperor. Frederick the Great of Prussia is a fine example. But you are right, it always goes wrong the moment a mortal gets even a modicum of power. Most people can't help themselves but to fill their bank accounts with as much cash as possible." I gave a light laugh to show that I should not be taken too seriously. I was a gun for hire not a Reader in Politics at a grimy red-brick university.

Guzman nodded. "You are right. Man is weak. We give in too easily to temptation."

"I've always made it a rule to give in to any temptation that comes my way," I said. "But then I'm not a politician and have no ambition to ever be one."

He looked out over the well-manicured gardens in front of him, rich with hibiscus and jasmine bushes, to the fields and jungle beyond.

"I love my country, Bill," he said. "My family have farmed here for hundreds of years. I owe it to our people to run for President, but I fear for my life and those of my family. Will you help me? They tell me you are a security consultant, and a good one."

"Good," I said, pouring myself another swig of the Suntory whisky, "but not cheap. My rate is fifteen thousand US dollars a week."

"I will not insult you by negotiating," he said. "I have much money, but only one family. In this country everyone's loyalty can be bought. That is my problem. When it comes to my safety, I do not know who to trust."

"I have one golden rule," I said. "If my employer doesn't cheat me, I never change sides once I take one."

"You strike me as an honest man," he said, shaking my hand. "I would be delighted to have you by my side."

The next three months were a crash course introduction to the curious world of Philippine politics. The best way to understand the country was to think of it as the product of half a millennium of Spanish colonial influence, followed by a century of American ascendancy. That vibrant mixture affected their political structures and sentiments. Eduardo Guzman's family had ruled his part of the country for eight generations so he called the shots. When he said jump, everyone jumped. When he said kneel, everyone kneeled.

We criss-crossed the country with the Senator. There were ten other candidates including my old acquaintance Charlie Santos. There were 33 million registered voters. Twice someone came after Guzman and twice they failed. They weren't particularly skilled assassins, but I earned my keep. The second man put up a fight and I had to break his arm. The first man took one look at me and ran for the hills.

In the end, Guzman's presidential bid ended in failure. But it had been fun and as some old soldier quipped, a close run thing. Eventually my contract was up and I said good-bye to Senator Guzman and his family retainers. A private Gulfstream would take me from Clark Airbase back home to Singapore.

"Thank you, Bill," he said. "I have made the last payment to your bank account in Liechtenstein. I have added a little extra."

"You didn't have to," I replied. "A deal is a deal. And you didn't win the big prize."

"Would you have come to work for me in Malacanang Palace if I had won?"

I shrugged. He understood that like the best birds of prey I was not comfortable in captivity.

"We shall remain friends. You will always have a marker with me, should you ever need help in my country."

Since then our paths had not crossed. Two Presidents had come and gone. Not much had changed in the country. The weather was either inclement or delightful. The economy stumbled along supported by remittances from the army of overseas workers. I spent much time on the beaches diving, drinking and dancing with the prettiest girls known to man. Sometimes I did a bit of work.

So this time around, when I found myself once again in prison, framed for murder and the murder weapon had my fingerprints on it, I wasn't too worried. I had a phone call that I could make.

2

There was a typhoon closing in on Manila and the ride had been bumpy coming in from Hong Kong.

The Philippines. A large country of small islands, over 7,500 of them. I was going to my holiday house in Puerto Galera on Mindoro, but first I planned on spending several days in Angeles City, north of Manila on Luzon. It had been a year since my last visit and I'd heard there were some interesting new venues on Field's Avenue.

I was coming to the Philippines for a few weeks to cure my soul through my senses. I had in mind some scuba diving and the consumption of beer and bar-girls in industrial quantities. I'd worked three jobs back-to-back and it was time to take a few weeks off. I'd finished a job in Surabaya a few days earlier - a factory owner's wife had wanted a quickie divorce and was willing to pay for it. I'd arranged for her husband to commit suicide at his mistress's home and collected my usual fee.

Rannie, my regular driver, was waiting for me on the other side of immigration with a grin and a cold can of Coke.

"Boss, how are you?" he said.

"All good. How's your family?"

His sisters and their absent husbands, his father's gout and his mother's glaucoma filled in the time while he pushed my trolley, loaded with two dive bags full of gear and clothes, to the car. He stashed it all in the boot of his Toyota and we set off to fight our way through the Manila traffic and get on to the E1 which would take us to Pampanga province and Angeles City. It could take anywhere between two and four hours.

Strictly speaking we were heading for Balibago, the nightlife district outside what had once been the front gates of Clark Airbase, a vast complex housing 15,000 American service men in its pomp. They'd required a lot of entertaining when they weren't polishing their bombs or fixing planes. In 1991 the Americans lowered their flag and handed the place back to the Philippine government. It had slowly reinvented itself as a free port and manufacturing location. The nightclubs had somehow survived on retired servicemen and tourists who descended on its fleshpots in search of a good time.

Rannie was a fine bloke and he drove safely so I nodded off and eventually he pulled up outside the Pacific Breeze Hotel. It was brand spanking new and highly recommended by my friends from Manila, the Galbor Brothers.

"Welcome, sir, welcome, sir," the three tiny Filipinas behind the reception counter greeted me. They were uniformly pretty, had raven-black hair down to their shoulders, red-hot luscious lips and warm, inviting almond eyes.

I handed Rannie three thousand pesos and told him I'd be in touch in two or three days. Then I completed the registration formalities, asked the ladies to have my bags sent upstairs to my room and headed in the direction of the pool where I'd spotted some familiar figures.

The pool was a decent size but not deep - in case some of the guests could not swim - and was set in a generously proportioned garden with an abundance of tables, chairs and recliners. The entire area was surrounded by a wall that gave it a feeling of being a secure compound. A special kind of Disneyland for middle-aged Western men. Wherever I looked they were frolicking with tight-bodied Filipinas. I figured some of the girls were in their twenties and early thirties, but most looked in their teens.

The three men I had spotted were sitting beside the azure water grinning at me in recognition.

"What brings you here?" James asked. He was an Australian in his sixties with a wispy moustache, a ready smile and a generous stomach. "We haven't seen you in Puerto Galera for a long time." The three of them owned shares in a house on a mountain that looked down onto the dive resort where I was heading later in the week. I owned the house next to them.

"This place must be a bit crap if they let blokes like Jedburgh stay here," Paul said with a smirk. He was a retired British merchandising director. When he wasn't kickboxing in the gym, he spent his time following rugby union around the globe. Competitive sport was Britain's contribution to the world. Only occasionally could we beat the world at it. In 2003 we'd all stayed at James' place in Sydney while the Rugby World Cup was on. My old history teacher, a bloke called Brian, was working with the England team and there were three lads from my old school in the squad. They were all twenty years younger than me, so I didn't know them, but I felt a sense of pride when Jonny kicked that drop goal over the bar that sealed Australia's fate in the Final.

I put my hand on Paul's shoulder. "Yes, and fuck you too, mate." I pulled over a chair from the next table. They all had squat bottles of San Miguel in front of them. I waved at the waitress to bring more.

"Stupid question, James," Paul said. "He's here for the same reason we are here."

"And what brings you sorry lot here?" I asked, wiping the rim of my San Miguel bottle with one of the tiny tissues provided.

"One of my bands is playing at 'Phillies' later," William said. He was Swiss and managed several rock bands in Manila. "It's their farewell tour. The lead singer has been signed by Journey. He's leaving for San Francisco next week and they're disbanding."

I raised my eyebrows in respect. "Journey as in the American arena rock stars?"

"*Don't stop believing...*," Paul started singing in a falsetto voice.

"What will the rest of the band do?" I asked William.

"I'm going to get them a gig in Hong Kong at a new place called 'Amazonia'," Paul said. "I know the owner. What they need are three really sexy female lead singers. We're starting the interview process now, here in Angeles, tonight." He smiled lasciviously.

I enjoyed the ice-cold sugary taste of the Philippine's second most important export product as it chilled the inside of my throat. "Can I be on the interview panel?"

Paul gave me a stern frown. "Not sure your standards are high enough. There is a rumour that you have been seen running around town with the occasional dog."

"That's the problem with you," I said. "For you, everything is on the surface. You never delve into the deeper more meaningful aspect of a woman's personality. You just judge a woman on the basis of her physical appearance."

"I always suspected that you were one of these men who actually talked to women," Paul accused me.

I shrugged. "Guilty, but only on occasion, of that charge."

"This is my suggestion," said William, "if Jedburgh promises to buy all the drinks for the first two hours, we shall let him join our panel of interviewers." He looked at the other two men.

"Mate, that's a fair deal," said James. He winked at me. "You'd be a fool not to take it. You wouldn't want to go around the bars by yourself. You might get raped or drugged or have your wallet stolen."

Slowly I nodded in agreement. "Yes, I was really worried about being lonely tonight in a place full of willing available women. It's sad travelling around the country on your own without folk like you three to guide me."

"Less of the sarcasm, Paul said, "or we'll make you pay for the first four hours."

Five hours into our evening, somewhere between 'Brown Sugar' and 'Lancelot', I lost Paul and James. We'd lost William much earlier as he'd stayed on to drink with his band. 'Phillies', an open-air sports bar, had been packed wall to wall and up to the rafters. The band had run through all the great rock staples and played them pitch perfect. The country had some amazing bands and that evening one of them had been playing. The entire nation seemed to be singing along, wishing the young man well in his exciting new adventure.

It was like a fairy tale. Arnel, the lead singer, had put a few songs up on YouTube and one day he'd received a phone call from someone who said he was Neil Schon, Journey's guitarist, asking him to come for an audition. At first he thought it was a hoax but it turned out to be the real deal.

I was introduced to him during one of their breaks. "You used to play in 'Grammy's' in Hart Avenue, didn't you?" I said.

He nodded.

"I used to go there after they'd thrown us out of 'Rick's Café'."

He laughed. Those would have been tough times for him, probably playing six nights a week, six sets a night, until six in the morning.

"You deserve it. Don't take Americans too seriously. They are mostly full of shit."

Balibago was a strange entertainment quarter. Along Field's Avenue, and the shorter roads that ran parallel and at right angles to it, there must have been a hundred bars, restaurants and nightclubs. It was raucous and dusty. The acrid smell of passenger trikes burning low quality gasoline got into your nose and from every open door, loud music pumped into the night. There was no beach near here. This was no seaside resort, no tourists came here except men who wanted to party. It was like Tijuana but without the Mexican food. It was like Soho but all the girls were younger and prettier, and fewer of the men were gay.

In every venue there were four or five girls to every man. They had come from the poor villages around the province, and farther afield, to earn money by dancing, chatting or serving food and drink. Occasionally other pleasures were on offer, but for that a man had to buy the girl out of the bar, compensate them for the time she would be missing. It was called 'BF-ing' a girl, paying her bar fine.

If you were so inclined, you could work your way from one bar to the next all night. A drink in this place, one or two drinks for the girls who came over like butterflies to flutter around you, then on to the next place. You might linger slightly longer, if the music was good or if a pretty girl caught your eye and moved particularly well up on stage.

I got hung up in a club called 'Dollhouse' for a while because there were just so many butterflies that caught my eye. These were not hard-nosed hookers. They were country girls raised on American television shows and a dream that perhaps marrying a foreigner would be the most wonderful thing that could happen to them in the world. And many of their sisters did marry foreigners and left their country to live in small towns in exotic states called Minnesota and Missouri or counties like Lincolnshire and Leicestershire.

It must have been around 2 a.m. when I staggered into the 'Voodoo Bar'. I was on my way home. Just around the corner, not many careful steps away, was my room with the comfortable bed and a bathroom that contained a jacuzzi.

I ordered a San Miguel. Rihanna was warbling on about her umbrella and three pretty ladies in pink bikinis were doing their best to dance like the dusky Barbadian singer. I smiled crookedly at the one in the middle whose breasts were perkier than those of her two colleagues.

There were two empty bar stools between me and an obese white man in a funky striped shirt. It was the size of a tent.

"How ya doing?" the large man said.

"Yeah," I replied because it was too much effort to come up with anything more complex. An opinion at this time of the night was hard to formulate.

He reached across the bar stools and held out a big hand, "Fred Sonnenstein, where you from?"

If I just had a dollar for every time the question had been asked already that evening. But it was a fair question. This was a multinational town.

"British, but I've been in Asia for over twenty years. You?"

"Toronto, working on setting up a factory over here in Clark Airbase."

"How's that going?" I asked.

He shook his head with an air of frustration. "About as fast as a tortoise with a broken leg."

"You have to pay the right people to get stuff done here," I said, speaking from experience. "Do you have a local Filipino partner who has the contacts?"

The Canadian frowned. "He says he knows all the big shots."

"When you are paying the right person the right amount of money in this country," I said, "everything moves really fast. If you are not talking with the right person then it's like running through three feet of water. What's your factory going to make once you get it up and running?"

"We're going to make something called a smart phone. Have you ever seen a Palm Pilot?"

I nodded.

"It's the same concept. You'll have a big screen and be able to access the internet and your emails. It's going to be the next big thing."

I thought about that for a moment. "Don't think that will ever take off," was my comment. "Why would you want a big phone when you can have a little itty bitty one." I pulled out my Nokia from my jeans pocket and placed it on the bar next to my beer.

"What about you? You here on business?" he asked and leant forward to tell the barman to get us two more beers.

I shook my head. "Nah, just here to party. I'm on my way to a place called Puerto Galera to do some scuba diving."

"Are you married?" Sonnenstein asked.

"Hard to get married in Asia with all this temptation around you." I pointed at the next set of girls that had gone up on stage and the twenty others lounging about the dark bar.

A figure in a Hawaiian shirt appeared between me and the Canadian, sliding onto one of the empty bar stools. "Bill Jedburgh, drunk as a fucking skunk if I'm not mistaken."

"Dickie Goodyear," I said and gave the man a punch on the arm. "I thought you might pop up somewhere if I stayed out late enough."

Dickie was medium height with closely cropped hair and the lean face of man who took fitness seriously. We'd served together in SDU, the specialist anti-terrorist unit of the Hong Kong Police. Then he'd been thrown out of the Force for running up gambling debts and getting too friendly with some local Triad money lenders. He'd moved to the Philippines and set himself up in business. When we bumped into each other and shared a few drinks, he was rarely specific about what type of products he imported and exported. With former coppers, if a man didn't volunteer details it was rude to ask too many questions.

"What are you up to?" I asked and introduced him to my new Canadian friend.

"This and that. Ducking and diving. I've got a share in this bar. Just a little one, so I keep an eye on things when I have time."

"Time with women, if I know you," I said. "How many have you got on the go at the moment?" A look of concern passed across his face.

"A couple, here and there," he said. "They're getting more expensive, so I'm working hard on the day job."

"Dickie here," I said, leaning across Goodyear and addressing Sonnenstein, "is a good man to know. He might be able to check if you are talking to the right people about your smart phone factory."

"Is that so?" he replied and appeared pleased.

"We used to work together. When we were young and innocent. In the Hong Kong Police."

"The Royal Hong Kong Police," Goodyear corrected me.

"Dickie's's right, we both left before the Queen gave up on the Force and our little colony," I said, noting a tiny twinge of melancholia rearing its head somewhere. That was ten years ago now. I pulled myself up sharply. When a man became maudlin, I told myself, it was time to get to bed and sleep until noon.

"We must catch up for a chat. Lunch or dinner tomorrow?" I said to Goodyear. "Where do I find you?"

He handed me a white card with his name and mobile phone number printed on it.

"Where are you staying?" he asked me.

"The new place around the corner. Pacific Breeze."

"Tell the manager you know me and he'll give you a bigger discount."

"I'll give you a call," I said and stood up, placing a five hundred peso note next to my beer bottle. "It's been nice talking to you, Sonnenstein. Good luck with your smart phone idea. It will never take off. Small is beautiful. Might see you around tomorrow."

3

A furious banging on my bedroom door and a man's voice shouting my name dragged me back to consciousness from the depths of a drunken stupor. My Rolex told me I'd only been asleep for a few hours. I flicked on the main light and staggered over. I stopped long enough by a mirror to discover I had fallen asleep in my clothes. That happened sometimes when I'd been drinking.

The voice was still yelling and even in my post-alcoholic haze it sounded familiar. There was a peephole in the door and when I looked through it I recognised the Hawaiian shirt, so I unhooked the chain and turned the lock.

Dickie Goodyear fell through the doorway. I caught him as he slumped towards me and helped him over to the bed. There was blood all down his arm and now there was blood all over my sheets.

"They shot me, the bastards," he said. It started as a snarl but ended up as a cough.

I knew a lot about gun-shot wounds. When you spend a life around bullets it's important to know not just how to inflict them but more importantly how to fix them. I'd done all the training until it was instinctive. When you were as hung-over as I was, that was when you needed to let the training kick in.

The most important thing was to apply as much pressure to the wound and try to stop as much of the blood from leaving the body as possible. Goodyear was a big bloke, so he'd have started with most of the regulation twelve pints. If he lost more than two pints, he'd start looking a bit peaky. I began pulling the cases off the pillows on my bed so I could roll them up and turn them into makeshift field dressings.

"Where's the wound?" I asked

"Shoulder," Goodyear groaned. I ripped his shirt off and found a nasty mess of flesh where his left shoulder had once been. Somebody had shot him with a high calibre handgun. One of the big revolvers or semi-automatics that fired a .45 ACP round. That was good news, under the circumstances. The damage from a gunshot wound depended on the muzzle velocity and mass of the bullet. .45 ACP was much less damaging than 9 mm, which is why the US military switched away from it in the mid-80s. The muzzle velocity was a couple of hundred feet per second lower and it produced less cavitation injury as a result. In layman's terms, cavitation was the hole made by the bullet as it passed through the body. The higher the velocity, the more secondary damage was done around the primary hole.

The second piece of good news was that the round used hadn't been a hollow-point. I always used hollow-points because they expanded inside the body and caused more damage. This wound looked like it had been caused by a conventional round. The next thing to worry about was bone fragments. I prodded around inside trying to work out whether the bullet had gone through bone.

"Fuck me, Jedburgh," Goodyear yelled. "Do you have to do that?"

"Checking on the damage, you'll thank me later. Hold this," I said, putting his hand on the big pad of pillowcases that I'd laid across his wound, "and press down hard." I tugged my belt out of the loops on my jeans and wrapped it around his shoulder. He winced in pain and bit into his lip as I pulled the buckle as tight as I could and surveyed my handiwork.

"We need to get you to a hospital," I said. "You live here. Where's the nearest?"

"Get me to the Angeles University hospital. They're the best in town for gunshot wounds," he groaned. I was already changing my clothes, grabbing a new Polo shirt which wasn't stained with blood and didn't stink of booze and sweat.

"How far is it?" I said.

"Down McArthur Avenue. My car's downstairs. I can't drive." He dug in his trouser pocket with his right hand and pulled out a heavy bunch of keys. The pillowcases were starting to soak up more blood and were turning from white to a dirty brown. A familiar metallic smell penetrated deep into my nostrils.

"Press down harder on the wound," I urged him. I managed to get him up on his feet and we walked, like a pair of drunks who were running a three-legged race, to the lift. The night concierge and the front security guard were two young Filipino lads. They helped me get him into the passenger seat of his pickup truck. He swore a lot under his breath and his face was getting paler, but I thought we were probably in decent shape if he could stay awake to give me directions to the hospital.

It was around 4 a.m., according to the dashboard clock. The streets were still busy for this time of the night. Not busy enough to hold me up as I gunned the Isuzu D-Max down the main road at a speed that was neither safe nor legal. We got to the hospital ten minutes later and I dragged Goodyear out and staggered with him into the emergency entrance.

The Emergency Room was shabby but clean. About thirty people were sitting about on wooden benches. They were the usual late-night mix of the sick and their families, mixed with the flotsam and jetsam of alcohol-induced car crashes and bar fights. I ran in shouting in Tagalog, just in case the staff were on their coffee break, that my friend had a gunshot wound which was still bleeding heavily. Three nurses and a doctor emerged and loaded him onto a gurney which they wheeled off into another room. I gave the triage nurse what information I had. I'd kept hold of Goodyear's wallet for safe-keeping and found his address on the driver's licence inside it. I also handed over one of his credit cards to make sure that there were no payment issues down the line. By the time I'd finished, the young doctor emerged - his name tag gave his name as Dr. Alfredo Lim - and asked me what had happened.

"I've no idea," I said, conscious that everybody probably said exactly that when they brought in someone who'd been shot. "He's an old friend and he came to my hotel room like that. How bad is it?"

"It could be worse," Dr. Lim said. "It's a mess but we've got him stabilised. You've had some First Aid Training?"

"Army and Police," I said.

He nodded. "Did you give him any kind of medication or drugs?"

"I didn't. I was drinking with him a few hours earlier, but he seemed relatively sober. I couldn't tell you whether he has any recreational drugs in his system, but he didn't seem high when he was in the bar."

"Good. We always have to be careful. He looks very fit. How old is he?"

"About my age, mid-forties. He was also in the police. In Hong Kong."

"Do you have any idea what kind of weapon he was shot with?" Dr. Lim asked, watching me carefully.

I shook my head. "Probably a surplus US Army or Air Force sidearm. One of the old .45 calibre Colts at a guess. There must be a lot of those floating around?"

He shrugged knowingly. "We get a lot of GSWs from those. Especially on Friday and Saturday nights when the men start drinking Red Horse beer and singing karaoke." He began to turn away, then said: "We must report this to the police of course."

"I expect so. I've left all the details with your front desk."

"We will continue to stabilise him then operate," Doctor Lim said, efficiently. "The bullet is still in there, but it seems to be in one piece. Maybe you want to go back to your hotel and get some sleep. There is nothing else you can do for him until we have finished."

I smiled. "That sounds like good advice. I'll be back in a few hours."

I took the truck back to the Pacific Breeze Hotel and parked it where it had been earlier.

"Do you know who shot Mr. Goodyear?" I asked the security guard when I reached the lobby. He was young, wearing a tight white shirt with a fake badge on his chest and a real revolver on his belt. It looked like a .38. Over 4,000 people died of gunshot wounds every year in the Philippines. It was common for security guards in places like this to be armed, occasionally with Armalites. Sometimes they even had the appropriate ammunition.

"No, sir. He just came around the corner, bleeding like that and asking for your room."

"Do you know him?"

"Oh, yes, sir. Everybody knows Mr. Goodyear in Balibago. He is friends with our owner and manager and everyone. He has been in Angeles for many years."

"What does he do for a living?" I asked

An uncomfortable expression slid across his face then vanished. "I don't know about his business, sir. Maybe a bar owner, or importing and exporting?"

"What would you export from Pampanga?"

"We have garment and electronics factories, sir. Especially now, Clark is becoming big for factories."

Something smelt a bit fishy, but I wasn't going to press him. He was terrified enough as it was. I told them they had done well and Mr. Goodyear was in safe hands now in the hospital.

"I need some new sheets and pillowcases. Can you get those from another room? And then don't let anyone disturb me until at least lunchtime."

4

It was nearly 1 p.m. by the time I had rolled out of bed and emerged from the shower into another warm and sultry afternoon. Paul, James and William were sitting at their usual table by the pool having brunch.

"Did you have a good one?" James asked. Paul was wearing a flowery shirt that was too bright for me in my current condition. William wore a black Polo shirt and the rings under his eyes were nearly as dark. He wasn't saying much, just staring at his coffee mug. The band's 'Last Waltz' had obviously continued to revolve for quite a while after we'd left him and moved on up the street.

I shrugged. "I guess we all had a wild night, one way or another."

A pretty little waitress called Maybelline bounced over and I ordered the greasy stuff that makes hangovers go away. "And make sure you bring filter coffee," I repeated, "none of that Swiss instant shit." She nodded and wrote it all down dutifully.

"Where did you guys end up?" I asked.

"We went to 'Blue Nile'," Paul said with a grin. "I BF'd a big black bird. Her Dad must have been the biggest, baddest, US Marine in the Navy. It was like wrestling with a super-sized Naomi Campbell."

James said, "No ladies for me. I'm saving myself for a honey in Manila when we get back there."

"A man of honour," I commented and he seemed pleased. He was in his early sixties but could still match us drink for drink. He owned a business in Australia that traded with China. Much of the time he spent in Asia was not strictly speaking required for his business, but he was the boss and he called the shots.

"Are you staying at your house in PG this time?" Paul asked. He had made a fortune in his previous job, taken early retirement at the age of 48 and divided his time between Hong Kong, the Philippines and visiting his kids in the UK.

"Yes," I said, "I'll be staying at the *Casa Azul*." That was the name of my holiday home because it had a dark blue roof and light blue walls.

A few years earlier I'd bought a plot of land from a lovely man called Josef and his Filipina wife after drinking in the Yacht Club. Together they'd acquired a mountain outside Puerto Galera town, received permission to parcel it up for development and I was one of the first people to buy. Sometime between the tenth or eleventh San Miguel I bought into the idea of owning land in the Philippines. It had cost me a million pesos, which at the time was about US$20,000. Two months later, Josef took me up the hill to show off the new access road he'd built - he was an engineer by profession - which was now the best road on the island. It had to be, because the mountain was steep. But once you got to the top, the views were glorious. He'd also flattened my plot of land so a house could be built on it, if I was so inclined.

Over a few beers in the Yacht Club I took a napkin and designed my house. It was very simple. It would have a three-metre-deep veranda that ran ten metres along the front of the house. The house itself would be ten metres by ten metres with two bedrooms and a generous airy *sala* living room and an open-plan kitchen at the back. Downstairs would be a garage and another guest room.

The next day Josef brought me the blueprints that he'd had a local architect rustle up. A few months and couple of hundred thousand pesos later I had accidentally built myself a house.

Josef's wife's sister took care of the house when I wasn't around. Her husband sprinkled the lawn at the back and planted flowers along the edges and made sure there was food and beer in the fridge when I advised Josef I was coming, which I did regularly to dive and enjoy the amazing view of ships crossing the channel to and from Batangas.

Shortly after my house had been completed, I'd introduced Paul to Josef. He and his mates bought the plot next door and built a huge swanky mansion which was great for pool parties. They shipped in guests and entertainers in industrial quantities from the resorts and bars on Sabang beach where the dive shops were located.

"We might be down there next week, the three of us," Paul said. "It's Rohan's 70th birthday so we thought we'd have a party down at the villa. We'll be bringing all the dancers from 'Squirt'."

Rohan was the club's owner. It was one of the best clubs on Makati's Burgos Street, famous for a troupe of perfectly choreographed professional dancers who filled the place wall to wall every night.

"Well in that case, I might have to force myself to come over, neighbour."

"Well in that case, we might need to put a few girls into your guest bedrooms," he said. "We've only got twelve rooms at the villa."

"Sure, send over the fat, ugly ones to stay with me," I said in a snarky tone. I knew where I stood in the pecking order.

"There are no fat ugly ones, as you are very well aware," he said mischievously, "but I think two of the dancers are billy-boys and I've heard you're a bit of a pervert…" He gave me a wink.

I laughed. "There's nothing wrong with men who think they are actually women born in the wrong body. Everybody should have a choice to determine their own gender."

"You are the very model of a fucking enlightened *Guardian* reader, aren't you?" Paul said lightly.

"Tolerance has always been my middle-name," I said. "Just don't send me any ugly ones with deep voices and bristly beards."

My food and coffee arrived. I tested it and said to Maybelline: "This isn't filter coffee, this is the Nescafé."

A look of guilt took hold of her face. "I'm so sorry, sir. I'm sorry. I forgot." She rushed off with the offending mug.

"The scrambled eggs look perfect," I said. "Shame the Chef forgot the baked beans."

"It's the Philippines," James said with a gentle smile. "If you want antiseptic anal perfection, go back to Singapore."

"Point taken," I replied. He was right. It was the custom of the country. The contrast between the amiable chaos of the Philippines and the sterile efficiency of the Lion City was one of Asia's great mysteries.

An hour later, after a bit more banter and finally getting my order right - including fried bread as good as any from a transport cafe on the A1 - I went to pick up some stuff for Dickie Goodyear. I assumed he'd be in hospital for a few days so he might appreciate a change of clothing and some reading material.

His Isuzu pick-up truck was where I'd left it. I'd copied down his address from his driving licence and had a map, with directions from the concierge, to find the house. It was about half an hour outside town in a modern, gated development.

The two security guards waved through Dickie's truck when they saw a white face driving it. They didn't even bother asking me if I was a friend of his.

I parked the truck outside Dickie's bungalow beside a big, heavy, Honda motorbike. All the houses in the development were in a similar style. There was a small garden in front and parking for three cars in a covered garage area. I guessed there would be swimming pools in the back gardens. It didn't look cheap, but it wasn't particularly flash either. Perfect for a decent quality of life if you were a retired serviceman living on a reasonable pension or an upwardly mobile Filipino family of accountants.

As was common in the Philippines, all the windows were covered in heavy ornate steel bars to deter burglars so I assumed there wouldn't be an alarm. Two of the Yale keys on the bunch he'd given me worked the locks on the front door. Inside, there was a short hallway which was empty except for a wooden table and a long mirror. The hallway led into a generous living room, much larger than the *sala* in my place in Puerto Galera.

There were three big sofas arranged around a large flat screen television. The room felt as if it belonged to a bachelor who didn't spend much time on home decoration. The only picture on the wall was of a buffalo in a rice field.

The buffalo looked out placidly over a room that had been completely trashed. Cushions had been sliced open, the drawers of a chest in the corner had been pulled out and tipped upside down. They were lying on top of each other like the dead in a Western saloon after a shoot-out.

5

Slowly and silently I walked through every room of the bungalow and checked that nobody else was in the house. I began to wish I had brought a gun, but I pulled a sharp knife from a block in the kitchen as the next best thing. The bedrooms had been trashed just as comprehensively as the living area. Someone had been looking for something and they were not reticent about how they went about it.

Sliding doors led out to the patio. The pool was wide enough for two people to swim alongside each other and about 15 metres in length. I walked around the garden briefly but saw nothing unusual. There were no big footprints amongst the flower beds, because there wasn't a flower bed. Goodyear didn't seem the type who would spend his afternoons weeding and watering plants. Grass cutting was probably included in his management contract.

There was a padlocked shed at the back of the plot full of gardening tools but when I checked Dickie's key ring I couldn't find anything that would open it. What I did find was a wide, heavy key which looked like the one I had for a floor safe in my condominium in Singapore. I went back inside, locked the patio doors and searched specifically for any hiding place that might conceal one.

It took fifteen minutes. The safe was built into the concrete floor under the bed.

You had to move the king-size bed first, then the fake oriental carpet on which the bed rested and then remove two large floor tiles, which I did using the knife that I'd taken from the kitchen. Beneath was the steel door to the safe. I slotted the key into the lock. It fitted perfectly but it didn't turn. There was a numeric keypad next to it. I guessed it wouldn't turn unless I tapped in the right code. Even if the men who had searched the house had found the safe they wouldn't have got much further than me unless they had the code and a copy of the key.

I replaced everything the way I'd found it and went back to what I'd originally come to the house to do. There was a sports bag in the cupboard and I stuffed in some underwear and T-shirts, then went to the bathroom and filled Goodyear's wash bag with his toiletries. I locked up but left the mess as I'd found it. Helping out a mate was one thing, post-search maid service required a different sort of professional.

When I arrived at the hospital a fresh group of people were sitting in the ER. There seemed to be less blood and broken heads at this time of the day and it had more the look of a family outing. The room was filled with limping kids and bilious grandparents.

"I'm sorry, sir. But Mr. Goodyear already checked himself out," the nurse told me at reception.

"What do you mean checked out?" I asked, puzzled. "Half his shoulder was missing when I brought him in last night."

She gave me a blank smile and repeated her answer.

"Is Dr. Lim working at the moment? He was the doctor last night. Can I speak with him?"

The reception regretted that Dr. Lim was long off duty and it was not possible to speak with any other doctor. Mr. Goodyear had paid his bill and left the building about an hour earlier.

"OK," I said and turned around to go back to the pickup truck. Maybe we'd passed each other on the road and he was already back home wondering how to get hold of me. I wasn't sure if I'd given him my phone number when we met in 'Voodoo'. That part of the evening was an indistinct blur.

I drove back to Goodyear's house. The security guards were getting used to me by now and waved me through without even slowing me down. I parked the Isuzu back in the same spot next to the big motorbike. This time there was a Yamaha Mio scooter standing behind it.

The front door was unlocked so I pushed it open and walked into the house calling out Goodyear's name. There was a girl kneeling in the middle of the living room looking under the sofa. She glanced up at me. A guilty expression slid from her face and was replaced with a crooked smile.

"Is Dickie back home?" I asked.

The girl was in her late twenties. She had blonde highlights in her long black hair, wore a tight pair of jeans, dangly earrings and a heavy gold chain around her pretty neck.

"Who are you?" she asked, using the sofa to push herself up.

"I'm a friend of Dickie's. And you are?"

"I'm Lillibet, his girlfriend," she said. "How you know Dickie?"

"From Hong Kong. We worked together for a while."

"Oh," she said, "in the police?"

"That's right. Did you know he got shot last night? I took some stuff to the hospital but he'd checked himself out." I held up the hold-all full of his things to demonstrate I was telling the truth.

"I got a text this morning. I came over, but he's not here," she said and shrugged.

"Where is he then?"

"I don't know."

"Do you know who shot him?"

She frowned and then said, "Maybe one of the Lapida Brothers?"

I took a few steps down the corridor that led to the bedrooms and glanced quickly into the rooms. The master bedroom door was open but everything appeared to be as I'd left it earlier.

"Who are the Lapida Brothers?" I asked. The girl had replaced the cushions on all the sofas by now. She sat down and lit herself a Marlboro Light. Her jeans, I noticed, were tightly wrapped around legs that were unusually long for a Filipina.

"They are gangsters. They sell drugs," she said. "They own some nightclubs and restaurants around town."

"Dickie involved with them?" I asked.

She shrugged.

"How does Dickie make his money?" I said.

"This and that," she said and took another puff on her cigarette then blew the smoke up at the ceiling the way she might have seen Lauren Bacall do it in an old movie.

"Was Dickie supplying these Lapida Brothers with something illegal?"

She shrugged her shoulders once more. "They've been arguing about business. I don't know what kind. I know he was angry last night. He texted me to say they could go screw themselves."

"Where were you last night then?"

"I was playing cards with some friends in Concepcion."

She was staring up at me as nonchalant as anything. I wasn't really buying her story, but I didn't want to come over all heavy. None of this was really my business.

"So you didn't go and see him in hospital?"

She shook her head. "I got the text from him this morning but I was still asleep. I tried to call him but he never answers unless he wants something." She crossed her legs and I got an idea of what Dickie generally wanted.

"Does he have any close friends?" I asked. "Close business associates?"

She shrugged. She did a lot of that.

"Mainly Mikey, I guess. I think they are doing some business together."

"Do you know his surname? Where does he hang out?"

"Mikey Tomkins. They drink a lot together. He owns a bar on Field's Avenue."

"That doesn't narrow it down much," I said, pressing her. "What's the bar called?"

"The Tighter Pussy." She gave a dry laugh and leered, watching for my reaction. I nodded, inscrutable. Nothing wrong with that. I'd once been in a bar called 'The Laughing Labia'.

"Try calling Dickie again," I said and watched as she did so. After a while she shook her head.

"Just voice mail," she said, her hand over the speaker, then she spoke into the phone: "Hello, baby, this is me. I'm so worried. Will you call me? I'm at the house."

I wasn't going to get any more out of her. Despite her obvious charms, I didn't take to Lillibet and it was time to move on. We exchanged phone numbers and I told her to keep me posted in case he turned up. I would be in town for another day or two.

"You might want to clean this place up and keep the door locked in case the Lapida Brothers turn up again," I suggested. Then I walked down the road to the security gate. The guards gave me the phone number of the local taxi company and five minutes later a battered Toyota turned up and took me back to the Pacific Breeze Hotel.

My hangover was gone and I needed alcohol, meat and the pleasure of my own company for a while. I was going to start off with a hearty meal at 'Piccolo Padre', my favourite Italian restaurant in town. A bottle of Barolo and Veal Saltimbocca would hit the spot, in preparation for another night on the town.

6

I caught up with Paul, James and William in the 'Champagne Bar' after I'd finished dinner. The lads were sitting on stools along the bar. Their heads were about knee height to the girls dancing in their bikinis on the stage behind the bar staff. Every four songs a new shift of girls came up on stage and the ten or so girls who'd been dancing came down to hustle drinks or sit in the far corner, if they were the shy sort.

James had two girls - not the shy sort - straddling each of his legs and they were feeding him lemons and tequila like half-clad wet nurses.

"Where have you been?" Paul said as I squeezed onto the vacant stool next to him. The music was upbeat rock and pop. The girls were mostly pretty and the bar had a nice, relaxed, jolly atmosphere.

"Taking care of business," I said and filled him in on my latest adventures.

"You know he's a drug dealer, don't you?" Paul said.

"Do you know, know, or are you assuming it the way I'm assuming it?"

He shrugged. "Guessing, but I could make a few phone calls and find out if you want. See if he's known around town."

I took the squat bottle of San Miguel that had appeared in front of me and wiped down the top of the neck with the napkin that had been wrapped around it.

"Leave it for now," I said to him. "The man's gone into hiding. It could be drugs or gambling or fucking another man's woman. I'll hang on for a while and see if he turns up. Then I'll head on down to Manila and on to PG. Might leave tomorrow actually."

Paul gave me an approving look. He knew his way around the Philippines and had an extensive network of contacts.

"Best walk away. Helping out an old mate is the best way to drag yourself into something that you don't want to be part of."

"You're not wrong," I said. "But I've still got his keys. Didn't want to leave them with the girlfriend. Something a bit dodgy about her."

"If he doesn't turn up, leave them with the manager of the hotel. He'll take care of them."

"That's what I'll do," I said firmly and turned my mind back to my own libido. A girl was standing next to me and smiling.

"How can I help you?" I asked.

Her hand made the universal signal of a glass going up to her mouth. She was miming that she was a mute but was keen to drink with me. She was average height which made her about 5 foot and pretty in the homogenous way that most of the girls were in this part of town.

"If you had a flat head, you'd make someone a perfect wife," I said with a gentle smile and asked the waitress to line up a 'lady's drink' – the ones the bar sold with no alcohol and a big price tag – which was how the girls and the bar made its money. The girls were working here because mostly they had siblings to support, and maybe a child or two whose fathers had fled the scene. It wasn't an easy life but they put on a smile and got on with it. The least one could do was support them and the local economy for an evening.

The girl had an ID card hanging around her neck which stated that she was a Guest Relations Officer and that her name was Annabelle. The waitress placed what looked like a Seven Up with lime juice in front of us and charged me the equivalent of a day's salary. Not mine, hers.

Paul, William and I laughed and joked while Annabelle sat quietly on my knee and I kept on buying her drinks. James was busy with his two cunning little vixens. They were matching him round for round. His bar bill was going up and his eyes were starting to glaze over. The girls were also getting rowdier as the sharp Mexican love juice kicked in. From my experience, the more practised girls could manage seven or eight tequilas but after that were pretty much useless for carnal purposes. A new girl's legs would turn to jelly by the third tequila. Best not to bring her back to the hotel under those circumstances because she'd throw up all over the bathroom.

One of these days, I thought, as I tapped Annabelle on her pert nose in jest, I'd have to write a manual on all of this. Might be useful for innocent tourists who accidentally wandered in off the streets into the raunchy nightlife here.

It was time to move on. I turned to Paul and said: "I'm going to go further down the road in search of 'The Tighter Pussy'. Will you join me?"

He shook his head. "We'll hang on here for a while and then William wants to bring us to a new place and check out a live band."

"Catch you guys at breakfast," I said and popped some money in the cup for my share of the bill.

After a gentle twenty-minute walk down Don Juico Avenue, politely evading the young ladies and ladyboys offering their massage services, I ended up outside 'The Tighter Pussy'.

A speaker hanging over the entrance was playing a slow rock ballad. A Filipino doorman with the obligatory revolver on his belt, greeted me with a warm smile and pulled open the heavy mahogany door. It was about the same size as the 'Champagne Bar'. The walls were painted black and the lighting was low. The room smelt mildly of lavender and strongly of Lysol antibacterial spray. There were about twenty girls in the place, three dancing in a desultory fashion and the remainder lounging around in the darker corners of the burgundy semi-circular booths. The nine customers, middle-aged white men and one Indian, were ignoring the totty and watching a cricket match on a big screen that hung at one end of the room. It was a pleasant enough place that deserved more business but it was far from the main drag and needed to rely on regulars and locals.

I pulled up a stool at the end of the bar, as far from the television as possible. Two girls immediately descended on me and began asking me my name, my country and my business. The skinnier of the two had a short bob haircut which I found appealing. Her friend was more than merely plump and had a wobbly layer of fat around her waist.

"Do you know Mikey Tomkins?" I asked the skinny one while putting my hand on her bum to hold her in place.

"Sure, sir, he's our boss," she said.

"What about my friend Dickie Goodyear? Do you know him?"

"He's a friend of Mikey. He always comes here," her friend said.

"Is Mikey around?"

The skinny one shook her head. "He didn't come in today. You maybe ask Mummy, she can tell you." She pointed at a hefty, middle-aged woman who was standing by one of the customers and chatting amiably.

"Will you bring Mummy over and introduce me?" I suggested.

The girl's eyes narrowed but there was a smile in them. "You have to pay for my services, sir."

"That seems fair enough," I replied. "What's your name?"

"Carla," she said and put her hand on my shoulder in a proprietary fashion. "Maybe you want to ask Mummy if you can bar-fine me when you talk with her?"

"Here's the deal," I said. "I'll buy you and your friend a drink each. Then she needs to run along so I can interview you more carefully about your proposal."

"What proposal?" Carla said with a puzzled expression.

"Your proposal to pay my bar fine," I said.

She shook her head as if I were a child that was getting the wrong end of the stick. "You have to pay *my* bar fine and then we can go somewhere and have dinner."

"But I've already had dinner," I said and glanced at my Rolex which told me it was around 1 a.m. "And it's a bit late to eat anything."

"Maybe," Carla suggested, her eyes narrowing again under her bushy brows, "you can eat me."

"Get the mama-san over here and then we can continue this conversation later," I said.

Carla told the barman to fix the drinks I'd agreed on and then ambled off to get the middle-aged lady manager. Carla's chubby friend didn't say anything. She sat and grinned and bopped her head to the low background music.

"Hello, sir, how are you. I'm Mummy."

"Pleased to meet you. I'm an old friend of Dickie Goodyear's and I know he's good friends with Mikey. Have you seen either of them this evening?"

There was nothing disingenuous in her eyes when she replied, so I believed that she was telling the truth when she said Mikey hadn't been in all day and they hadn't heard from him. Mr. Dickie hadn't been in either since a few days ago.

"Is Mikey usually here every evening?" I asked, dropping into copper mode.

"Yes, sir, he always comes at four in the afternoon and checks the liquor stock and then does the accounts."

"So don't you think it's a bit strange that he hasn't turned up today?" She stared at me as if my suggestion hadn't occurred to her.

"You know men," she leant forward and pinched my thigh, "maybe he has fallen in love and gone to Baguio for the weekend with his new girlfriend." I considered that.

"Does he have a new girlfriend?"

She shook her head. "No, I don't think so." She thought about it for a while and then put the entire matter aside: "I'm sure he will turn up later or tomorrow. I have the keys and I always take care of the bar. Is this the first time you've been to 'The Tighter Pussy'?"

"It is, Mummy."

"Do you like Carla here?"

"She's pretty hot isn't she?"

"She's skinny but she's naughty."

"She's naughty?"

Mummy assured me: "Oh, yes, she's very naughty."

"I'm going to spend a bit of time interviewing her on the exact nature of her naughtiness and then I might come and talk to you again later."

Mummy nodded gravely. "All our girls have an HIV test every four weeks. They are all very clean. But," she leant forward and whispered into my ear, "you must always use a condom. You don't want to have any babies, do you?"

I agreed with her. "Absolutely. I don't want to have any babies."

"How many children do you have?" Mummy asked.

"I don't have any yet," I said.

"I don't believe you." She turned to the girl. "Carla, maybe you should get pregnant with this guy and then he can marry you."

Carla thought that was wildly amusing. I pushed Mummy gently away and told her to leave us in peace.

"What is that you are drinking?" I said to Carla.

"Sprite in a champagne glass."

"How about a tequila to take the edge off?"

"I love tequila," she said and clapped her hands in delight. "Can my friends all have tequila as well?"

We romped for about an hour, Carla and I. It was thoroughly enjoyable. I have always been partial to the tastes and sounds of cunnilingus so I spent about twenty minutes with my head between her thighs and then, after she'd had a hip-shaking orgasm I let her climb on top of me – but not before donning the featherlight raincoat - and she rode me vigorously until she reached her second. I was tiring by then and ready to let slip the dogs of war into the wild forest of her passion. They yelped and howled with pleasure. Now, satiated by lust, she lay in the crook of my arm and I twirled her long black pubic hairs around my fingers as we made post-coital conversation.

She was a single mother who worked as best as she could to support her offspring. She had two children. An eleven-year-old boy and an eight-year-old daughter. For a twenty-nine-year-old she was in cracking shape. Her stomach was flat as a washboard, her tiny bum was firm and rounded and her limbs were long and lean like an elegant doe. She had no breasts to speak of, just little mounds with nipples, but that worked well with the rest of her shape. And, for a woman who had given natural birth to two children, she certainly met the requirements of her employer. She knew how to squeeze the muscles at that last vital moment when the man's eyes fluttered and ejaculation was inevitable.

She also had a fun line in banter and an unassuming personality that was easy to handle.

"No boyfriend anywhere?" I asked.

"Men are all arseholes," she said but with a smile that took any rancour out of the comment.

"No Americans who want to marry you and bring you off to a ranch in the middle of Kansas?"

"I am a qualified nurse. I would like to work overseas but I want to wait until my children are older," she explained.

"How often do you see your children?"

"Every week. It is close by and we have one day off. Mikey is a good boss. It's not a busy bar but the customers are all regulars and so you don't get any troublemakers."

"Does the bar make enough money? It didn't seem very busy."

She shrugged. "I think Mikey and your friend Dickie have other business. They own a motor boat, I heard them say. They go somewhere and bring back things and can sell them here in the market."

"What sort of things do they sell?"

She raised her head and rested it on the palm of her hand. My fingers were still twirling her pubes and she seemed to find that relaxing. "Are you sure you're not FBI or CID?" she said.

"You mean a policeman?" I said with an innocent smile. "Goodyear and I both used be policemen in Hong Kong, but not anymore, not for a very long time."

Carla gave me a searching look and then decided that I was probably telling the truth. "I think they buy mobile phones, Nokias, Motorola and Ericsson cheap in China and then they bring them here and sell. It's illegal, but only a little bit, isn't it?"

"What else do you think they bring in? Alcohol and tobacco?"

She nodded. "Mikey says you can't survive if you're a bar owner and buy whisky from the distributor. I saw them unloading Dickie's pick-up truck one morning. It was full of boxes of alcohol."

"What about drugs like marijuana, cocaine or *shabu*?" I asked, using the street name that covered all varieties of methamphetamines that had been knocking around the Philippines for years. In Thailand they called it *Yaba*. These days they were the cheapest and most common party drugs in Asia. Using cocaine was a bit like turning up at a club in your Dad's suit from the 1980s.

Carla's eyes became shrouded with concern. She wasn't comfortable having this conversation anymore and worried she might get herself into trouble. I decided to leave break off the questioning for now.

She said, "I think Dickie sometimes sells *shabu*. But only to his friends," she added quickly.

"Do you use *shabu*?"

"I don't," Carla said sharply, "but a lot of girls like it for fun or to keep awake if they have to work in the daytime and at night."

I'd got what I wanted and had a pretty good idea what I would do in the morning. Now I needed to sleep. It was time for Carla to go.

"Listen, my sweetheart," I said gently. "I'm a confirmed old bachelor and so it's really hard for me to have a good night's sleep with a girl in my bed. I also snore horribly. Why don't you go and have a shower? I'll put you in a trike so you can go home."

She gave me a long disappointed look but went off obediently for a long shower. Once she was dressed I slipped five thousand pesos into her handbag. It was much more than the usual rate but she deserved it. I took her downstairs, making sure she got into a decent motor-tricycle that would take her back to the boarding house that she shared with twelve other girls.

The next morning I felt sprightly. Two paracetamol and a cooked breakfast banished the hangover. In the lobby I bumped into Paul, James and William. It was shortly before noon and they were checking out, on the way to Manila.

"You've got a smile on your face," James said. He looked worse for wear so I assumed he'd had about as much sleep as me.

"Met a nice girl," I said.

"Good for you, mate," he said and patted me on the back. "Make sure you invite us to the wedding."

"Very funny, you Aussie prick."

"Send us a text when you get into town," Paul said. "Or we'll see you down in PG."

"I'll do that."

I gave the three of them an ironic farewell wave as their bags were loaded into their hired mini-van, and decided to go in search of the mysterious Lapida Brothers.

7

My new mate the security guard, whose name tag told me that he was called Ryan, was working the day shift.

"Hello, boss," he said cheerily. "Have you been to the hospital to see Mr Dickie? Is he getting better?"

"I don't know, Ryan, which is why I need some information," I said. He looked even cheerier when I held up a five hundred peso note for him to pocket. "Have you ever heard of the Lapida Brothers? I need to have a word with them." The smile on his face turned a somersault as soon as I said their name.

"Boss, they're gangsters. Everybody in Balibago knows them. Bad guys. You better stay away from them."

"I just want to know if they have done anything with Mr Dickie. He's vanished from the face of the earth."

"Be careful of the Lapida Brothers," Ryan pleaded with me. "They have the police in their pocket. Maybe even the Mayor."

"I'm always careful, Ryan, but I do need to know. Where can I find them?" He shook his head in one last attempt to convey the gravity of the situation, then gave me the information and the directions I wanted.

"They own the 'Happy Days' diner on Manuel Roxas Highway. It's about half a mile past 'The Tighter Pussy' bar."

Reason told me if you go poking around in someone else's beehive, you're likely to get stung. But the whole business with Goodyear was niggling me and until I could get his keys back to him and knew he was OK, I wasn't prepared to walk away yet. I patted Ryan on the shoulder and told him I'd be careful, then I waved at one of the trike drivers who was lounging about playing cards and told him where I wanted to go.

The 'Happy Days' diner was pretty much as you'd imagine. It was a good Filipino likeness of the restaurant from the sit-com series except there was no Fonz strutting his stuff. The chairs and benches in the booths were upholstered in a bright red vinyl and the floor was a chequerboard pattern. A long countertop ran along the right side of the room. The place was about half full, mostly with Western men and their Filipina girlfriends, but two of the booths were occupied by Filipino families having lunch.

At the far end, tucked behind the corner of the counter was another larger table. I couldn't see who was sitting there until I glanced up and noticed the angled round mirror that was hanging from the ceiling. It let me see the occupants of the hidden table - four Filipinos with beer bottles and burgers in front of them - but also allowed them to monitor everyone who walked in through the front door. Neat.

I slid onto a vacant stool about half-way down the counter and ordered a coffee from the machine. The waitress - dressed in a smart pale blue uniform - smiled as if I'd asked her to marry me and held out a laminated menu card. I shook my head. When she brought me the coffee I leant forward and asked: "Are those the Lapida Brothers?"

She frowned, glanced sideways in the direction of the recessed table and nodded.

"Are they available for a little business discussion, do you think?"

"I will check, sir." It looked like acting as their receptionist was part of her job description. A few minutes later, having leant over the end of the counter for a quick conversation, she told me I could go down there.

I brought my coffee mug with me. It was thick pottery and the best I could do for a weapon at short notice. There was a vacant chair at the head of the table. Two men sat on each side.

The two men on my right were thin, weasel-like creatures who hadn't been hired for their intellect. One wore a red baseball cap on his head and a vacant expression on his face. The cap was embroidered with the letter 'B'. His friend had a moustache and the logo on his baseball cap read 'Dodgers'. I doubted that either of them had been to Boston or LA. They wore identical green sleeveless shirts outside their jeans with the words 'La Salle' on them in cursive script. I could see the tell-tale bulge of a revolver beneath the fabric of Boston's shirt. The other seemed unarmed, but I guessed he'd have a knife in his boot. I gripped my coffee cup tighter.

The Lapida Brothers were identical twins. At least they would have been identical except that the one closest to me had a white left eye and a nasty scar that ran down across from the bottom of the eye all the way to his ear lobe. Both men had short cropped grey hair, wide brown faces that were not quite clean-shaven and had waistlines that looked as if they spent a lot of time in the diner sampling its wares.

"Who are you?" the man with the white eye and scar asked.

"I'm Bill," I said, "a business associate of Dickie Goodyear."

The right hand of the other brother was missing two fingers - the index and the middle finger. The stubs were neatly rounded off, as if the fingers had been cut off with a bolt-cutter but a competent doctor had sewn up the mess afterwards. He drummed the remaining fingers on the table and said something in Tagalog to the two baseball-capped boys which made them sit up straight. The lad who liked the Boston Red Sox made his hands disappear under the table.

"Where is Goodyear?" the man with the scar said.

"You are the Lapida Brothers?" I asked in turn.

He nodded slowly. "I am Alvin Lapida. This is my brother Marcial. What is your business here?"

I made a vague gesture with my hand. "Dickie promised to introduce us," I lied. "We know each other from Hong Kong. I've been supplying him with some products. This and that." Taking a little sip from my coffee, I continued: "The thing is, someone shot him last night and now he's disappeared. I wonder, if you might know where he is?"

Marcial, the brother who was missing two fingers, leant forward and scrutinised me. "Why the fuck would we know where he is?"

I smiled at him pleasantly. "I heard that you did some business with each other."

"Maybe we do," Marcial said, "but we don't know who the fuck you are."

"As I said, I'm a friend of his and I can't get hold of him. I need to go back to Hong Kong tomorrow so want to wrap up a deal we were working on."

Alvin said: "We want to talk with Goodyear. If you find him, you let us know. He owes us some money."

"He owes you money?" I repeated and took another sip of coffee. I looked over at the weasel with the Red Sox cap to make sure he wasn't going to do anything that would make me nervous.

"What sort of deal were you doing with Goodyear?" Alvin asked, suddenly interested.

"It wasn't booze or phones," I said and watched for a reaction. Their three good eyes gave nothing away. They were good at this game.

"Well, If you don't know where I can find Dickie then I won't be bothering you gentlemen any further." It must have been the first time anyone called these fellows gentle. Alvin stared at me as if he couldn't make up his mind whether I was a fly to be swatted or a wasp that might sting.

"Where are you staying, my friend?" he said.

"The Blue Nile Hotel," I lied smoothly. "But here is my local mobile number." I took a yellow post-it note from my wallet on which I'd written the number of my Philippine's SIM card and passed it to Alvin. The card didn't mention my surname. He looked at it and pushed it over to his brother.

"How long have you been doing business with Goodyear?" Marcial asked. "If you have interesting product you don't need to work through him. We control all of this part of Angeles City."

"That's why I wanted to meet you." I glanced at the man with the Red Sox baseball cap. He'd been staring at me unflinchingly all this time like a Cocker Spaniel waiting for his master's instructions.

Alvin said something to his brother and his brother seemed to agree.

"What is the specific nature of the product, my friend?" Alvin asked.

"It's chemical and used by people who want to feel happy," I said obtusely and with an oleaginous smile.

"Where does it come from?" Marcial asked.

"Shenzhen, just across the border from Hong Kong."

"We know people who might be interested in buying that type of product," Alvin said. "But we don't know who the fuck you are so let's get to know each other first."

"You've got my number," I said, "but I'm going back home tomorrow." I stood up. "Call me if Dickie Goodyear turns up."

Alvin's eyes narrowed and he nodded slowly. "Be sure to tell us if you find Goodyear first. He knows why we want to speak to him."

I pushed the chair I'd been sitting on back under the table and gave them a mock salute. Then I fixed the Red Sox fan with a firm stare and said: "Next time we meet be kind enough not to have a gun pointing at my stomach, or I will take it away from you and shove it up your arse." Marcial burst into big heavy guffaws while Alvin smiled in mild amusement at my brazenness.

I walked along the length of the counter keeping them in sight with the mirror on the ceiling, popped a hundred peso note in front of the waitress and told her to keep the change, then walked out into the hot afternoon sun.

So much for rattling somebody's cage. Let's see if any monkeys would fall out and follow me. I grabbed a trike and told the driver to get me back to the hotel where I got changed into my shorts and T-shirt and walked around the corner to the Fitness Connection Gym.

"Hello, boss," said Trinity, the owner. He had won Mr. Pampanga a few times under the careful tutelage of an Englishman called Longfield. "Long time no see, you're looking a bit skinny."

I spent two hours in the gym and then dragged my tired arse back to have a gentle swim in the hotel pool.

8

At 6 p.m. precisely my bedside phone woke me from my nap. Fifteen minutes later I found Carla sitting in the lobby. She looked charming in a bright yellow dress and two-inch high heels. I'd called her earlier and suggested we have dinner together and to let Mama-san know that I would pay the bar fine for her to take the evening off.

"That's a very nice dress," I said, kissing her on the cheek.

"I bought it with some of the money you gave me," she said.

"Good investment. What sort of food do you fancy?"

She shrugged. "I like any Western food."

"How about Swiss?" The 'Swiss Chalet' restaurant was just around the corner. I'd eaten there before and the food was first-rate. My exercise had left me hankering after a fondue with a big pot of molten cheese. I was paying and if the girl wasn't into cheese there were plenty of classic dishes on the menu.

Hans, the owner, wasn't around but Herbert, his Austrian Chef, was rattling the pots personally in the kitchen, so I was hoping for a treat. We were given a nice table with a mural of the Alps and I asked for the 'secret' wine list. The waitress nodded knowingly and brought me a small printed card. This was wine from the owner's special collection, for friends, regulars and cognoscenti. I hoped I was at least one of the three.

I choose a 2003 Louis Bovard 'Medinette' Dezaley and wasn't disappointed. My friend Dominic Tweddle had introduced me to the wines of the Valais which we drank in copious quantities when I visited his ski chalet overlooking the Rhone, but I still preferred the ones from Vaud, harvested from the Lavaux terraces that clung to the hills above Lake Geneva. The Swiss are precise and understated in everything they produce, from watches to wines. Not forgetting that fine range of handguns made by the Schweizerische Industrie Gesellschaft, otherwise known as SIG, even if a lot of their product was now being made in America.

"Did Mikey Tomkins turn up at the bar today?" I asked Carla after we'd ordered.

"He hadn't come in when I left. Mummy was getting worried."

"Anyone think to call the police?"

She shook her head. In the Philippines insouciance was a national sport. "Maybe he went to Manila with Dickie and some other guys and they're getting really drunk."

"Surely you'd tell your manager that you were going to be out of town?" I said.

"When Mikey starts to drink, he can't stop," she explained. "Once he was gone for five days and they found him in a hotel in Subic with a hangover and no money."

I smiled. In my time I'd come across men like that who lived with the demon drink riding on their shoulders, claws deep in the flesh, unable to stop putting the glass up to their lips.

"Where is Mikey from originally?" I asked.

"He's Australian. Or the other place. I can't remember its name."

"New Zealand?"

"That's the one. Is it the same country?"

"Not exactly," I said. "But they sound the same when they speak to the rest of us."

"Why are you not married?" she asked. I wasn't going to answer that question truthfully but it was a common enough question from any girl and I had a commonplace set of answers.

"I've been so busy working hard," I said, "and I am always travelling."

"What do you work?" she asked me as we tucked into the first course of Goulash soup. Judging by the speed she was putting it away Carla was enjoying it.

"I'm a consultant, I said. "I give people advice on how to solve their problems. Mostly it's about security and what they call risk management."

"I don't understand. You mean you train security guards?"

She was trying hard and it wasn't a bad stab at interpreting what I wasn't saying.

"Something like that. That's a good example. I might go to a big hotel and see if they have good procedures in place, if they have enough guards. I ask them to imagine the worst things that could happen and how they would deal with it."

"What is the worst that could happen in a hotel?" she asked with sudden morbid fascination.

"How about if you had a big hotel in Manila, like the Mandarin Hotel in Makati with 500 rooms and one of your guests came down with a terrible disease. Suddenly the whole hotel might be sealed off and nobody would be allowed to leave, even if other guests were dying from the disease."

"Could that sort of thing really happen?" Carla asked and pushed her empty soup plate away.

"Sure, it happened in Hong Kong a few years ago. Something called SARS. Do you remember that? It all started with one hotel in a place called Mong Kok."

"I don't really remember exactly."

"My job is to remind companies of what might go wrong and give them a plan on how to handle it. Here in the Philippines it might be a big typhoon or a military coup. Hotels need to plan for those to keep their guests safe."

"You must work very hard. Do you work for a big company?"

I shook my head. "Just me. I am a one man band."

"Don't you feel lonely?" she wanted to know.

"Not really. I've got a lot of friends all over the place and I'm too busy most of the time."

"But you need to have one person to be with," she insisted. She wasn't really trying to sell me the concept of a serious relationship with her. In her world it was just a truth universally acknowledged, that a single man in possession of a good job, must be in want of someone to share his life with. It had been drilled into their heads as children. Nobody could live a life alone and be happy.

"When I get older, I will settle down and have children." I gave her a consoling smile. "Perhaps."

"You must," she countered in all seriousness. "You are not so young anymore."

"But not old enough yet."

"I had my first child when I was eighteen," she said.

Our conversation continued in this manner. She tried the melted cheese fondue and pronounced it to be excellent and worth trying again sometime. I drank most of the wine myself but restrained myself from ordering a second bottle and had a double espresso instead. I planned to stay energetic for a few more hours enjoying her company.

As we finished dinner and stepped out from the restaurant, two familiar faces were waiting outside on the street for me. They hadn't changed out of their basketball vests and baseball caps. Red Sox, clearly the alpha weasel, pointed at me:

"Your name is Bill?" he asked.

"Yes, we met earlier."

"Where have you been?"

"Why is that any of your business?" I said putting a pleasant smile on my face. I told the girl to go back into the restaurant and stay there until I was done.

"We've been looking for you." He seemed upset that it had taken them a while to find me.

"I gave my phone number to your boss. He could have called me." I glanced around. Three trike riders were sitting by their vehicles and watching with interest. A group of girls in tight shorts walked past and they'd stopped, sensing an altercation that might break up the monotony of their evening. From the open door of the Eden Karaoke bar, music of an indeterminate nature filled the air.

"You said you were staying in the Blue Nile Hotel," Red Sox said, making it sound like a complaint.

"I must have been confused," I said.

"Tell us where Dickie Goodyear is?" Red Sox said. His partner, Dodgers, stood slightly behind. He had a toothpick in his mouth and was trying to look artful and failing. On consideration I came to the conclusion that they looked less like weasels and more like ferrets.

"I have no idea where Goodyear is. That's why I came to see your bosses."

"You know where he is," Red Sox accused me. He hitched up his basketball vest, which was an undertaking since it reached to the top of his thighs, and produced a snub-nosed revolver. It was a Smith & Wesson Bodyguard .38 Special, the one with the shrouded hammer. He pointed it at my face holding it sideways after the fashion of rappers and Los Angeles gang members. He was about five metres from me so I took a few steps closer, which disconcerted him, but he didn't budge.

"They know how to hold a gun properly in Boston," I said. "Maybe you should give it to your colleague if you want the full LA gang member look." He scowled.

"Tell me where we can find Dickie Goodyear and we will let you go," he said, squinting down the barrel at my face.

"Didn't I tell you that the next time you pointed a gun at me I'd shove it up your arse?"

With this model revolver, Red Sox didn't have the option of pulling back the hammer, and the double action on a Bodyguard .38 Special, fresh from the factory, had a trigger pull of around 12 pounds. That's quite a bit of squeezing before the gun goes bang.

I looked sideways, waved at the group of girls, and shouted: "Hello, help me."

It was enough to distract Red Sox for the split second I needed to cover the final few metres, grab the muzzle of the revolver and twist it out of his hand. I then slapped him left and right across his face. Hard slaps, not punches, but he went down anyway, holding his face and whimpering.

I pointed the gun at Dodger. He held his hands up high above his shoulders.

"I know you've got a gun," I said, using my best policeman voice now. "Take it out and throw it down at your feet."

He pulled an identical Bodyguard revolver out from his waistband and dropped it in the dust of the road. Red Sox was still trying to work out what I'd done to him.

"Now piss off, both of you. Tell your bosses to leave me alone. I'm on holiday now. I don't know where Goodyear is and I'm leaving town tomorrow. Figure it out yourself."

I watched them, gun in the firing position, as they receded into the distance glaring malevolently over their shoulders, until they rounded the corner. Then I bent down and picked up the other gun. They were in good nick, relatively new and well maintained. Both had five rounds in the cylinder.

Carla appeared behind me. "That wasn't a good idea, Bill. They will come after you. They work for the Lapida Brothers," she said. I smiled.

"You're safe with me, dear, I'm a security consultant." I said, as nonchalantly as I felt. "Let's go back to the hotel. We can go skinny dipping in the pool."

9

Carla's face was buried in the pillow and I was holding on to her lean haunches as I thrust vigorously into her from behind. She was exhorting me to push harder and faster and I was trying to oblige despite the sweat dripping down my chest from my forehead.

I was put off my stride when my mobile buzzed twice with a message and fell off the bedside table onto the tiled floor.

Ten minutes later we were done for this round and I reached down to pick up the phone. The Nokia 5210 was water resistant and designed to bounce and still keep working. I always carried a few spare because I had different SIM cards depending on my location, plus a few burner SIMs if I needed total anonymity.

The message came from an unknown number but I had a good idea who had sent it: 'SORY 2 DISAPEAR. NEED UR HELP. USE KEYS. SAFE UNDER BED BRING CONTENTS 2 ME. D.'

The second message read: 'THIS NUMBER', followed by an eight digit numeric code which might have been Goodyear's grandmother's wedding day in reverse or an entirely random sequence of numerals.

I texted back. 'WHERE ARE U? ARE YOU OK?'

A few minutes later he replied: ALL GUD. TEXT AGAIN SOO."

It was just after midnight. I was feeling wide awake and charged with an energy that came from curiosity. I wanted to know what this was all about. I could have a lie-in tomorrow morning before setting off to Manila and then Puerto Galera and it was only half an hour to Goodyear's house.

Using a mnemonic trick they'd taught us during my time in the Intelligence Corps - each number is an image and you make a mental picture stringing the images together - I memorised the number then deleted both text messages.

Carla had snuggled up with the sheets wrapped all around her legs and was half asleep. She wasn't best pleased when I explained that I'd received a message from one of my friends who wanted to meet for a drink so we'd have to get out of bed. I jumped into the shower to wash off the musk of our exertions and put on a clean shirt. Then I put enough money on the table to support her family for a month and told her to let herself out when she was ready as I didn't know what time I might get back. I gave her a long kiss on the mouth and told her she was gorgeous.

Downstairs I rustled up the night manager and got him to open up the safe where I deposited one of the snub-nosed revolvers I'd taken off Red Sox and Dodgers. I kept the other in case they were hanging around outside or anyone else wanted to give me trouble.

The security guard on the door whistled up a trike from further up the street. The night was busy and music was booming from all the bars. Groups of men and gangs of girls patrolled the streets and then we turned into a more sedate part of town and took the road that led towards Goodyear's gated community.

Once again the security guards recognised me or perhaps just trusted my white face. If they'd given me any trouble I would have shown them Goodyear's keys and persuaded them that I'd been sent by him. The house was in darkness. I gave the trike driver two hundred pesos and told him to wait. I shouldn't be long.

Goodyear's car was in the drive where I'd left it but there was no scooter so the girl wasn't here. She obviously had a key but wasn't living permanently with him. Goodyear had been married to a Thai woman once who was hard as nails and bitter as angostura. They had a grown-up son who was studying in America now. That first marriage had put him off any kind of serious commitments. If you kept your wits about you - which meant not getting a girl pregnant - it was possible to remain footloose and fancy free in Asia while still enjoying most of the benefits of having a relationship.

I unlocked the front door and entered the house. I felt my way along the hallway and went into the living room, where I flicked on the light.

Facedown on the floor between the solid wood coffee table and the television stand, was the body of a man. A pool of dark brown liquid had gathered around his chest.

"Dickie, you fool," I said to myself and advanced cautiously. This was a crime scene so I had to be on my best behaviour from now on. I crouched down and tried to get a better look but without lifting up his face I couldn't be sure if it was Goodyear. In the kitchen I used a tea towel to open the drawers and found one that contained discarded plastic shopping bags. I turned two of them inside out, and used them as makeshift gloves to raise up the body and get a closer look at his face.

It wasn't Dickie Goodyear. It was a middle-aged Western man with bruising on his face. I let the body fall back into the pool of blood without splattering myself. He'd been shot three times in the chest. I patted him down and found a wallet in the back-pocket of his jeans.

Inside the wallet were a few thousand pesos, credit cards, old receipts and a driver's licence identifying the dead man as Michael Tomkins. The photo was a close enough match for the face of the corpse on the floor.

"Pleased to meet you, Mikey," I said to myself. "I guess someone else will have the pleasure of possessing 'The Tighter Pussy' now."

I paused to think. This was all wrong. Mikey hadn't been here during my last visit and whoever had dumped him here might be coming back.

I supposed it was possible that Goodyear killed his friend and business partner. But unless he was disturbed and had to get out of the house quickly, I didn't think he would be stupid enough to leave the body in plain sight. It also didn't make sense that he would have come to the house when I had the key to access the safe. I supposed it was possible that he'd had a spare set of keys but was disturbed by Tomkins, killed him and had to flee the scene. Which was why he then sent me a text asking me to go and retrieve the contents of his safe.

These thoughts ran through my head as I moved rapidly to the bedroom. Now I had to hustle. I pushed the double bed aside and tried without success to use my fingernails to lever up the loose tiles that concealed the safe beneath. I was about to return to the kitchen to find a knife when I heard the front door smash open. It was the sound of an Enforcer battering ram which the police use to get into a building without a key.

Not good.

I pushed the bed back into its original position and made sure the carpet was straight and all was in order. Then I dropped the Smith & Wesson Bodyguard into Goodyear's bedside drawer. The next moment two men dressed in black were pointing assault rifles at me. They wore helmets and protective goggles and their body armour proclaimed SWAT in big white letters.

"Don't move, police," they yelled at me and I raised my hands as high above my head as they would go. They didn't take long to find the gun in the bedside table. They had me on the floor and handcuffed in a jiffy. I wondered what they thought was so dangerous about me that they had to deploy a SWAT team of eight men.

Outside there were several regular uniformed police officers and a few in plainclothes. Some of the neighbours, dressed in shorts and T-shirts, had come to watch. I was bundled into a police van which stank of ancient vomit and we passed an ambulance that must have been called to pick up Tomkins' body and bring him for an autopsy.

For the Philippines it all felt incredibly efficient.

They brought me to Angeles City Police Station 1 and put me into a holding cell by myself. There was a rubber mattress on the floor and an empty bucket in the corner. A roll of toilet paper sat on the window ledge. The window was just above eye level, covered by six steel bars and missing any glass. I had an idea it would become very sweaty once the sun came back up.

After an hour a man in civilian clothes - black slacks and a baggy, grey-collared, shirt was let into the cell. He sat down on a folding stool that he'd brought in with him and said: "My name is Police Captain Archie Francisco and I'm the arresting officer in your case."

"Nice to meet you, Captain."

"We have arrested you for the murder of one Michael Tomkins, Australian citizen," he said evenly and waited for my response.

"That's what I assumed."

Captain Francisco handed me a bottle of mineral water and watched as I took a few swigs.

"We found a Smith & Wesson revolver in the bedside drawer with your fingerprints on it. Is that the weapon you used to kill Tomkins?"

They'd fingerprinted me on arrival so that had been fast work. I was impressed.

"No, it is a weapon I had with me when you guys arrived on the scene. I admit trying to hide it."

The Police Captain gave me a quick smile and asked me: "Do you confess to the murder of Michael Tomkins?"

I shook my head. "I didn't kill him. I've never met the man and I had just found him dead on the floor a few minutes before your colleagues broke the door down."

Francisco was a man in his early thirties. I had an idea he was going places, career-wise. He seemed a clever man with whom I could have a sensible conversation. As an interrogator he'd started well. Rather than coming over all heavy-handed he'd tried to empathise with me, if not by what he was saying at least with his body language.

"I worked with Dickie Goodyear in the Hong Kong Police many years ago. He asked me to come over to his house this evening and pick up some stuff. When I got there I found Tomkins dead."

"You are a policeman?" His eyebrows had shot up.

"I left the police over ten years ago. I'm a security consultant working for big corporations now."

"What was your job in the Hong Kong Police?"

"Mostly VIP Protection and Anti-Terrorist work. I was in the Special Duties Unit."

He nodded. "I know about that. I've done a secondment to the Hong Kong Police. Have you ever been a detective?"

"Not really," I said. If he'd been seconded to Hong Kong he must be a bit of a highflier from a well-connected family, selected for the fast track.

"So you are saying, you did not kill Michael Tomkins?"

"Correct."

"Why were you carrying a gun? Don't you know that is illegal without a permit in the Philippines."

"I'd been threatened by someone earlier in the evening. I took the gun off him and was still carrying it when I came here."

He smiled. "That seems like an unlikely story."

"Do you know who the Lapida Brothers are, Captain?" I asked and took another swig from my bottle of water.

He nodded sadly. "We know who they are."

"They are looking for Dickie Goodyear, in fact they may have tried to kill him last night and I helped him get to hospital. You can check that out if you want."

"Continue," he said.

"They sent two of their boys after me because they thought I might know where Goodyear is hiding."

"And do you know where he is hiding?"

I shook my head. "He sent me a text asking me to go to his home and get some of his things and then he'd meet me later."

"Tomkins and Goodyear were business partners," Captain Francisco said. "Maybe they had a falling out and Goodyear killed his partner then he tried to set you up for the murder." He gave me a sly look. "Does that sound like a possible scenario?"

"It's possible but I don't think Goodyear would do that to me."

"But Goodyear could have killed Tomkins?" He grabbed at the theory and tugged at it. I thought it prudent to play along.

"It's possible. I just don't believe an ex-policeman like Dickie would be stupid enough to leave a dead body lying on the floor of his house."

"They could have argued. Things got out of hand, tempers flared, a few shots were fired?"

I shrugged. It was possible but it felt all wrong. What was clear was that I'd been set up to take the fall for the murder of Mikey Tomkins. Someone had called the police the moment I walked through the front door of the house.

"How come you deployed a SWAT team to come and arrest me?"

He gave me a sly look. "We were told that you were armed and dangerous." He nodded slowly. "Now that you tell me that you were in the famous Flying Tigers of the Hong Kong Police, it proves you can be dangerous and we also know that you were armed."

"Touché," I conceded.

"So you are a logical suspect. Why did you kill Michael Tomkins?" he asked again. He was a good interrogator. The golden rule of interrogation was that you spun your suspect around and kept asking the same question from different directions until they forgot what they had told you. He wasn't going to catch me out, because I was telling the truth.

"I didn't kill him, and nor did Goodyear in my opinion."

"So who did, then?"

"I suspect one of the men who works for the Lapida Brothers." My racing mind had already worked out what Captain Francisco was going to say next. I suspected the bitter irony wasn't going to do me any favours.

"Tomkins was killed by three shots to the heart from a .38 calibre weapon. Our firearms expert believes it was a gun like the one you hid in the drawer of the bedroom. He also believes from examining the barrel that it has recently been fired and not cleaned." He gave me what might have been a pitiful look. "Tomorrow we will send it to the lab and be able to confirm if the bullets that killed Tomkins came from that revolver."

"Is your ballistics lab that efficient? How long does it take them to turn this sort of case around?"

"We haven't had a foreigner murdered in Angeles for two years. This is a high-profile case and they will give me the results within 24 hours."

"Suddenly the Philippines has become incredibly efficient. I'm not used to that."

"We are not perfect, but we are much better than you imagine."

"Somebody must have tipped you off to come and arrest me," I pointed out.

The Captain smiled. "That is true. We had an anonymous phone call. Two phone calls as a matter of fact, one reporting a body and the second saying the murderer had returned to the scene."

"Doesn't that smell a bit fishy to you?"

"We get much information from anonymous informants. It is very common in our country. When they want money, they tell us their names."

"In this case you didn't get a name?"

"Mr. Jedburgh, I will not comment on this matter any further." He cocked his head to one side and asked me: "Do you confess to the murder of Michael Tomkins? It will make it much easier for you later if you confess now."

"You know I didn't kill the man. I'm not bloody well going to confess to anything."

"Very well then, my friend." He stood up and folded up his stool, then walked to the door and banged on it three times. "Enjoy the rest of your night. Tomorrow, we will charge you."

"What about my phone call to a lawyer?"

The Captain smiled and managed to look marginally apologetic. "In the Philippines you don't get a phone call unless the police permits it. If you don't confess, then I will not permit it."

10

It could have been worse. The foam mattress was thick enough and I managed to get a few hours' kip although it was sweaty. The cell could have benefited from a decent ceiling fan. The noises from the street and the police station never stopped. Eventually the sun came up and I thought I'd do some press-ups and sit-ups to wake myself up properly.

A uniformed police officer came an hour later and brought me a bottle of water and a bowl of rice with some morsels of pork on top. For a while I debated if it was worth the risk. I had no idea how clean the kitchen was and I didn't want stomach cramps or the galloping trots. I was sure that the average Filipino accused of murder would not be given a cell to himself. I was getting favourable treatment. Finally I compromised by eating the rice and leaving the pork. They'd taken my watch and belt so I couldn't be sure of the time and had to hitch up my trousers as I walked around the cell. The room smelt of urine because I'd made use of the bucket a few times during the night.

About an hour later my new friend, the Captain, appeared.

"I have decided to permit you a phone call," he said with a dry smile.

"That is very kind of you."

"Are you sure you will not confess to the murder of Michael Tomkins?"

"I've given this some thought," I said, "and have come to the conclusion that the Lapida Brothers killed Tomkins as part of a business dispute they were having with him and Goodyear. They then dumped his body and decided to frame me by tipping you off anonymously. They are hoping to pressurise me into revealing where Goodyear is hiding."

"That is a complicated theory," Captain Francisco said. He was standing by the door and had a cell phone in his hand.

"What is your theory then?" I asked.

"Being a detective is like going shopping with your wife," the Captain explained. "She tries on different dresses and some look nice but don't fit. Others, they fit but they don't look nice. Eventually she will find a dress that fits and it also looks nice and then she is happy and then I will pay."

"So how many dresses are you trying to fit on me at the moment?"

"The one with you as the murderer looks very nice to most of my colleagues and also to my Chief but somehow I don't think it fits you at all," he admitted with a friendly chuckle.

"I'm pleased to hear that."

"Do you wish to call a lawyer?" He held out the phone to me and I took it. The number was one I had memorised years ago, but it still worked. It was answered quickly and I spoke briefly and explained my predicament. The Captain took back the phone and gave me a sly look.

"You are an interesting man, Jedburgh," he said and banged on the cell door three times to be let out.

Perhaps an hour later Attorney Reyes arrived at the police station. The cell door was opened and - like St. Peter whose chains fell off as the angel led him out of prison - Captain Francisco told me I was free to go and that all charges had been dropped.

Reyes was a fat, bald fellow wearing an exquisitely embroidered *barong tagalog*, the traditional formal shirt for Filipino men. He was signing a stack of documents while a police officer handed back my belongings. I snapped the Rolex onto my wrist, threaded the belt back onto my trousers, checked the contents of my wallet, pocketed the bunch of keys and felt happy to be a free man again.

"You should check the movements of the two men who work for the Lapida brothers," I said to Captain Francisco as he held the front door open and waved me out as if he was a hotel manager and I'd been a treasured guest.

"Names?" he asked.

"No idea. But they were both wearing green La Salle basketball vests the last time I saw them."

"That narrows it down to about a million men in Pampanga province," he said.

"They won't be hard to find," I said.

"We will think about your advice," he said.

Attorney Reyes led me over to a smart BMW 320i that was parked next to a police cruiser.

"Did you have any breakfast, sir?" he asked, opening the rear door for me to get in. The inside smelt of polish and Merino leather.

"Not really. I could do with something to eat and a large coffee."

"We could stop off at the 'Jollibee' and get some burgers and French fries?" he suggested.

"Why not," I said and slid into the plush interior of the Beemer. I ended up with two bacon, cheese and egg breakfast sandwiches and a large coke. They hit the spot. The drive was about fifty minutes, Attorney Reyes explained, so I popped my head onto one of the fluffy pillows and snaffled up some more shut-eye.

"We have arrived," Reyes said, waking me up. I stared out of the tinted windows as security guards with shotguns slung over their shoulders opened a tall steel gate. On either side of the gates, a wall topped by barbed wire extended into the far distance. The compound was around 400 hectares. I had run round the perimeter once and it had taken several hours.

Reyes drove the BMW along a winding road, past lakes on either side and what might have been part of a golf course until we arrived at the Spanish-style Hacienda.

Reyes parked up next to a row of other expensive German automobiles and opened the door for me. He then shook my hand, wished me good-bye, did a U-turn on the gravel and drove away.

Another man, also wearing an elegant *barong tagalog*, stood at the top of a set of steps waiting to receive me. "Welcome, sir," he said. "The Senator is waiting for you in the breakfast room. Did you have a pleasant journey?"

"Thank you, Julio," I said, "the day has improved the more it has gone on. It's nice to be back."

Julio's family had worked for the Guzmans for years and his role in the house reflected that. He was still quite young, but had watched too many movies that featured butlers, which he tried to emulate. To be fair to the chap he did pull it off nicely. He led me through several connecting *salas*, all the size of volley-ball courts, decorated mostly with plush rattan furniture. The veranda was the size of a football pitch and sitting by himself at a table that had room for fourteen people was Senator Eduardo Guzman. He was now in his fifties and the pale blue *barong tagalog* covered a paunch that had thickened since I had last seen him. He gave up on the grapefruit that he'd been digging into and stood up to greet me.

"My dear English friend, Bill," he said pumping my hand and slapping me on my shoulder. He waved for me to sit and a servant appeared, placing a glass of freshly squeezed orange juice in front of me.

Senator Guzman and I had history and when I'd called that morning asking for help he'd sent his angel to help me walk free from prison.

"What is this nonsense about murder?" the Senator asked me.

"I don't know. It's some vendetta I've got myself involved in for no apparent reason."

"You are not working at the moment?"

I shook my head. "I'm on my way to go scuba diving in Puerto Galera. Met up with a few friends here." I spent ten minutes giving him the full story of Goodyear and Mikey Tomkins.

He shrugged, when I'd finished. "The Lapida Brothers I know well. They are in my debt, but very powerful in these parts. If you had asked my advice I would have told you: best not to cross them; best not to do business with them." By implication he was more powerful and he'd plucked me from their sights now. I thought that the younger Senator Guzman would have been less happy to accommodate gangsters like the Lapida Brothers. But in the Philippines everything was a complicated spider's web of patronage that would put Republican Rome to shame. Only locals truly could understand it. Most of the time we foreigners bobbed on top, like cream on a vanilla milk shake, oblivious to the harsh, complex world around us.

"That matter is sorted out now," Senator Guzman said with finality. He waved it away as if it were a pesky mosquito. "My granddaughter is getting married in Manila next week. I would be honoured if you could be there?"

"As a guest or would you like me to work?" I said.

"Could you be there as a guest," he said his face revealing nothing, "but also to keep a special eye out for any troublemakers?"

"It would be my pleasure, Senator," I said. Senator Guzman suggested I freshen up, have a swim and then join him for lunch. He wanted to introduce me to his brother-in-law.

I was shown to a charming guest room that overlooked the swimming pool and found some clothes that I could change into later and a baggy pair of trunks in neon yellow. I had a long shower to wash the dirt of the prison cell off my skin and out of my hair. Then I grabbed one of the towels, shucked into a dressing gown and made my way down to the pool. Nobody else was around except the butler who asked me if I needed anything to drink. He strode off to get me a coffee while I jumped into the water.

It wasn't quite Olympic-size but the pool was long enough. I spent ten minutes thrashing up and down using the Australian crawl, then sat on the edge dangling my legs in the cool clear water while I drank coffee and then got back into the water for another twenty minutes of crawl. By the end of all that I was starting to feel the burn. One thing was certain, if I turned in the wrong direction on the Kilima Drift I'd need all the power in my legs to keep myself from shooting off into the deep blue yonder at six knots. Puerto Galera was famous for its drift dives but some of them could be seriously wild.

Julio had placed a jug of ice-cold water in the shade at the side of the pool, so I had a few glasses of that then I dropped back in and swam up and down using a steady breaststroke, the nautical equivalent of a leisurely stroll around the park. When I got bored of that I flipped over to backstroke and did another half hour staring up at the azure, cloudless sky. The sun was starting to crank up now and I was feeling the heat on my face.

I ran through in my mind the events of the last few days. Something was not quite right. I wasn't clear what Dickie had done to annoy the Lapida Brothers but I was pretty sure they had killed Mikey Tomkins. I figured that Dickie was probably in deep hiding and I would have bet money on the fact that all was not as it appeared between himself and Lillibet. I figured there was some other women that he was hiding out with. Truth was I was annoyed that I'd been dragged into a mess that was none of my business. I was on holiday. At least in this pool, in the sunshine, I was beginning to feel human again.

11

Lunch was planned for 2 p.m. so I went back to my room, showered off the chlorine and donned the white *barong tagalog* that had been laid out for me. It was no coincidence that everyone in the household wore the strongly nationalistic Filipino garment. The black trousers were a bit short and stopped at the top of my ankles but the waist was fine.

Senator Guzman welcomed me in one of the other rooms. It was decorated as a gentleman's lounge with plush burgundy leather armchairs and sofas. The air-con was quietly humming away so the atmosphere was pleasantly cool.

A man in his twenties stood up to shake my hand. Sonny Guzman was older but no more appealing. He shared a similar facial structure to his father. His skin was pallid and his eyes bloodshot, making me suspect he'd been partying hard the last few months and some of the late nights might have involved substances that were not strictly legal.

"Do you remember, Bill?" Guzman asked his son. "You went to college in the States shortly after he started working for me."

"Are you now back in the Philippines permanently?" I asked the young man.

"Kind of," he said with a strong American accent. The look on his face seemed to imply that he wasn't sure he wanted to be back home and maybe was missing his friends or his dealer.

"Where did you go to college?"

"I was at Vanderbilt," he said.

"That's in Nashville, isn't it? What did you study?"

"A bunch of stuff, mostly fine arts," he said evasively.

"How was your swim?" Senator Guzman asked and led me over to a table with an open bottle of white wine.

"Refreshing, just what I needed," I replied and took the glass he had poured for me. The door opened and another man entered. Whereas Sonny was wearing a black and silver Dolce & Gabbana shirt this man stuck with the theme of the *barong tagalog*. His was a beige, almost translucent, colour with a white T-shirt visible underneath.

"This is my brother-in-law, Ricardo Fernandes," Guzman said to me. The man accepted a glass of wine then grasped my hand firmly for a shake. He was in his late thirties. He was deeply tanned, steely-eyed and there was a military aura about him. He was tall and carried himself well, his back straight and his chin high. He felt like a man one might consider following into battle.

"Ricardo is based at Camp Tecson in Bulacan, not so far from here," said Guzman, sounding proud of his sister's husband. "He is with the First Scout Ranger Regiment."

I gave him a respectful nod. "Counter-terrorism and urban warfare, am I right?"

Guzman said: "Bill here was in the Hong Kong Police's Special Duties Unit."

It was Fernandes' turn to give me a respectful smile. "We did some training with your guys in Mindanao. There was a crazy South African guy, I remember. Big chest, big laugh, big belly."

"He's still around," I said. "Although I heard he's about to leave and join JP Morgan to head up their security team."

"Could that guy drink," Fernandes said and shook his head in wonder.

Later we sat down for lunch and enjoyed the best of Filipino food. We had *Sisig,* we had *Lechon* and we had *Pancit Palabok*.

Guzman waved a greasy finger in my direction as he addressed Ricardo, "Bill here is coming to the wedding. I've just invited him. You will take a few days break from your scuba diving to party in Manila, won't you?"

"It will be my pleasure, Senator," I said.

Fernandes had spent some time interrogating me on my work and my experience and I'd given him the sort of answers that would impress him without providing much substance. Sonny sat quietly and sullenly opposite me and picked at the food. It was as if he'd been ordered to attend by his father and really wanted to be somewhere else. The Senator had obviously been mulling something over in his head during lunch. When we moved on to coffee he got to the point.

"This wedding will be a grand affair and many of the great and good of Philippines politics will be there. This President is no better than the previous one. You were a great help to me then. I hope you can be again."

"So are you planning another run at the Presidency?" I asked. "The election is still a few years away. I'd be happy to help you again when the time comes."

"My dear English friend," he said looking over at his brother-in-law who gave him a conspiratorial smile. "This is the Philippines. Our democracy has never run smoothly. I don't expect the next few years to prove any different."

"Let me show you my unit this afternoon," Fernandes suddenly said. "I would like your professional opinion."

"Is it far?" I asked. Travelling anywhere by road in the Philippines was a taxing experience. I had no desire to spend hours in an army vehicle to see men marching up and down. Fernandes' unit had a fearsome reputation, but I had been around enough army camps in my life, and I was on holiday after all. However I sensed from the energy in the room that this was important to Guzman and his brother-in-law. Fernandes' next words made my mind up for me.

"Not by helicopter," he said.

It was funny, I thought. I hated flying on jets but I loved helicopter travel. The Bell UH-1H had been a workhorse of the American Army since Vietnam. Coppola had filmed 'Apocalypse Now' in the Philippines because they had so many old Hueys knocking about. The Huey on the Senator's helicopter pad was a utility aircraft in camo colours, not a VIP runaround. I was glad that I was in a canvas jump seat not sitting on a tin helmet over the Quang Tri province in Vietnam. Fernandes had changed into the combat fatigues of a colonel in the Philippines Army, complete with obligatory Rayban Aviators. He clearly came from money but he appeared a serious soldier. His uniform was well-laundered but showed signs of having been used on manoeuvres that involved more than paperclips. I strapped in and put earphones on my head.

"Camp Tecson is near San Miguel," I heard Fernandes' voice crackle through the intercom after we had dusted off. So about 70 kilometres from Angeles City. It took us less than half an hour. We landed on a helicopter pad where we were met by a smart young lieutenant and shown onto a jeep.

"I want you to see the Scout Ranger Training School," Fernandes said, "I think you'll be impressed." As we entered the compound we passed a fountain in front of which was their logo of a commando knife with the motto 'We strike'.

The Americans had heavily influenced the Filipino military so if one squinted one could have been on a US army base in the deep South. Everything was well arranged and buttoned down, as the Yanks liked to say. Soldiers were running in squads, calling and answering in the American fashion. We came past the obligatory assault course on which a group of cadets in grey-blue DPM uniforms were crawling underneath tracer spitting from an FN Minimi machine gun.

I followed Fernandes into a long briefing room where about fifteen men in uniform were gathered. Around their necks they all wore bright red scarves. Their bronzed faces were young and earnest. Their hair was shorn to the scalp. Fernandes introduced me to the more senior officers:

"This is Major Ramos, 7th Company, motto: *In Hoc Signo Vinces*. This is Major Gerardo, 11th Company, motto: *Pericoloso*. This is Major Somera, 4th Company, motto: Final Option. This is Captain Dagupon, 8th Company, motto: *Destruere Hostis Deus*." The Colonel paused and gave me a quizzical smile. "Do you understand Latin, Bill?"

"I learnt some at school. 'Under this sign you will conquer', 'Dangerous', 'Destroy the enemies of God'. I'm getting the theme."

"Each company has its own sense of identity. The men are proud to be part of the Regiment, but the company is the main unit of loyalty."

I nodded and said to the men closest to me. "I was in the British Army for a while."

"Mr Jedburgh was in the Army, yes," Fernandes said, "but he was also in the Special Duties Unit of the Hong Kong Police. He has worked with our good friend Senator Guzman."

They paid attention to that. I found it surprising. Guzman might have been Fernandes' brother-in-law but they seemed to be very familiar with him.

"The Senator is a patriot," Major Ramos said approvingly. "We are all patriots here."

"I would expect nothing less," I commented. "To serve your country is an honourable profession."

"If only our President was as honourable," Major Gerardo interjected. I said nothing. My golden rule was never to express a political opinion in a foreign country, but it seemed to me that Ricardo Fernandes had brought me here for a reason beyond simply showing off his crack regiment. I got more of an inkling a few minutes later.

"Bill," the Colonel said, "I understand from the Senator that you won a famous shooting competition at Bisley." When he mentioned the name 'Bisley' there was another audible reaction in the room. Wherever army people meet, the name is synonymous with target shooting. The famous Imperial Meeting was inaugurated in 1860, with Queen Victoria donating the first prize. It had been held on the Stickledown Range at Bisley since 1890. I still remembered the goosebumps I had felt standing on the top and looking 1200 yards downhill to the butts beneath me. I could hit the target at that distance, but now I rarely shot at anything greater than 500 metres. The complexities of wind, bullet drop and muzzle tremor become exponentially greater the further you have to shoot. But in those days I had been young, clearsighted and one of the best rifle shots in my regiment.

"The Conan Doyle, yes," I said. "At 900 yards – about 820 metres."

"That is impressive," the young lieutenant who had greeted us at the helipad said. He was dark haired, like many of his people, but taller than most. He had cold, slate-grey eyes. His uniform was slightly too tight, I imagined that was deliberate, because beneath it you could tell that he worked out and had a six-pack that would make the ladies swoon.

"Lieutenant Obregon is the best shot in the regiment," Fernandes said. "We do not have a range that long – ours is only 750 metres. Perhaps you might be interested in a small competition?"

Everything that afternoon had been leading up to this question, I surmised. He wanted to know how good a shot I was. I could have ducked the challenge. I was on holiday, I could have pleaded an injury or a prior engagement, but I was curious. Ricardo Fernandes commanded a highly sophisticated special forces unit. He had any number of trained snipers at this disposal. But he wanted to know how good I was. I was minded to find out why.

"As long as there is a suitable prize," I said. "Your Lieutenant…"

"Francisco," the young man said, interrupting me and shaking my hand in a steely grip, "Francisco Obregon."

"…Francisco," I continued, "can shoot for the honour of the Regiment, but what prize can I have if I beat him?"

"We will let you and the Senator decide that at the wedding," Fernandes said. "If you win, I think you will be very happy."

"In which case," I said, hoping the bridesmaids were going to be pretty, "I will let Lieutenant Obregon choose the weapon."

"The Barrett M52 would be too easy for us," he said. "What about an SR-25?"

"That's not a rifle I'm familiar with," I lied. I knew more about sniper rifles than I wanted him to know.

"It's American. Designed by the creator of the AR-15. Chambered in 7.62 NATO. It's our standard intermediate range sniper rifle."

"Sounds good," I said. "Scope or iron sights?" The young man laughed.

"You are getting on, old man," he said. "so I will let you use the scope they are fitted with. You may dispense with the suppressor if you choose."

"Your choice," I said. "The Senator may think you made a bad one though if I beat you."

"I doubt you will," Obregon said. The smile on Colonel Fernandes' face showed that he thought the Lieutenant might live to regret that.

"Then let's keep the length of shot to 450 metres, to give me a fighting chance," I said.

Out on the range. I examined the SR-25 I'd been given. It was an excellent weapon, modelled on the AR-15 but with the benefit of a free-floating 20-inch barrel. The original rifle had a 24-inch match target barrel, but this was the special forces version and was designed to have an integrated suppressor. I had fired this model with and without it, and in this instance, since sound was not a factor, I was going to remove it. I noted that Lieutenant Obregon had chosen to leave his on. I figured that made sense for him. This was probably his standard weapon and muscle memory was at least as important as overall accuracy.

I didn't intend to lose. I had rigged matters in my favour as far as I could. I was comfortable at 450 metres. It was my preferred distance for long range assassinations. I had fired this weapon before and I had a scope.

The standard Leucon scope was relatively straightforward and the Mil-Dot crosshairs made it relatively easy to adjust for wind and range. The reticle on a Mil-Dot scope had four 1 mm dots on each of the four sides of the crosshairs. At 450 metres each dot would represent 45 centimetres. Each click of the windage and elevation turrets represented 0.1 of a mil, so a tenth of that. At that distance I needed to allow for the bullet falling 1.8 metres, or around six feet – that meant I needed to be aiming that distance above the target. Wind variation would account for the lateral adjustment. I looked at the range flags streaming at intervals down the range. This was what made match target such a complex and challenging discipline.

"I will act as umpire," Colonel Fernandes said when Obregon and I were ready. "You each have a magazine containing 15 rounds. You will get five rounds at 100 metres to zero your rifles, then we will commence the competition. If the competition is tied after ten rounds, we will count back the number of V bulls. If it is still tied, the nearest round to the centre on a tie-break round will win."

The competition began in earnest once we were zeroed. I felt good. I was breathing calmly. I had found the biting point on the trigger and my last three rounds had taken out the direct centre of the zeroing target. We tossed a coin for the right to choose whether to fire first or second. I won. The only way to influence your opponent was to put pressure on him. That meant hitting my own bulls and forcing him to make a mistake.

The butts system on a range hadn't changed in over a hundred years. The large targets were hauled up on pulleys with a paper target with concentric circles in the middle. After each shot, the spotter in the butt placed an orange circle on the latest shot and then patched up the previous one.

Obregon and I were in adjacent firing positions. My first shot was just outside the bull, at 4.30 on the clock face. His was just inside. I was a point down immediately and my plan was in tatters. Now the pressure was on me.

I calmed myself. Your miss always tells you what to allow for height and windage so I adjusted my scope and prepared to go again. You could only kick the ball in front of you. For the next eight rounds we matched each other more or less shot for shot.

I had a stroke of luck. The flags on the front and rear of the range started to move in different directions. This was the sniper's nightmare. It was like putting on the most devious of golf greens. But I'd seen this fluctuation before. On the day I won the Conan Doyle trophy. It was a sign. My shot hit the dead centre of the bull.

Now it was Obregon's turn. I could tell he was rattled. He knew what he needed to do. Simply land his shot in the bull to win. But the time he took was a sign he didn't know how to handle the gusting wind. After fifteen agonising seconds he fired. And shot just wide.

We were tied now on 49 points apiece. It would all come down to the number of V bulls, the tiny inner bull on the F Class targets we were using. A scurrying sergeant brought them to Colonel Fernandes. He looked at them and smiled broadly.

"Jedburgh, you have five V-bulls. Obregon, you have scored only three."

Match Rifle. The one discipline where experience and age could almost always trump youth.

12

The Colonel lent me his driver, so I returned to my hotel that evening in a military sedan. I dozed on the way back. I had been required to have a few drinks with the Colonel and his senior officers to celebrate my victory on the rifle range. Victory had felt good.

"You are an excellent shot," Ricardo had said to me as I took my leave. "I believe you have taught Lieutenant Obregon an important lesson. He allowed you to control the terms of engagement. In battle that is fatal."

"I would probably still have beaten him at a longer distance, but it would have been much harder," I admitted.

"The important point," Fernandes said, "is that the Senator's assessment of your abilities was correct."

"Are you going to tell me now why that matters?"

"All will be made clear at the wedding," he said, and shook my hand. "The Senator also asked me to make it clear that you would be best to leave Angeles City and the Lapida Brothers to their own devices now."

"Excellent advice, which I intend to follow," I said. "I want to get to Puerto Galera as soon as I can."

"Puerto Galera," he said. "I know it. "The Regiment has a diving school just up the coast."

"That's why I am going there. I love diving the fast drifts there."

It took me twenty minutes to pack up all my stuff when I got back to the hotel. I had called Rannie from Camp Tecson and he was waiting downstairs with a big grin and his dusty Toyota taxi. I paid my bill, emptied the safe, slipping the Smith & Wesson Bodyguard I'd taken off Dodgers into my dive bag, hidden beneath the lime green Mares fins and wrapped in my Henderson Lycra wetsuit.

"Manila, boss?" Rannie asked once I was settled in the back.

"I need to pick up something from a friend's house first," I told him and gave him directions.

Despite having seen me carted off in the back of a police van, the security guards at Dickie Goodyear's compound waved us through. I guess they reckoned if the police had let me go that obviously meant I must be a good guy. Nevertheless I asked Rannie to keep a look-out and alert me in case anyone appeared suddenly. He didn't find that was odd. We'd known each other for a long time and his resumé included some interesting previous occupations.

In the bedroom I was now well-practised at moving the bed, pulling aside the carpet, and levering open the tiles with a knife from the kitchen. This time I had the key and the code number. The key turned and the safe door opened upwards. Inside, held together with red elastic bands were stacks of US dollar notes. The bundles were of different denominations but I guessed it was around 50,000 dollars.

This was obviously Goodyear's running-away stash and I was pleased the man trusted me with it. There was a canvas shopping bag in the safe which contained nothing but a silver and black metal box. It had the name 'Seagate' on the side with a couple of cables attached and I guessed it was an external hard drive. I threw the money into the bag on top of it. I'd expected to find a couple of fake passports as well, but the safe was now empty. I guessed that if he needed to leave the country – and frankly I would be concerned about him doing so using his real name with the Lapida Brothers and the police potentially looking for him – he would use the money I brought him to purchase a good quality counterfeit. In Manila everything could be had for a price. I could recommend a man in Mabini who had access to the real deal through a relative at the Australian embassy. I locked the safe again, returned the carpet and bed to their original position and left the house.

"All good, boss?" Rannie asked.

"So far so good. Take me to Manila and don't spare the horses."

"I don't understand?"

"Drive at your usual excellent speed," I said.

"Traffic might be bad," he said. We may have missed the evening rush hour but Manila never sleeps.

"Sometimes in life, we can't fight the inevitable," I told him and settled in to get a few more hours of shut-eye. A soldier slept whenever he got the chance and that was a useful habit in my line of work as well. As I slept my unconscious brain kept on working, turning over the disconnected pieces in my brain. Dickie, the Lapida Brothers, the Senator and his brother-in-law. I woke up no less enlightened but with a good idea from whom I might seek more information when I reached the capital. When I awoke, I sent a text. A few minutes later I had my answer.

We arrived in Makati, the business district of Manila, shortly after 10 p.m. The roads were still water-logged from the typhoon and so were as clogged up as the drains.

Before leaving Angeles City I'd sent a text message to Goodyear's burner phone. I wrote: 'GOT YOUR STUFF. CALL ME. J' He hadn't called or texted back by the time we arrived in the Makati district. That didn't mean he was dead but it meant I'd have to hang on to his things until he surfaced.

I did get a call from Carla. I'd sent her a text saying I had to leave town in a hurry on business and was heading to Manila. She told me she would miss me. I promised her I would come and see her again as soon as I had a chance. Then I asked if she'd heard anything about the owner of her bar. Mikey Tomkins still hadn't turned up, she told me, but the police had been there earlier talking with the Mama-san.

They'd find out sooner or later that their boss was dead. I wondered if there were any other partners or if Mikey had left a will. A girl like Carla could get a job in any of the places up and down the road so even if 'The Tighter Pussy' closed she'd still be able to support her family.

I also made one other phone call as we were driving along.

These days I liked to stay at the City Garden Hotel which was on Makati Avenue within five-minutes' walk of the nightlife on P. Burgos Street. It was newly built, clean and an Executive Twin Room cost less than fifty bucks. I dumped my bags upstairs, had a quick shower to freshen up, asked the hotel manager to place my rucksack with its high value contents in the big safe at the back, then headed straight out again.

The Alba restaurant on Polaris Street had been around for ever. It served the best Spanish food in Manila and it was a regular haunt of mine. I wasn't hugely hungry but some tapas and the *Sopa de Ajo* - the garlic soup - always hit the spot – even if the wine list was pretty hit and miss. More importantly it stayed open late. I got a table in the corner as far away as possible from the three-man guitar band who were working the room playing old time favourites. Eventually they'd get to me. I always asked for the same two songs. 'Stardust' by Hoagy Carmichael and Richard Roger's 'My Funny Valentine'. The girl they reminded me of was long gone, but the songs put a melancholy smile on my face.

The waiter greeted me as if I were a long-lost friend. He didn't know my name but he recognised my face. I was the man who always came for dinner by himself.

"Have you got this Rioja?" I said pointing at the wine list. He frowned, then nodded and went off in search of the bottle.

But this evening I wasn't going to be dining by myself. Or at least I would not be drinking by myself.

The man who entered the restaurant and pulled out the chair opposite me looked a bit older and greyer than the last time I'd seen him.

"How's the food here?" asked Hank Petersen.

"I like it," I said. "Are you eating?"

"I've already had dinner about two hours ago. I'll have a San Miguel."

I'd got to know Petersen many years earlier in Danang. We'd crossed paths in a good way a few times since then. These days he headed up the Philippines office of the DEA, the United States of America's Drug Enforcement Administration.

"How have you been, Hank?" I asked, "and how's Mona?" Mona was Hank's wife. She looked like butter wouldn't melt in her mouth but played a mean hand of pinochle.

"I've been in hog heaven," he said and smiled. His Southern accent was as smooth as a glass of Jim Beam strained through a lump of honey. "They love partying in this country and no party is worth a bean without a big supply of *shabu* and his little brothers and sisters. I'll be lucky to get a posting back to the States before the next decade. I asked Mona to join me here, but she's having too much fun on Broadway. She's doing some crazy Limey show called 'Spamalot'."

"Do they make the *shabu* here or do they import it?" I said.

"Mostly they import. And they import a whole bunch from the States which is why yours truly is here along with my team."

"How many people do you have in the country? Or is that a secret?"

He shrugged to show that it didn't matter. "I've got eighty-three special agents in the PI."

"And are you the big boss of all of them?"

"I am the big boss."

"What's your title then?"

"Deputy Administrator," he said and turned to order his drink from the waiter who'd just uncorked my bottle of wine.

"Not a very cool title."

"We have really boring titles in the DEA."

"How much money do you make in a year?" I asked.

He gave a chuckle. "That's none of your fucking limey business, I'm a US federal employee."

"Nothing wrong with asking a question. Sometimes people are not so touchy about answering."

"I earn good money and I have a good pension," he said. "Any others?"

"Isn't it about time you retired?" I said with a cheeky smile.

"I'll retire when you do, Jedburgh. I think I'll have one of those meatballs you're having."

"They're called *Albondigas*," I said.

"And the *Calamares Fritos*. Do you know how many years I was stationed in Colombia?"

"No idea," I replied and blew on my spoonful of garlic soup.

"Long enough to know my way around the Spanish language."

"Good for you."

We bantered for a while and caught up on gossip. Then I told him most of the story of Dickie Goodyear and Mikey Tomkins.

"Their names don't ring a bell but I can run them through the computer," Petersen said. "The Lapida Brothers, now, they've come up a few times in our investigations. Evil pieces of shit. Linked to a bunch of homicides. Both of them have done time in prison but not as long as they should have."

"I've come to the conclusion that it's basically a drug deal gone bad. Tomkins and Goodyear are bringing stuff in from China or Hong Kong and somehow things have gone wonky. Maybe the quality wasn't up to standard. Maybe the Lapida Brothers wanted to squeeze down the wholesale price."

Peterson nodded at my assessment. He was on his third bottle of San Miguel and I'd nearly finished my wine.

"I really don't know why I'm mixed up in this shit," I said. "I'm on holiday and resting between engagements."

He gave me a long, knowing look. "You're mixed up in this shit because it's what you do. There are dudes who go through life without anything ever happening to them. Then there are dudes who just step into dog shit every time they walk out of their front door."

"Is that a fact?" I said.

"Yep. I've got to level with you. You're just one of these dudes that always finds crap on your shoe."

"I don't mind trouble as long as I get paid for it."

"No, Bill, you prefer to get paid for it. When push comes to you, you just lap it up, any which way it comes to you."

"Are you going to join me bar hopping some girlie joints on P. Burgos Street?" I asked him.

"Naw, I'm too old, too tired and too married for that nonsense. You can buy me a cigar and I'll smoke it with you next door. Then I'm going home. Mona will be up shortly in New York and I'm going to try and interest her in some of that there phone sex."

13

After a Cohiba with Petersen I decided I had no appetite for anything else and went back to the hotel for an early night.

It was late in the morning when the street noises finally penetrated my sleep and I lay in bed staring at the smoke alarm for ten minutes. Finally I rolled out of the white sheets and stood in the shower for as long as I could stand the cold water.

My intention was to spend one more night in Manila. Maybe I'd catch up with Paul, James and William in 'Squirt' or one of the other places they liked to frequent. I'd give Goodyear another day to turn up and then I'd head on down to PG. It was probably a wise idea to stash the money and his other belongings in a bank vault. There was no benefit in bringing it down to the dive resort where security would be much slacker.

I went to the 'Filling Station' for breakfast and had a vanilla milkshake with my eggs. This was another American-themed diner and they'd done a great job of it with 1950s signage and other Rock'n'Roll paraphernalia. There were life-sized models of Superman, Batman and Elvis, a rack of Shell and Esso gasoline dispensers and two pool tables. A genuine blue

Cadillac happened to be parked in the middle of the dining room.

From my booth I could look down onto P. Burgos street and watch it slowly waking up. This was another one of those discreet Asian red light districts where every building contained a bar or a club with funky names that hinted at the delights and debauchery on offer within. My favourite name was 'Crawdaddy's'. That conjured up all sort of wickedness but was in fact a restaurant. The street closed down once dawn arrived and the nightlife had a lie-in but by noon the bustle started up again. The beer deliveries arrived, the cleaners did their work, the managers came to bring the money to the bank.

My mobile rang. It was Lillibet, Goodyear's girlfriend.

"Is that Bill?" she asked.

"That's me."

"Have you seen Dickie?" she asked.

"No, he hasn't turned up. But his business partner Mikey Tomkins did. Somebody shot him slightly more successfully than Dickie. He's dead."

"Oh," was all she said at the other end of the line. "But Dickie isn't dead?"

"No evidence that he is so far. He was still alive a couple of nights ago. I got a text." As I said it, I had to qualify that in my own mind. I assumed the message had come from Goodyear but was not absolutely certain. It could have been someone else who knew the combination of the safe. On balance I still thought he was alive and keeping his head below the parapet.

"I guess Dickie hasn't been in touch with you either then?" I said.

"I left Angeles. I was too afraid. I came back to my parents' home in Quezon City." That was an urban sprawl Northeast of Manila and geographically part of the extended capital.

"I have some big problem," the girl continued "some people knew I am Dickie's girlfriend and they follow me here and ask for money he owes them."

I rolled my eyes at my reflection in the Coca Cola mirror. I thought I could detect a tremor in it that was the start of a shakedown. "What kind of people?"

"They are two guys here with a gun. I have to find Dickie and tell him to give them their money."

"Are they two skinny guys wearing baseball caps, one's a Red Sox and the other is a Dodgers fan?"

There was a longer silence this time, then she whispered: "How do you know?"

"We've met before. Where are they now?"

"Here in my home in Quezon City. Please come and help me."

"And how much do they claim Dickie owes them?" I asked.

"They say $50,000 US. Can you help me?"

"How do you imagine I could help you?" I asked, trying to think it through as we were talking. I was probably being set up, but sometimes attack was the best form of defence.

"Can you come and pay them money?" she suggested. "I think they are going to hurt me." She said it with as much emotion as a hooker who couldn't be bothered to fake an orgasm.

"I'm not in the habit of walking around with $50,000 in my wallet."

There was a longer silence as she probably put her hand over the phone and consulted. "They say they will take five thousand dollars from you and then they won't harm me." Now she sniffed as if there were tears welling up in her eyes. "They might rape me, Bill. Please come and help me or find Dickie."

"Dickie doesn't want to be found at the moment," I suggested.

"I know he had a secret hiding place where he kept the money and other special things. Do you know where it is?"

"Your new friends ransacked the house and couldn't find it. How would I know?"

"You are an old friend," she pointed out.

"And you're his girlfriend," I turned the notion back at her.

"You must come and help me. They are bad men. I am afraid they will kill me." She added a few expert sniffles.

I finished the last dregs of my vanilla milkshake, sucking it up through the red and white striped straw and made up my mind. "I will come and speak with those two guys. Tell them I will bring five thousand dollars and not to harm you."

"Thank you, thank you, Bill," she gushed.

"Send me the address by text. I have to go and get the money first. It's now noon. I will be there at 3.00 p.m."

"Please come quickly," she said. I grunted and cut the connection. I was going to be there much more quickly than I'd said. Surprise is always your friend.

The text message with the address came through within a minute. I expected a taxi driver would be able to find the place, although road and house names were not always entirely precise in the Philippines. I needed supplies. Back on the street I went to the Seven Eleven and one of the pharmacies. A visit to the hotel safe was my final stop, then I hailed a taxi on the other side of the big junction, by the petrol station.

It was a convoluted drive through mostly ugly parts of the city. Potholes filled with water made the journey slow and laborious and took us around an hour. They were saying there was another typhoon on the way. That was about par for the course. During typhoon season they often came hard and fast. There was only just enough time to clean up and then the roof was blown away again or a landslide took out half of a hillside and buried the flimsy homes built on it. For a bit of tragic variety, once in a while a volcano would erupt spewing ash and misery over entire provinces. Mount Pinatubo had last blown its load in 1991 which coincided with a major typhoon. The Taal Volcano near Tagaytay, south of Manila was overdue for a good outburst but everyone prayed it wouldn't happen.

Lillibet's house was in the Payatas *barangay* which felt more impoverished than the other quarters we'd come through. The taxi driver indicated a two-storey house with a tin roof and loose electric wires flapping in the wind, barely attached to a utility pole. I told him to drive past and park a few hundred metres further on. I gave him five hundred pesos and told him to wait. If I didn't return after half an hour he should call the cops and get the hell out of Dodge.

There was no activity on the street. No kids playing football. It felt like one of those Western towns that had lost its sheriff and was waiting for something bad to happen.

The steel gate was open and I stepped into a courtyard. The cement was cracked and weeds grew between the cracks. It didn't feel like a busy family home but perhaps the parents were at work and the kids were scattered all over the world earning a living. Much of the Filipino economy was driven by the remittances transferred by daughters working as domestic helpers or nurses and sons labouring as sailors or construction workers.

I looked in one of the barred windows and saw Dodgers sitting on a sofa watching a soap opera. There were squeals coming from the room next door. Framed like a porn star in the window of the room next door, Lillibet was energetically straddling Red Sox on a crumpled bed. He was still wearing his baseball cap and had a goofy smile on his face. It wasn't rape. The only thing she needed to be scared of was venereal disease.

The front door was open so I knocked and entered. Dodgers looked up in surprise. I was early. He flicked the sound off when he saw me and yelled through the open doorway into the room behind. A few minutes later Lillibet was pushed into the room. She had a gun to her head now and Red Sox was trying to look menacing. But she didn't appear half as scared as she should have done in the company of these two gangsters. I was certain now they were part of the same crew.

"Ill met by daylight," I said grimly. Red Sox grinned at me. His new gun was a big fat semi-automatic. I didn't want to jump to any conclusions, but it looked like the sort of gun that had taken out a chunk of Goodyear's shoulder. The sort of gun he might have borrowed from his employers the Lapida Brothers after he had his own taken away from him.

"Did you bring the money?" Red Sox asked. "We will kill this girl if you don't give us five thousand bucks and tell us where Dickie Goodyear is."

"I know this is starting to sound repetitive but I have no fucking idea where Goodyear is hiding."

"You are his friend. You must know," Red Sox said.

I pointed at Lillibet. "She's his girlfriend. Why hasn't he been in touch with her?" I stepped further into the room and gave Dodgers a friendly smile. He started to smile back but then realised he wasn't supposed to be friendly.

"I will answer that myself," I explained. "It was because Dickie didn't trust Lillibet here. He might have had an idea she had sold him out."

A hint of guilt dashed across Red Sox's face as he tried to work out how I could possibly have known that. "Here's the five thousand I've brought you to let the girl go free," I said, slipping the rucksack slowly from my shoulder and removing the bundle of greenbacks. They were mostly grubby $20 notes with President Andrew Jackson's face on them that I'd grabbed from Dickie's stash.

"Dickie owes our boss $50,000. And he stole some documents," Red Sox made his point again. The dead horse he was flogging now looked like a skeleton.

"I simply have no idea how I can help you. Take this money and let the girl go. Dickie has abandoned her. Or give her the money and she'll probably let you keep her."

Red Sox still had the gun's muzzle pointing at the girl's bare midriff. As far as he was concerned she still had to appear to be the hostage in their narrative. Dodgers didn't seem to be armed although he now stood up and produced a set of handcuffs.

"You are coming back to Angeles City with us," Red Sox explained.

"I don't think so," I said and shot him between the eyes with the Smith & Wesson Bodyguard. Then I shot Dodgers twice, because the first round only went through his cheek and that doesn't always kill right away. Finally I shot the girl. That was easy because she'd frozen in terror and hadn't moved. I put a round into her larynx which generally takes out the cerebral cortex if the angle is right. Stops them twitching faster.

I paused and studied the tableau for a few seconds. There was very little I wanted to change about it. Two men, a girl who'd recently had sex, a gun. It could easily be read as a crime of passion. I pressed the little revolver into Dodgers' hand then squeezed the trigger so that a bullet lodged in the wall behind Red Sox and the GSR ended up on his hand. Then I tossed half of the bundle of dollar bills on the floor to confuse the scene a bit. Maybe the first person on the scene would be tempted to pocket the money and upset the forensics team even more.

I ambled casually outside. The taxi-driver was waiting for me at the end of the road. He hadn't heard the shots or maybe 500 pesos for fifteen minutes work meant he was happy to pretend he was hard of hearing. But he heard me perfectly when I asked him to drop me off at the airport.

14

A straw hat and sunglasses from the Seven Eleven had obscured most of my face. I tossed those in a rubbish bin at the airport as I walked through it to switch taxis for the drive back into town. Then I had myself dropped off at the Peninsula Manila Hotel, which was about a mile down Makati Avenue from the City Garden. I was wearing surgical gloves and a cheap plastic mac which I had bought in the pharmacy. I disposed of those in a dumpster in a back alley beside a restaurant on the walk back to my hotel.

There's a lot of guff talked about gunshot residue, but if they did find any they were going to find it on Dodgers, not me. When a gun is fired, small particles are emitted from the back of the weapon and the muzzle during the gunpowder explosion. These particles fly onto the hands, face and clothing of the shooter. A competent investigator will use dilute nitric acid to swab for these particles which are then subjected to atomic absorption analysis to identify the characteristic elements of antimony, lead and barium. That was the theory.

In real life though, it was never as simple as when the CSI did their stuff on television. In practice the swabs didn't always pick up the particles, the AA machines weren't calibrated properly, the investigators were rarely competent and cross-contamination confused the findings, especially in countries where people owned and fired a lot of guns.

As a professional I took calculated risks. You practised a lot, and you prepared as carefully as circumstances permitted. When I returned to my hotel room, I had a long hot shower using a bar of carbolic soap I'd bought at the pharmacy. One of my chemist friends had explained to me that it was very good at scrubbing particles off your skin.

An hour later I was ready for the first beer of the evening. I stank of green Polo Ralph Lauren, which was one of the most potent eau de cologne's known to man and masked any lingering odour from the carbolic soap. But first I needed to visit an Internet cafe.

There was one opposite the liquor store on P. Burgos Street. I paid for half an hour of time and sat down in one of the cubicles. The PC was using the new Windows Vista. All I wanted to do was check the contents of the external hard drive I'd taken from Goodyear's house. I used these myself, so I was familiar with how they worked. Using them was safer than keeping information on computers, because you could lock them away from prying eyes. It must have something important on it if it was in the safe. I suspected it would contain files showing money paid and owed. Maybe even some stock keeping or possibly contact details of clients and suppliers. Any of that information would be risky in the hands of the wrong person. Or the police if your business was trading contraband.

I unwound the cables and plugged the hard drive into a USB port on the computer. I listened to it churning into life and saw it come up as an F:\ Drive on the system. I clicked on the icon so that I could view the contents. I clicked on it and a dialog box popped up: 'Enter password.' I'd expected that. There was no guessing what Goodyear might have used except the same number that had opened his safe. That was my first choice and it didn't work. Several guesses later the dialog box told me that I had run out of attempts and to come back twelve hours later. That was an interesting request. The software I used to encrypt my confidential data would have erased the entire disk. Maybe I was more paranoid than Goodyear or he had something on this disk that he didn't want to lose by accident. I undocked the drive and cables and put it back in the bag.

I took the opportunity to check my emails. I punched in a string of numbers which brought me to the servers of my Hushmail account. It was an encrypted email service that I'd started using when my friendly Indian tech guy had explained that Firemail's days of anonymity were numbered. This one used the dark web and had been created by a couple of Russian former spetznatz operatives in London. Not even the FSB could hack their systems, and I knew they had tried.

There were several messages that I quickly deleted. I'd stopped replying these days. In the past I'd sent back the word 'declined' signing it RM if I didn't want to pursue the offer of a job. These days I just ignored anything I didn't like. People got the message. It didn't stop them from coming back. When you have a reputation for excellence you don't need to go hunting for work.

There was one message I lingered on for a moment longer. "Fuck you," I muttered under my breath but it was a light-hearted curse. I was on holiday. Why couldn't the man leave me alone?

The email came from someone calling himself Thanatos. It simply read: "He wants to see you."

I deleted everything. There was no trash box so the system wiped everything completely clean the moment you told it to. I still didn't trust it completely but it was more efficient than using the phone with a voice changer or placing an ad in the newspaper, which was how I'd operated when I first started out. Technology had moved on a long way in fifteen years. I logged out, told the manager that I was done with the computer and stepped out on to the street.

It was a bit early for 'Squirt' but I'd start there anyway. I'd sent Paul a text that I'd be around and about and to let me know where they were hanging out. So far he hadn't replied so I assumed he was still in his four bedroom penthouse apartment trimming his nose hairs, dancing around in his underpants and listening to Bob Seeger.

'Squirt' was billed as a cabaret. The impressive dance troupe continually came up with new routines but what gave it the real edge was the inventive flair of the costume designer. It was still a girlie dancing bar but it had a style that set it apart.

I sat by the edge of the dance floor and had a San Miguel. The girls were half way through a cracking rendition of 'You can keep your hat on'. Then they rolled into 'Big Spender' and 'Hello Dolly'. The girls all had longer legs than the average Filipina and they strutted around stage with enthusiasm and passion, belting out the numbers. When the set ended a new gaggle of girls came on stage in matching orange miniskirts and boob tubes. The DJ cranked up Beyonce's 'Irreplaceable' and they began grooving to the music.

I checked my watch and my phone. No reply from Paul yet so I thought I'd walk down to 'Dimples' which was a smaller more intimate club where the girls normally had more clothes on.

The street was getting busier, men were trying to sell fake Viagra and Cialis. Now that it was dark, the ladyboys were beginning to show themselves in greater numbers.

I got a table at the back of 'Dimples'. There were only three girls on the small dance floor. They were wearing black evening gowns with slits up the side of the leg providing an enticing glimpse of thigh.

The waitress had just asked me where I was from when the curtain covering the front entrance was pulled aside and Larry Lim entered. His eyes adjusted to the darkness, then they found me and he slid onto the bench next to me.

"This is the part where you are supposed to say: how did you find me?" Larry said. He was a muscled-up Chinese Singaporean and although he had become more self-important as he had risen through the ranks of the SID, he was a good buddy of mine.

"Do you want a beer?" I said instead.

"Go on humour me," he said and waved at the waitress.

"Okay, how did you possibly find me, Larry?" I said, putting on a falsetto voice.

"I'm very glad you asked me that," he replied then told the girl he wanted a Chivas Regal topped up with soda water. "I asked myself, where can I find Bill Jedburgh?

And the answer came to me. If I went to every sleazy bar in Manila, sooner or later I'd bump into him."

"It would be very funny," I said, "if I didn't know that even you, with your beautiful wife at home, enjoyed the fleshpots every bit as much as I do."

"For men in our profession, we are a bit predictable," he commented. "There was me thinking what amazing powers of deduction I have."

"I'm on holiday. If someone is on holiday at a beach resort it's hardly being Sherlock Holmes if you find him lying on the beach."

He frowned at me and scratched behind his right ear. I rummaged in my pocket and took out one of my Nokia phones. This one had a light blue waterproof casing on it. "You have this number and you've plugged into the PLDT network to get the location of my SIM card."

Larry said, "But a cell phone only puts you within the zone of a cell tower so that's not accurate enough. I still had to find the right bar."

"You know I like 'Dimples', 'Squirt' and 'Rogues'," I said.

"I went to 'Rogues' first," he confessed. His Chivas arrived and he took a long swig. Half of the tall glass was ice so it must have been refreshing with barely a bite of booze.

"What are the girls like in 'Rogues' at the moment?"

"They are short and they have long black hair."

"You are a very boring Singaporean man," I said.

"I'm married and despite your earlier insinuations, I only have eyes for my wife."

I shook my head in despair at this and asked: "What are you doing in Manila?"

"Unlike you, I am not on holiday."

"Obviously."

"Did you not get my email?"

"I did."

"Then you know why I'm here."

"I have no idea why you are here. I thought you and the old bastard were in Singapore and you wanted me to come back."

"The old bastard is here in Manila."

"I suspected that when you walked through the door," I said. There were three new girls up on stage now and the one in the middle had an interesting face. There was something about her cheekbones that drew my attention. She was singing and dancing along enthusiastically to Christina Aguilera's 'Ain't No Other Man'.

"We have need of your expert services," Larry said, watching me as I stared at the girl in the middle of the dance-floor. She was wearing a green satin evening dress and four-inch high heels.

"Is that so?" I said, aware he was watching her as well out of the corner of his eye. "What's so special that makes Brigadier Wee get on a plane and come to the Philippines?"

"He'll tell you all about it."

"Why don't *you* tell me?" I suggested. I had a nasty feeling that this was the end of my evening chilling out. I hadn't even decided what I was going have for dinner yet.

"It's not up to me to tell you."

"What do you think about that girl in the green dress?" I asked him, cocking my head at the dance-floor.

"She's short and has long black hair," he said.

"She's not short."

"She'd be short if she wasn't wearing those high heels."

"I suppose so but," I took my last mouthful of the sweet Filipino beer, "in the dark all girls are tall."

"Did someone famous say that before you?"

"Benjamin Franklin. Although I think he was talking about cats and older women not Filipina bar girls."

Larry put down his empty glass of Chivas and peeled off two hundred pesos in notes from a roll he'd produced.

"Let's go," he said.

"Where are we going?"

"To see the old man. He's staying at the Shangri-La Hotel."

"Now?" I said, trying to sound annoyed even though I'd seen it coming and was actually looking forward to seeing the old man. I had worked for him for well over a decade now and I enjoyed our meetings as much as they frequently irritated me.

"Better go now before you get drunk. He doesn't like you when you are drunk."

"I like myself very much when I am drunk. And all the girls think I'm a brilliant dancer when I am drunk."

"These girls think any man with a job and a bank account is a brilliant dancer, even a middle-aged Englishman like you."

"That's insulting to the girls. Makes them sound shallow." I stood up to leave. "And besides I'm not middle-aged. I'm in the prime of life."

"Life expectancy for men is eighty," said the pedantic Singaporean, "and you're over half of that. Makes you middle-aged."

"You'll be middle-aged soon," I fought back.

Larry told the waitress she could keep the change and we walked out of the dim, dark club. I threw one last look over my shoulder at the girl in the green satin dress with the interesting cheekbones and wondered if she would still be around when I returned from my business meeting.

15

Brigadier Wee had taken a pleasant suite that looked out over Ayala Avenue. I hadn't seen him for a while. His date of birth was shrouded in the mists of time. He never changed. I suspected that he was in his seventies by now but he could have been ten years older. He was bald, apart from a few wisps of hair over his ears, with liver spots on his face and hands. He rarely smiled and when he was amused he did something with his face that appeared to be a scowl but actually wasn't.

We'd had a long association and it had been fruitful for his organisation and lucrative for my purse. Most of the time. Occasionally he gave my testicles a hard, vicious but thankfully metaphorical squeeze to remind me who was calling the shots. I didn't like that much but somewhere in my complicated psyche I admitted to feelings towards him that were approximately filial. I hated him as much as I respected him.

"A glass of champagne, Bill?" the Brigadier said holding up a bottle of Vilmart. It crossed my mind that there must be a Frenchman in charge of the Shangri-La Hotel who knew the difference between Reims and Rilly-la-Montagne.

"Don't mind if I do," I replied and took a glass from him. He indicated that Larry and I should sit in the two armchairs opposite the couch on which he was sitting.

"Are you fit?" he asked, his eagle eyes contracting as he surveyed me like an army draft doctor ready to pass me fit for service in Vietnam.

"As a butcher's dog, sir." I hated myself for the habit, but I couldn't help the last word slipping out.

"You're looking a bit fat," he commented. A chunky Panasonic Toughbook in a magnesium alloy protective case sat closed on the desk by his elbow.

"I'll have lost ten pounds by the end of next week from scuba diving," I said.

He nodded and made an indeterminate grunt. He took a sip from his champagne glass and I took a sip from mine. Get on with it, a little voice at the back of my head was saying.

"I don't want to spoil your holiday…," the Brigadier said.

"… But?"

"No, there is no need to cancel your holiday. I simply want to put you on stand-by for a job. A very important job."

I nodded at him with a resigned smile. "Are you paying full rates?"

"When do we not pay your full rates, Bill?"

"You are working off an old rate card," I said – this was a regular tennis rally between me and the Brigadier. "The one from fifteen years ago."

"I consider that represents our special relationship discount. Isn't that right, Larry?" Wee glanced over at his factotum and pushed his face into a shape that could have been a smirk. The Brigadier was dressed in a light blue cotton shirt and a pair of dark grey suit trousers. He'd removed his tie but he still had his gold cufflinks in. On his feet were a pair of corduroy slippers that marked him as being from an older generation.

"Who is it?" I asked. Wee took another sip from his glass and waved with his other hand to indicate that he would be coming to that, in good time.

"When do you go down to Puerto Galera for your scuba diving?"

"I was hoping tomorrow."

He nodded in agreement. "That's fine. Oriental Mindoro is not so far from here. When we need you, we can get you back within a few hours."

"In twenty minutes if we send a helicopter," Larry said.

"I'm in Manila," the Brigadier said, "because Singapore Airlines Engineering has just signed a multi-million-dollar deal to provide maintenance services to Philippine Airlines." His face moved to its smug position. "We are taking the contract away from Lufthansa Technik."

As was common in the Lion City, Singapore Airlines was largely owned by the government. That accounted for the involvement of SID, the Security and Intelligence Division that Wee headed up.

"Would any bribery have been involved to win this kind of contract?" I asked casually.

"You should know better than to ask a question like that," Wee snapped at me.

"I'm not on top of all the latest details, but I know the Philippines. Rumour had it that the former President was in Lucio Tan's pocket or vice versa." I knew PAL had gone bankrupt after the Asian Financial Crisis in 1998 but was now out of receivership and had just been named 'Airline Turnaround of the Year'. I'd read that in an in-flight magazine. Tan was the Chinese-Filipino billionaire who had been the Chairman and major shareholder of PAL for many years.

"It is illegal in Singapore for anyone to solicit or pay bribes. Especially government ministers, as you well know," the Brigadier made his point. "We won the tender based on a better price and a closer relationship with the current President."

"I suspected that crony capitalism would be in the mix somewhere," I said.

"Relationships are everything in Asia," Wee said firmly. "It is the reason we have had such a long and mutually beneficial involvement with you for example."

I shrugged. "As long as we are all making money, it doesn't make any difference to me, one way or the other."

In fact it did sometimes but that was neither here nor there.

"This is where you come in," Wee went on. "The deal has not been finalised; the contract has not been signed yet. Nothing must happen to the President of the Philippines in the next six weeks."

"What's wrong with the Presidential Security Group?" I said.

"The PSG is perfectly competent. We don't need you to help in that regard." He reached for the bottle of Vilmart and poured himself another glass. I stood up so he could top mine up as well. Larry put his hand over his glass to indicate that he was fine. He'd probably spent longer in 'Rogues' than he'd let on and he had a limited capacity for alcohol as I'd proved on a few occasions.

"We have received intelligence," the Brigadier continued, "that there is another military coup being planned to oust the President and to replace her with someone else. Someone who may not be in favour of our deal or wish to sign it."

"That's an occupational hazard in the Philippines," I said. There had been about six or seven coup attempts since President Marcos had been deposed in 1986 and it was hard to keep count. Not all of them had been successful.

"We want you to take out the designated leader of the plotters to remove the risk of the coup being successful."

"The old 'cut the head off the snake before it strikes' manoeuvre," I said.

"Correct," he said.

"Wouldn't they have someone else to step into the breach?"

"Possibly, but we think taking out this particular officer will stop the revolt in its tracks. From past experience we know they are prone to fizzle out."

I nodded in agreement. "There was one in 2003 wasn't there? They all marched back to their barracks and were made to do 50 press-ups as punishment."

Brigadier Wee smiled. It was a bit more complicated than that, but that was how the press had reported it.

"The fellow is holed up at an army base outside Manila but he's coming into town for a big wedding. There'll be lots of people, celebrities, politicians and captains of industry, along with their bodyguards and lots of confusion. That seems to be the best opportunity," Wee said.

"A wedding in Manila?" I repeated.

"That's right. Is that a problem? You are looking at me as if you swallowed a fly in your drink." I had a sinking feeling in my stomach I knew who the target was going to be. But the best way to deal with these situations, was to keep quiet, act professionally and wait for time and events to unfold.

"No, weddings are good," I said. "Either for a sniper shot or a walk up with a silenced weapon. Any idea of the venue?"

"The Manila Hotel," he said.

"That figures. Lovely old hotel."

He placed his empty glass on the table and said, "Now, we may not go ahead with this. There are a few other moving parts. So if we call you, we want you to do it quickly. Or we may not call you. Is that clear?"

"Crystal clear," I said. In life - some bloke with a big brain had once written - there are no coincidences, just synchronicity. I picked up the canvas bag with the external hard drive in it. I'd grabbed it from my hotel after Larry and I had left 'Dimples'. I might need a bargaining chip if I ended up having to finesse the endgame.

"I wonder if you could do a little favour for me? A friend of mine gave this to me for safe keeping and now he's disappeared. I can't get past the password. Could your tech people crack it for me?"

The Brigadier stared at me, perhaps mildly irritated that I appeared to have changed the subject. "Is this important?"

I didn't want to tell him the entire story about Dickie Goodyear and my night in jail so I simply said: "It's important to me. I think there is some information on here that might be helpful with something that I'm working on." That was getting Bill Jedburgh out of an increasingly smelly tub of manure. Maybe Hank Petersen was right and I couldn't helped rolling in the stuff. But I really had just wanted to be left alone to holiday in peace.

"Fine," he said. "We'll have a look at them for you. Hand them to Larry he'll have one of our cryptologists at our embassy open them up."

I leaned back, holding the bag above my head and Larry took it from my fingers.

"Can I go now?" I asked. The night was still young and I wanted to enjoy some of it. I was starving. A vision of a steak with a side of mashed potatoes was floating over Brigadier Wee's head.

"I haven't told you who the target is yet," he said sharply as if I was being impatient.

I shrugged. "I thought you'd tell me closer to the day."

Wee said: "Larry, pass him the file."

My friend handed me a thin brown file which contained several pages and a large photo of Senator Guzman's brother-in-law.

"That's Colonel Ricardo Fernandes. He's with the First Ranger Regiment. A tough cookie and a charismatic leader, I am told," the Brigadier commented.

I didn't let on I knew the Colonel. It didn't surprise me that both sides of this coup seemed to want my services as an assassin, because that was surely the purpose of the audition I had passed the previous day. I wasn't ready to tell the Brigadier, but I had no real desire to shoot anyone at the moment, even for good money. I'd already killed three more people on this trip than I'd expected.

"Right," I said and handed the file back to Larry. "I'll make sure I've got the right kit close at hand then."

"Let Larry know if you need anything special. We've just got a new shipment of those Israeli Meraglims that you are so fond of. The new Mark VI."

That made me sit up straight with excitement. "Could I have one of those? Pretty please?" They were a favoured handgun of the Mossad Kidon units who specialised in sanctioned political terminations.

The Brigadier gave me his odd smirk and nodded like a parent who reluctantly agrees that his son can have a top of the range air rifle.

16

From Makati to Batangas was about a hundred kilometres down the E2 highway. Like any journey in the Philippines it could be quick or it could be slow.

Rannie had picked me up from the hotel at 10 a.m. the following morning. I'd not pushed the boat out too much after taking my leave of Brigadier Wee. Larry had joined me for dinner at the 'El Gaucho' steak house and we'd talked about the meaning of life, the universe, and everything. We came to the conclusion that the answer probably wasn't 42 but it wasn't far off.

After two bottles of excellent Santa Rita 120 Chilean Malbec, most of which I drank – Larry was definitely the worse for wear - I was feeling far too tired to look at nubile young wenches in bikinis contorting their bodies to the sounds of American soft rock and so went to bed shortly after midnight.

The next morning I walked down to the United Coconut Planters Bank on Makati Avenue and deposited the remains of Goodyear's money in a safe deposit box that I kept there. When or if he turned up again, I'd return it and his belongings. But where was the bloody man?

The drive down to Batangas was generally smooth once we got out of the Manila urban sprawl. I slept until Rannie pulled up at a Starbucks and we got ourselves some iced lattes, after which we talked about music, which was his great passion, until we reached a beach at the end of a dirty road, south of the city of Batangas. From here the private *banca* boats ferried the more affluent tourists who wanted to get to Puerto Galera without slumming it on the public ferry.

A *banca* was a form of canoe with bamboo outriggers which provided stability in rough waters. This one had a bamboo roof and could seat six people in relative comfort. The crossing was as smooth as an ice rink. The sky was a startling blue and the sun beat gloriously down on us. There was no sign of a typhoon, although this was the Philippines, so the next one wouldn't be far away.

"Safe diving, boss," Rannie said after I paid his fare and told him I planned to be in PG for the next ten days unless something came up. He gave me a wave as he walked off. The two crewmen had already loaded my two dive bags onto the *banca* and all I had to do was manage not to fall off the thin gangplank that ran from the sand into the bow of the wooden boat.

The old man at the wheel grinned cheerfully. All the *banca* crews knew me because I was a regular with the Sabang Beach dive shops and had been for many years. This time he was taking me to Puerto Galera pier from where I'd hitch a ride up to my house. He put the noisy old diesel engine into gear and we started chugging across the strait. It rarely took more than three quarters of an hour, but I'd had a few hairy crossings during bad weather and then it could take a lot longer. Like any journey in the Philippines, nothing was predictable except uncertainty.

I sent a text message to say that I was on the way and sat back on the plastic cushions enjoying the sea breeze. Puerto Galera had been discovered by the Spaniards in the 16th Century as a natural harbour protected from the often inclement weather of the region. The name meant 'Port of Galleons'.

The town itself was a cheerfully grubby place no different from most of the country. A population of thirty thousand souls made a living from the sea - mainly driven by tourism. The quality of the sand on White Beach was outstanding, only rivalled by one with the same name on Boracay Island. On Sabang Beach, thirty or so dive shops competed for business. Diving had grown exponentially over the last twenty years because the coral, within five minutes boat ride from Sabang, was gorgeous and the strong currents that forged along the seabed made drift diving fun and challenging.

Three thousand expats, of all shapes, sizes and nationalities, had made Puerto Galera their home. They owned dive shops, hotels, restaurants or were simply making their pensions go further in a country where food was cheap and the weather mostly sweltering hot. Many of them had married, or shacked up with, local girls.

One of these expats was Josef, the Swiss developer who had built my house. He was leaning against the bonnet of his pickup truck, which was parked on the pier. He was a tall man, burnt brown as a hazelnut. He was always charming, good company and, even though he had no desire to return to its snowy mountains, upheld his nation's reputation for efficiency. He had settled in

PG many years ago and learnt how to navigate the bureaucratic complexities that the locals threw into the path of the unwary entrepreneur. As a result, he'd become the premier developer of property being sold to foreigners. It helped that his wife was a distant relative of the Mayor and one of her cousins was the Chief of Police.

"You made good time," he said with a welcoming smile. Like many from his country, he spoke perfect English, inflected with Germanic undertones. He spoke English with his wife, he spoke English with his friends, he spoke English with his customers. It was a wonder that he could still speak German. Of course his native tongue was the incomprehensible *Schwizerdütsch* that sounded like a glacier raping a mountain bear.

Josef drove us through town, past the mini-mart, the bank and onto the coastal road that led to Calapan, the provincial capital of Oriental Mindoro.

"Are you staying long?" he asked.

"I hope so," I replied. "What's happening up at the mountain?"

"We are building three more houses at the moment, but nowhere near you."

"Who owns them?"

"A gay Yorkshireman with his Filipino boyfriend." Josef gave me a quick sideways glance as if to check for any reaction. I had none. "He's a retired pig farmer. Then there is a retired US Navy Commander. Nice guy. His wife's twenty-one and she's pregnant."

"Good for him," I said.

"And a French banker who lives in Manila and wants a weekend place to bring his mistress."

"Sounds like an interesting bunch. Paul and James are threatening to come down soon and have a wild party in their house. Have you been told yet?"

He nodded as he manoeuvred the chunky Toyota around a tricycle that must have contained no less than four women clutching their plastic shopping bags. The trike was belching out black smoke but the driver had the throttle wide open as if he was late for church.

"How's the family?" I asked.

"Getting bigger. My wife's cousin had twins. My wife's brother's wife had a baby. My wife's auntie had a baby." He glanced sideways again. "You know how it is."

"Fecundity is a much-admired quality around here."

"One of the fastest growing nations in the world."

"So many mouths to feed," I said wistfully.

"And how's your business?" he asked.

"It's good. I'm getting paid."

"When are *you* getting married?" he asked and overtook another trike. This one only contained one passenger and was nattering along steadily, occasionally missing a beat.

"You are starting to sound like a Filipino," I accused him. "You are going native on me."

He gave a loud laugh.

"This country can drive you crazy sometimes. Never come and live here permanently. Only visit. The way you do. I've lived here for nearly ten years and I still understand nothing."

"You are being unfair to yourself, Josef."

He shook his head at my comment, then steered the pickup truck off to the right onto a smaller side road. The quality of the tarmac instantly improved. I had helped pay for this access road to the mountain, along with all the other owners. It had been built under Josef's rigorous supervision and to his punctilious standards. He dropped down into second gear because the road increased dramatically in steepness. It was a long way up but the tyres gripped the ridged surface.

Ten minutes later, after passing a few residences of varying designs we pulled up in front of my pretty blue *Casa Azul*.

"Will you come in for a drink?" I asked him.

"Just one little beer," he conceded. I crossed the small garden to the front door and unlocked the heavy steel gate, then the wooden door behind it. The Spanish tiles on the living room floor still showed damp patches from having been mopped earlier, the air smelt vaguely of lemon and the sliding doors that led to the veranda had been opened to allow a cooling breeze to circulate. It was nice to be home.

17

Lately I'd been using Action Divers on Small Lalaguna Beach. Roscoe, a canny New Zealander, had been running the place since shortly after Noah ran his boat aground on Mount Ararat.

It was 7 a.m. and I was feeling peachy, after a bowl of corn flakes and a mug of English breakfast tea. The weather was as calm and sunny as my disposition. The hassle and complications of Dickie Goodyear and Ricardo Fernandes had been washed away in the night and I was ready to dive. I ran through the contents of my dive bag, grabbed a spare mask from the cupboard, switched weight belts to a bright yellow one with pouches, then carried the bag down to the garage.

There stood my little baby, a lime green Kawasaki KLX250S. It was perfect for travelling on muddy tracks when it rained. It wasn't too heavy to fling around and had enough power to get up the steep road, even - as I had discovered - with two girls sitting pillion. I checked the tyre pressures and made sure the tank was full, wheeled it out into the sunlight and closed and locked the shutters on the garage. I popped on my Harley Hightail helmet and shucked the dive bag onto my back, like a rucksack.

The Kawasaki's engine gave a welcoming rattle when I brought it to life and flicked the throttle a few times. The sound made me feel free, as if I were riding a mustang on the range. I spun the wheels in the dirt as I shot up and over a little hump that brought me onto Josef's access road, then I sped past the other houses and down the steep incline, dropping gear to keep control and make sure that the bike didn't overbalance with all the weight on its front wheel. At the bottom of the hill I turned left onto the main road and headed for Puerto Galera town. I passed the usual trikes and two jeepneys - the joyously coloured buses that were unique to the country - filled to the brim with people going to market. As I entered town I took a right fork and headed in the direction of Sabang Beach.

The road was appalling. During the rainy season the *banca* men did good business transporting customers from PG to Sabang Beach by sea, so they made donations to the appropriate decision makers which kept new construction on the road down to no more than a hundred metres of tarmac a year. That's why riding a dirt bike made sense, because I hardly had to throttle back through the jungle foliage as my knobbly tyres bounced over the potholes and rocks until I finally reached the outskirts of Sabang. You couldn't ride all the way down to Small Lalaguna Beach so I left the bike outside one of the burger restaurants. They kept an eye on it for me in exchange for a daily fee. It saved me from chaining it up. A bike like that drew attention. It wasn't outrageously fancy, but it was handsome and only a few months old. I'd cheerfully kill anyone who stole my new bike, but you couldn't tell people something like that. They wouldn't believe you.

Action Divers was a ten-minute walk along a path that ran through a rabbit warren of buildings. There were dive shops, convenience stores, a string of bars which were still shuttered, guest houses and restaurants. You rounded the point by El Galleon, where they ran instructor courses, and then you reached the next beach. The other side of Small Lalaguna was the imaginatively named Big Lalaguna beach. These were not pretty like White Beach. The sand was coarse and grey but beyond it and beneath lay an amazing underwater world.

Roscoe was standing at his counter staring at the computer screen. It was not a large dive shop but it was tightly run and the team knew their stuff. The front gave on to the beach with two freshwater cleaning tubs that you could dunk your gear into after a dive to get rid of the seawater. At the back were the equipment room and an office. The compressor that filled the dive tanks was behind the building to keep the noise down.

"Josef told me you'd got in last night," Roscoe greeted me. "How was Manila?"

"Messy," I said. "Good to be back on the beach."

"The coral is in great shape," he said.

"Have you got a lot of customers?"

He shook his head. "We've got a German couple. They're doing their Open Water course and a small group of young Filipinos who turn up once or twice a day. They're staying over at White Beach."

"So I guess Heinrich is teaching the Germans? Who's going to take me out?"

"Bill," Roscoe said, shaking his head, "by my estimation you've done about five hundred dives here. If you get lost around the reef I can't feel sorry for you."

"I'm a PADI Staff Instructor so I take the buddy system very seriously," I said, laying on the gravitas.

"You can dive with Rico," he said, laughing. "He's not had a lot of customers lately, so he'll enjoy keeping up with you in the Canyons."

"Sounds good to me," I said. Rico was a young local Divemaster who'd worked his way up from boat-boy. He was keen, smart and a natural underwater. One of these days he would make it to PADI Course Director if he could save up enough money for the expensive training. His downfall was a fondness for Tanduay Rum - made from fermented molasses - which meant that when he got a decent payday he struggled to hold on to his earnings. As a Divemaster he was paid a basic salary for helping out around the shop and then got a commission for every customer he took out on a dive. During peak season, when a group might be up to ten divers who stayed one or two weeks, he could earn serious money by local standards.

"Bill, how's it hanging, man?" Rico said emerging from the back lugging two steel 12-litre tanks. The tanks contained compressed air. If you tried to dive on oxygen you'd be dead pretty quick. Oxygen was used by technical divers to flush nitrogen out of the system after a long deep dive.

One of the world's greatest technical divers, John Bennett, lived and taught in Puerto Galera. In 2001 I'd watched as he surfaced from a depth of 308 metres. I'd handed him an oxygen tank at six metres and then kept him company for two hours as we waited for the seconds to tick by on his final decompression stop. The entire dive had taken over nine hours and set a new world record.

"Rico, the smoothest tongue in Sabang," I said and took the two tanks off him so he could fetch two more, lining them up at the front. We would strap a tank into the BCD - the inflatable jacket that served as a Buoyancy Control Device.

"Canyons should be pretty fast this morning," Roscoe said consulting the tide tables. Flying along in a fast current was the closest thing an ordinary mortal got to feeling like Superman.

Rico and I prepared our gear. I pulled on the thin full-body dive suit that protected me from coral scratches. Then I prepared my mask with Johnson's baby shampoo, the best de-fogging solution a grown-up could ask for.

"How are things with the ladies?" I asked.

"Not good," he said, giving me a sad look.

"Why's that? Got someone pregnant?"

"Worse than that," he said as he tested the pressure in his tank by opening the valve and looking at the gauge. "I promised two girls I'd marry them and now both of their fathers are after me." His face had a look of abject misery. He was a handsome lad with a cheery face, long legs and broad shoulders. You could tell that the ladies liked him. He wasn't looking forward to settling down, whichever father caught him first.

"An abundance of blessings," I said. "You'd better become a Muslim, then you can marry four girls."

He shook his head. "I'm a good Catholic."

"If you were a good Catholic then you wouldn't be sleeping with any of them before marriage."

"But that's impossible," he said, frowning as if that were a novel notion. "I can't be celibate. Life wouldn't be worth living."

"Youth is wasted on the young," I said, meeting Roscoe's eyes who'd been half listening to our conversation.

"They grow out of it soon enough," he commented and went back to answering emails.

A pretty girl appeared from the steps that led up from the beach. She was wearing a baggy pair of white shorts, a pink top and flip-flops. Her black Asian hair was cut in a bouffant bob, one side longer than the other and shaved at the back of her neck.

"Hi, there," she said in greeting and came to stand in front of Roscoe's counter. As she passed me, she gave me a warm smile and the scent of lilies curled into my nostrils. "I hope I'm not too late for the morning dive?" she said with an Americanised Filipino accent that indicated she came from a wealthy family who could afford to send their offspring overseas.

"You're just fine," Roscoe said cheerfully. "This is Bill, he's an old customer and won't mind waiting a bit while you kit up." He waggled his thumb at Rico to fetch another set of gear from the equipment room. "Bill, this is Michelle Arupe. She's been diving with us for a few days with her friends from Manila."

Michelle gave me a little wave by way of greeting. She looked more Chinese than Filipino with very light-brown skin. I watched as she walked to the bench, turned her back and stripped off her shorts and shirt, leaving her in a one-piece virgin white swimsuit. I admired her back and the firmness of her thighs as she took down her wetsuit, which was hanging on the peg above. She shucked into it, then glanced over her right shoulder at me and said: "Will you zip me up, Bill?"

"Gladly," was all I could manage to say. The fragrance of lilies assailed me again as I pulled the wetsuit zip to the top, then tucked the string down the back of her collar which was standard practice.

"Where are you from?" she asked, taking a Cressi Big Eyes mask from her peg.

"I'm English. But I've lived in Asia for over twenty years."

"What do you do?" she said as she busied herself with a small bottle of de-fogging liquid. She was obviously an experienced diver and went about her preparations diligently. Rico emerged from the back room with a BCD and an Aqualung Titan regulator set.

"I'm a security consultant. How about you?"

"I work in Marketing in Manila for an American company called Monsanto."

"And you're on holiday?"

"Kind of," she said and looked me straight in the face. There was an unasked question there, but it was too early for me to give, or her to expect, an answer.

"Boat's ready," Roscoe said.

The three of us picked up our fins and walked gingerly over the rocky sand, waded through the shallow water and pulled ourselves into the small dive *banca*. The boat-boy sitting in the stern would drive us the ten minutes out to the drop off point for the dive site.

18

We surfaced from the Canyons dive and paddled backwards to the *banca* where the boat-boy helped pull our BCDs and tanks up. We could then grab the gunwale and pull ourselves over it into the boat. It needed a bit of practice and sufficient strength in the arms, but Michelle had no issue with it.

"That was fast," she giggled and took off the cap she'd been wearing to hold her hair in place. At thirty metres huge shoals of fish had been feeding in the current. We'd dropped in nearly a mile early and then dive bombed along the reef until we got to the spot where we hung around for as long as our air permitted.

"You're an excellent diver," I complimented her. She laughed at that.

"You are not so bad yourself, Bill."

Rico said, "Bill goes to America and does cave diving there."

"Do you?" Michelle eyed me with a pinch of fascination. "That must be scary. Do you do deep technical diving as well?"

"I've done some here." The boat-boy was gunning the engine now heading us back towards Small Lalaguna.

"Where do you go in America for cave diving?" she asked.

"Suwannee County, it's a few hours south of Atlanta in North Florida. Did you study in America?"

She nodded. "At BC - Boston College."

"Did you study marketing?"

"No, I'm a chemist," she explained. "The company I work for does agro-biotechnology. Pest control and all the rest. If you do marketing they like you to understand the big words and how the product works."

I nodded. She sounded like she had her shit together.

"I've been back home for a year now," she said, "and sometimes I miss the States. Most of the time I don't. The Philippines is an amazing country but there are such extremes of wealth and poverty." She wore a sad expression and ducked as spray hit us. "If only our politicians weren't so corrupt then everybody could become wealthier."

We were back in the dive shop within ten minutes cleaning off our gear and hanging it up to dry. It was good practice to take a two-hour break between dives to allow the body to work off the accumulated nitrogen. The second and third dives would generally be shallower than the first dive.

"Are you going to do the dive at twelve?" I asked the girl.

She shook her head. "No, I'm going back to White Beach to wake up my friends. They were still fast asleep when I left."

"Another fast dive tomorrow morning?" I asked, running my towel down my legs to get them dry before I put my shorts back on. I didn't shower between dives.

"Maybe," she said with her warm smile. "Depends on how much we party tonight." She turned to button up her blouse. "Do you know where White Beach is?"

"Sure," I said. I'd told her on the way out to the dive site that I travelled alone and had a house up on the mountain.

"If you feel bored this evening why not come over and have a few drinks with us? We usually go bar-hopping after dinner. We'll be easy to find."

"I might just do that," I said. She gave a cheery wave good-bye to all of us and bounced off up the beach towards Sabang where she had left her rental scooter.

"Fine figure of a woman that," Roscoe said with deadpan Kiwi understatement. Compared to the Australians, New Zealanders considered themselves cultured.

"A bit bloody gorgeous in my considered opinion," I said.

"Her dad owned half of Ilocos Norte, the half that's not owned by the Marcos family," Roscoe commented.

"Owned?"

"Died a few years ago, I think. Her mother is still alive."

"I do love sexy and smart heiresses from shockingly rich families," I said wistfully.

"You know how the Philippines works," Roscoe said, noting something down on his clip board. "That sort of lady you're better off looking and not touching."

"You're not wrong there."

"She's invited you to have a drink with her," he said and glanced up from his paperwork.

"I can resist everything except temptation," I said. "I'm going to the 'Full Moon Bar' for a bite to eat. See you at twelve."

"How do you fancy the Alma Jane Wreck?" he asked. "I've got two Yanks who want to dive it."

"Sounds good to me."

Diving makes you hungry, so I sat in the restaurant next door and had a full English breakfast, although they'd run out of baked beans. That was the second time on this trip. I wondered if there was a national shortage. I was on my second cup of coffee when my phone rang. The number was withheld.

"Is that you, Bill?" Goodyear asked.

"Dickie. Glad to hear you're still alive," I replied.

"It was touch and go for a while. I had to get out of Angeles City faster than a speeding bullet."

"Where are you now?"

"Somewhere. I can't say."

"And you're OK?"

"Shoulder's getting better. Thank you for helping."

"It's what you do for old mates," I said. "Your friend Mikey Tomkins is dead."

"I know."

"The police tried to frame me for his murder," I said. "I found his body at your place."

"Those fucking bastards," he said.

"The Lapida Brothers?" I asked.

"Yeah. They were the ones who shot me that night."

"I've met them," I said.

"Bill me lad, did you get my stuff from my house?" he asked and there was an anxious note now in his voice.

"I did. I got the whole lot. It's all safe and sound. But I left it in Manila."

"You are a superstar. Need a job done, you can rely on Jedburgh."

"That's what some folks say about me," I said, smiling at the unintended irony. I checked my Suunto dive watch to see how much time I had before the next dive. Still plenty. Over in the distance some dark clouds were forming. It felt like the weather might be turning.

"Where are you now?" Goodyear asked. I hesitated for a moment but figured he was calling from a pay-as-you-go SIM card so it was unlikely anyone would be listening in to our call.

"I'm in PG. What took you so long to get in touch?"

"I'd run out of load on my phone and I had some other issues. Had to go and see someone. I'll explain it all to you when we meet."

"What do you want to do?" I asked.

"I'll be in touch. Now that I know you've got my money. I might come down and see you there. I've got a motorboat moored by the Yacht Club."

"Just let me know. I'll be here for a few more days."

"How much money was there?" he asked and there was the strain in his voice again.

"I didn't count it but I thought about $50,000. The Lapida Brothers told me it was theirs and were keen to find you."

"Fuck them," he said angrily at the other end of the line. "I earned that fair and square. Take care of it for me and I'll be in touch soon." Then he cut the line before I could ask any more questions. I stared at the screen of my phone. His number had been withheld so I couldn't even call or text him back if I wanted to. At least he was alive and he'd come and pick up his stuff sooner or later. Which meant I had to make the next call.

I took out a different phone from my rucksack and punched in the numbers I'd memorised. Larry Lim picked up after a few rings.

"Are you still in the Philippines?" I asked him.

"I am," he replied.

"Is the Old Man?"

"No, he's gone back to Sing."

"Any luck with the hard drive I gave you?" There was a longer pause than I liked from him then he said:

"It's encrypted. We got past the security password but the data is unreadable until we can crack the encryption, which is a mutating algorithm. There look to be a variety of different files on the hard drive: spreadsheets, documents and photographs as well. Someone has gone to a lot of bother to protect it. It doesn't seem like the sort of thing your friend might have done by himself. It's very advanced stuff."

"That's interesting," I said to myself just as much as to him.

"We're still working on decrypting it," he told me. "The guys think they should be able to figure it out in a day or two."

"I need the drive back soon. The rightful owner has turned up and so I will have to return it."

"What is this about, Bill?" Larry asked, his voice sharp now. Before I felt there was an evasiveness. I knew him far too well for him to be able to pull the wool over my ears.

"I don't know. This old buddy of mine got shot up, I suspect because of these files, so I want to know what the big deal is. He's surfaced again so I could ask him directly, but I have a feeling he won't tell me."

"Curiosity killed the cat," Larry warned me.

"That's a silly thing to say for someone in your job - an intelligence operative is professionally curious."

"I'll call you when we know what's on the hard drive and get it back to you. Where are you now?"

"Down in PG enjoying dancing with the mermaids," I said. "Oh, another thing. Can you give me everything you know on a girl called Michelle Arupe, apparently her father was a big shot in the Northern part of Luzon?"

"It will cost you," Larry said. "Is this personal or business?"

"Personal. I hope. I'll give you a ten percent discount on my next job."

"Fifteen," he said and I could hear the smirk in his voice.

"You drive a hard bargain Mr. Chinaman."

"You old racist."

"I'm not afraid to be called a racist. I happen to have a penis that a black man would envy."

"I have no idea why I am friends with you," Larry said with a chuckle.

"Because I take care of my friends. That is a rare quality in this day and age. I will need the hard drive back as soon as you can."

We cut the connection and I called for the bill and wandered over to the dive shop for my next session.

19

After the final three o'clock dive I washed off all the gear, hung it up to dry and then took Rico for a drink in the Full Moon Bar. He had a Tanduay and Coke while I nursed a San Miguel.

"I hate trigger fish," Rico said.

"She was gunning for you," I replied. "You know what they say, scuba diving is 98% total relaxation and 2% absolute terror."

Trigger fish were unbelievably aggressive when they were protecting their nest and would take a chunk out of any diver given half a chance. We'd disturbed one on the last shallow dive and Rico had to fin as hard as he could to save his skin.

Rico nodded and changed the subject. "How do you like that Scubapro you're diving with?"

"It's good, super smooth, but not as nice as the Apeks."

"They don't make the TX100 any more do they?"

I shrugged. "I haven't checked lately, but John Bennett had about thirty of them in his storeroom. He might sell you one."

He laughed sadly at that. "I can't afford it."

"Stick with the Titan for now. It's a great classic regulator. If you really want an Apeks, I'll see what I can do. I've got two in Thailand that I don't use much."

His face lit up at that. Made in Blackburn, Lancashire, Apeks were the pinnacle of technical excellence, representing everything that had been great and good about British design and manufacturing even if it was now part of the American Aqua Lung corporation.

I asked the girl to get him another Tanduay and Coke. When I was scuba diving I didn't drink much. Two or three beers were my limit. I finished my San Miguel and told him I'd see him in the morning and we'd decide on a dive site then.

My Kawasaki was where I'd left it. There was no dive bag on my back so I rode faster than in the morning. I got back to my house in less than half an hour, rolled the bike into the garage and let myself in. I filled the oversized bathtub and lay in the hot water luxuriating and feeling the work my body had done during the day. When the skin on my hands started to prune, I got out of the bath, put on a fresh pair of shorts and a T-shirt and went to sit on my veranda. I had several teak steamer chairs lined up facing the view. The steamer chair allowed you to stretch your legs and recline at the same time and was ideal for chilling out. I'd made myself a cup of tea and a ham and cheese sandwich.

From my chair I could look over the balustrade and had a 180 degree view: below me was jungle, on the far left Puerto Galera town, in the middle distance the blue sea and the dive sites and in the far distance the city of Batangas.

I must have nodded off for a few hours. By the time I opened my eyes it was dark and the lights twinkled below me in the valley. I could make out the lights around the pool from Paul and James' house next door.

The caretaker would be there getting things ready for their arrival in a few days' time.

It was shortly after eight in the evening. I decided to go down to White Beach, have a pizza and then go looking for Michelle Arupe and a bit of intellectual banter. I had no other expectations. As Roscoe had reminded me, a girl like that was danger on legs.

I played some old music on my CD player - Santana's Moonflower - while I shaved, splashed some Paco Rabanne over my cheeks, told my reflection that I was still as handsome as ever and then chose a collared burgundy linen shirt and white linen slacks that made me appear mildly patrician.

White Beach was the other side of Puerto Galera town and took me just over half an hour on my Kawasaki. I pulled it up on its stand next to a row of other bikes and scooters and unfurled the heavy chain that locked the front wheel. Always better safe than sorry.

A while later I found Michelle sitting with two other young people outside one of the bamboo bars. They had a bottle of Johnny Walker on the low table between them and a carafe of coke. She'd changed into a simple white cotton top and soft light blue brushed denim jeans. She was wearing light brown leather loafers. Two large diamond stud earrings sparkled like her eyes when she saw me.

"Hey, you made it," she said.

"I was bored and I was lonely," I said. She waved me to one of the available chairs.

"This is my friend Angelika," she indicated the girl who had long black hair, luscious lips and wore big, round glasses. "This is Lorenzo Pineda. He thinks he's an actor, but he read chemistry at university like I did. Now he works for Orica in Bataan, when he isn't partying with me. Angelika is in IT in Manila, but she used to work in England."

"She's probably been to England more recently than me then. I've been in Asia for twenty five years and I rarely go back. Where were you?"

"The Cotswolds, near Cheltenham. It was very beautiful."

"And very wet and cold." She nodded in agreement.

Michelle said, "This is the guy I was diving with this morning. He used to be in the Hong Kong Police. Isn't that right?"

"A long time ago now," I said. "I've been clean for years."

"Did you get to shoot anyone in the police?" Lorenzo wanted to know. The lad was handsome and obviously came from good stock.

"Not really. Everyone's so well behaved in Hong Kong. It's not like you see in the movies."

"I love shopping in Hong Kong and the food is so yummy," Angelika said. She had the same strong Americanised Filipino accent as Michelle while the lad's tones were more purely upper-class Manila.

"How do you guys know each other?" I asked.

"School, parents, ballet class, usual shit," Michelle said.

I turned to Lorenzo. "You good at ballet?"

"Are you kidding?" Angelika said. "He's like John Travolta on the dance floor."

"Do people still watch Saturday Night Fever?" I asked with astonishment.

"Pulp Fiction, dude," Lorenzo explained.

"Cool movie," I said and took the bottle of San Miguel from the waitress who'd brought it over from the bar. "Are you diving tomorrow?"

Michelle said, "I told them they should come on the morning dive with us."

Lorenzo shook his head. "It's too early, man."

"So you're not really here in PG for the scuba diving?" I suggested.

"Kind of. We're here on an intervention," the young man said and raised his eyebrows at Michelle who shook her head at him. "Michelle is our best buddy and she is feeling down and so we thought we'd take her away from Manila and just chill out for a couple of days."

I glanced over at Michelle. "I feel there is a story here but maybe it's not my business to ask."

She giggled. "It's nothing. They're just making it a bigger deal than it is."

I smiled and said no more. The beach was pristine white and from every bamboo bar shack, pop music could be heard. The tide was out and the dark sea melted into the star-lit sky.

"Michelle is having some relationship issues," Angelika explained into the gap in the conversation. "She disappeared for a week to sort them out and came back miserable. We decided to come down here to cheer her up."

"Ah-ha," I said.

"Not worth boring you with, Bill," Michelle said quickly and leaned forward to mix everyone another round of drinks from the whisky bottle.

"Better we don't talk about love," I suggested. "How about politics or religion?"

"I don't believe in God," Lorenzo said kicking the ball into play.

"Why not?" I asked.

"The world is so screwed up, how can there be a God?"

"The problem of evil. Always a difficult one to explain."

"Are you religious, Bill?" Angelika asked.

"I can't explain why the sun and the moon are so beautiful. Why flowers blossom and how nature can be so perfect when mankind is so fallible. Maybe there is an afterlife. I've not met anyone so far who's come back from it and warned me to cease my evil ways. Met plenty of evil people down here though."

"So you don't believe in God either?" Lorenzo said.

"I always felt that it was very brave to declare oneself an atheist. To categorically deny the existence of a superior form of being. It's a lot easier to be an agnostic. Just ignore the question and pretend it doesn't matter."

"You didn't answer my question," the young man challenged me with a friendly smile.

"I don't know the answer. So call me intellectually lazy. There might be a God. I just don't spend much time thinking about him."

"Have you ever seen a ghost?" Michelle asked.

"No."

"Have you seen a lot of dead people?" she asked.

"I've seen some," I lied.

"I've seen the ghost of my dead grandmother," Angelika commented, her eyes widely serious.

"Did she talk to you?" I asked.

"No, she just looked at me and held out her rosary, then vanished."

"Sounds like someone came back to remind you to lead a better life," I said.

"Do you think so?" she said earnestly.

Michelle laughed out loud. "You better stop having sex with your boyfriend. Your grandmother will come and watch you."

"That's so gross," Angelika told her friend.

Half an hour later we'd moved on to politics.

"The President stinks," Lorenzo said, slurring his words by now.

"That's the problem with our neo-colonial Spanish power structure," Michelle jumped in. "All the same wealthy people just take turns in raping our country."

I gave her a long look because she didn't seem to mind the irony that her family must be part of that system.

"What does your father do?" I asked Michelle.

For a second there was irritation in her eyes. "He's dead now. He was a senator," she conceded.

"Did you like you father?"

"I loved him. I admired him. But his business got him into trouble," she said. "When Marcos was deposed he discovered that friendship in politics is a fickle thing. That made me realise that we need to rely on our own efforts not our family connections." She swirled the ice around in her glass pensively.

"There's the problem of the Philippines. A fundamental dichotomy. You are torn between the traditions of the old world and the yearnings of the young and the bold."

Lorenzo leant forward held up his half empty glass of whisky and coke and pointed a finger at me. "You are very philosophical for an ex-cop."

"Benefits of a good education paid for by the army. I let most of it go to waste." I turned back to Michelle. "Do you consider yourself a socialist?"

"Not socialist. We believe in capitalism for the benefit of us all. We are nationalists. We believe that our country could be better. We have been holding ourselves back."

"So you admire the structures of democracy?"

"Of course," she said and her two friends nodded in agreement.

"Is the American system of democracy that great? There are millions of starving men and women who are on minimum wage and have no health care. There are countless billionaires who don't know what to do with their money and spend it on foolish trinkets."

Lorenzo said, "It's true. American democracy has not been that great. And we Filipinos always want to copy everything that is American. We fought so hard to get rid of the Spanish and then we let the Americans keep colonising us commercially." He reached over to the bottle of Johnny Walker and slopped a few inches into his glass without bothering with the Coke. "The Scandinavian systems of democracy are the ones to copy. They pay high taxes but have a great quality of life and everyone is equal."

I shrugged because I had a different view on that. "Asian countries must find their own style of democracy. Your cultures are used to strong, paternalistic government. You just need to find the right leaders who don't always fall into the trap of wanting to enrich themselves. Singapore has done well in that regard."

We talked for another half hour about different political systems and the challenges faced by the Philippines. It became more obvious that they were passionate, disgruntled and frustrated. But their hearts were in the right place. Eventually I got up and said it was time for me to get back home. I'd had five beers and needed a full night's sleep if I was to challenge myself properly on the next morning's dive. Michelle seemed disappointed. She stood up, put her hand on my shoulder with slightly more pressure than necessary and chastely pecked me on the cheek, smiling shyly. Normally I would have taken that as an opening, but I really just wanted to dive the following day. I figured there would be plenty of time for temptation in the future.

My bike was where I had left it and the night air was now brisk. I gunned the engine and the tyres squealed on the rough tarmac road. I rode fast through Puerto Galera town. Most people were in bed and the street lights were few and far between.

Ten minutes out of town I drove through one of the villages. I wasn't paying attention - my mind occupied by thoughts of the sultry Michelle - when a dark shape suddenly lunged at me from the side of the road. My instant reaction was to slam on the brakes. But my reflexes were slow and they were wrong. My hand tightened on the front brake instead of both brakes simultaneously. The front wheel locked and I went flying over the handle bars into the middle of the road. My arms helped cushion me but my head still hit the ground hard.

20

It had been a dog. A big black stray dog who'd come bounding out of the darkness from behind one of the huts on the side of the road. He'd run off with a loud yelp as my bike had tumbled over itself.

I picked myself up from the road. My right arm felt heavily bruised and it hurt when I tried to rotate the wrist. My head rang from the concussion. Thankfully my Hightail helmet had taken the brunt of the blow.

As I picked up the fallen bike and checked it in the moonlight for mechanical damage, I delivered a torrent of swearwords. Mostly I just repeated two, over and over again.

The bike was fine. It was designed to take regular beatings. Nobody rode muddy country trails without losing traction frequently, slipping, sliding and banging into trees. The engine came to life immediately and I gingerly completed the journey home. The steep section of the mountain was the toughest bit because there was a searing pain in my right wrist and forearm as I turned the throttle.

I took a long hot shower. I took some painkillers. I examined every part of my body and found only bruises and abrasions on the exposed skin. I cursed my stupidity some more and went to bed.

The next morning I felt marginally better but I knew I'd have to let a doctor take a look at my right arm. It was either heavily bruised or something was broken. My head throbbed and, having been concussed many times in the past, I knew that it would take time to go away. It was probably a good idea to make sure I hadn't fractured my skull.

I called Roscoe and told him what had happened and that I would not be diving today.

"Was the motorbike very drunk?" he asked kindly.

"Not drunk at all."

"Was there a woman involved?"

"I was coming back from White Beach."

"Was there a certain lady diver involved?" he asked with a chuckle

"No, just me being stupid. Not paying attention. I'm going to see a Doc and then take it easy."

I rode gently down to the medical centre and had myself checked over. If you really had a medical problem the nearest hospital was over the water in Batangas. They didn't even have a defribrillator in PG, let alone a hyperbaric chamber if you got a decompression hit while scuba diving.

The medic reckoned I'd escaped with a mild concussion and the X-rays showed no broken bones. He handed me a baggy of drugs and reminded me not to drink and drive. Drunken tourists were obviously a large part of their regular business.

Roscoe had told me the next typhoon was coming and there would be no diving for the foreseeable future until it had passed by. You roll with the punches, as the man said. When I got back to my blue house Josef's pickup truck was out the front and he'd used his spare keys to let himself in and park himself on one of my steamer chairs. Sitting next to him drinking a can of Sprite was Larry Lim wearing a pair of khaki shorts and matching shirt.

"Look what the cat dragged in," I said and went to get myself a Sprite from the fridge.

"There is this rumour going around town," Josef said, "that you were so drunk last night you fell off your motorbike and can't go diving."

"Don't you just hate village life where everyone knows each other's business," I said light-heartedly. He must have been talking to Roscoe.

"I met this man on the pier," Josef explained, jerking his thumb at Larry, "who said he was a friend of yours and I called Roscoe to check on your whereabouts before I brought him up here."

"And what are you doing here, you smug Singaporean?" I asked Larry.

"Returning some property that you left with me by mistake," he said. I'd suspected as much but hadn't expected him to come all the way down here, simply leave the hard drive in the safe at the Shangri-La in Manila. I could have then directed Goodyear to pick it up from the concierge.

"That's nice of you. Did you bring your scuba gear?"

He shook his head. "You can buy me lunch and then I need to head back to the big city."

With Josef still there the conversation veered off into other directions. I didn't want to ask Larry why it was so important for him to personally come and see me until the two of us were alone. We talked about the direction and strength of the typhoon and some issues Josef was having with the water supply to the mountain. Nothing that a small donation to the tennis club couldn't fix, but it was irritating his punctilious Swiss soul.

"So what did the doctor say?" Larry asked.

"I was attacked by a vicious dog. The Hound of the Dulangan Barangay."

"Really?"

"No, I'm just making that bit up. My arm's bruised but apparently nothing's broken."

Josef left after finishing his San Miguel. I got Larry another Sprite and asked him what was up. He reached down into the rucksack that was on the floor.

"The hard drive," he said and handed me the canvas bag I had given him at the Shangri-La.

"That's a long way to come. You could have posted them or left them for me in Manila," I pointed out.

"Have you ever used the Philippines' postal service?" he asked me with a raised eye brown. "Explain precisely, not leaving out any small detail, how you came into the possession of this hard drive."

"It's like that is it?" I said.

"You tell me the story and I'll tell you what's on them."

I considered for a few seconds. There was nothing to hide from Larry or his boss. They knew all of my secrets, even the clean ones. So I recounted the entire story of what had happened in Angeles City, right up to Dickie Goodyear re-surfacing on the phone the day before.

"What's on them? I assume from your behaviour that it's not just drug dealing accounts and customer lists?"

Larry moved his head from side to side to indicate an element of prevarication. "Some of that is on there. Lists of customers, some well-known, some not. Details of shipments of Ecstasy, fake alcohol, cigarettes, standard smuggling stuff."

"Accounts?"

"Yes, those as well. He and his business partners were making a living but not hitting the big time."

"But none of that is the reason you've come all the way down here to have a chat with me?"

"Correct," he said with a funny smile. "You've stumbled across something very interesting here and we need you to give the hard drive back to Goodyear as soon as he turns up."

"That's it? That's all you want me to do?"

"For the moment, yes."

"What about the other thing? The Ranger Colonel you want me to take out?"

"That project is still on-going. We haven't finalised timings and we are waiting for some other information."

"So what's on the fucking hard drive, Larry?"

He gave me a conspiratorial look, leant forward - as if anyone could possibly hear us at the top of my mountain - and told me what they had found.

Sometime later Larry sat on the back of the Kawasaki and we rode down for a bite to eat in Tabinay. It wasn't great but we sat looking out over the beach trying to ignore what he had told me earlier and shot the breeze. Then I took him back into town and put him on the next ferry back to Batangas. He had a car waiting for him there.

The sky was overcast and you could sense something threatening in the air. Everyone was scurrying around getting ready for the next big wind. No-one expected a typhoon to hit us directly, but they regularly came skipping down the channel picking up speed. They were like a fat man late for a wedding who would knock over your wine glass as he rushed by your table, his coat tails flapping.

The locals were used to that. It was the Philippines. Houses would lose their roofs and there would be injuries from flying debris. In Hong Kong they closed the city down. Everyone stayed at home for 24 hours, played *mah jong* and got drunk. Then it was over. The buildings and windows were designed to handle the onslaught. Not so in the Philippines where many buildings had flimsy tin roofs, even if the walls were usually made of cement.

I bought several days' supply of eggs, bread, beer, pasta and minced beef, slung the rucksack on my back and returned home. I went around the back of the house to check the generator and topped up the petrol tank. Since the electricity often went down even on a normal sunny day, most houses that could afford it had a back-up generator. You needed the electricity to power your air con or your ceiling fans. Until I could crank up the generator, I placed candles around the living room, bathroom and bedroom and fitted a new battery into my Maglite torch.

All my windows had steel shutters that could be drawn down in case the winds became too strong, but I liked to sit on the veranda during a storm and to dare the vaunt-couriers of oak-cleaving thunderbolts to singe my head.

Watch the all-shaking thunder smite flat the thick rotundity of the world. Blow winds and crack your cheeks. I was ready for cataracts and hurricanes, which were just what they called typhoons in the Atlantic. Although we'd feel it more up on the exposed hill-top than down in the valley, as long as you had enough beer in the house, and no wicked daughters, it was all bearable.

I read my book for an hour and supped on a San Miguel. It was late afternoon and by now there were gusts of wind and spats of rain. My arm and my head ached but not unduly as long as I didn't move around too much.

It was dark outside now and I had finished my third beer, so I went inside and located a special box that I kept under my bed. My humidor was largely stocked with Cubans and Dominicans but I was in the mood for an Alhambra, a light, mild and sweet Filipino cigar. The Spaniards had brought cigar manufacturing to the country in the 16th Century and its small output was wildly underrated.

I opened a bottle of Armagnac from the drinks cupboard and fired up the tobacco while nature commenced its overture. The typhoon would be closest in the late morning so the night should not be too wild.

At about 10 p.m. the lights went out everywhere. The main electricity plant in Calapan must have gone down. Looking out from the veranda into the valley, all I could see was darkness. My ears filled with the howl of what in another age might have been considered evil spirits crying for attention. I lit a few candles, had another Armagnac, finished off my cigar and went to bed.

21

The typhoon raged around the house for all of the next day. I did nothing except eat, drink and read. The house creaked and shuddered but I had confidence in her. Josef had supervised the builders carefully and everything was sturdy.

Sitting on my veranda I had an omelette for lunch. At this distance the sea appeared calm but I knew the waves would be several metres high and only a madman would be out on a boat. Nothing moved. Everyone was at home. And if your roof was made of flimsy tin then you crouched in the back room and told the beads on your rosary.

The following morning all was serenely calm. The big wind had passed by and life could resume as normal, once the clearing up was done.

It was as I was walking around the house inspecting the walls and the roof for any damage that my phone rang. The electricity was still not working but the GSM masts that relayed the cell phone network had clearly held up.

Dickie Goodyear was at the end of the line. "I'm coming over to PG as soon as I can get a boat," he informed me.

"I've got your hard drive," I said, "but your money is in Manila in a bank. If you need it in Puerto Galera I'll have to make arrangements. We've had the typhoon here, so things are going to take a few days to get back to normal.

"That's fine," he said languidly, "provided you can spot me enough cash to get by for a few days. We'll talk about it when we meet."

"I'm at my house outside of town," I said, "but I can ride down anytime. Where do you want to meet?"

"Let's meet at the Yacht Club, if it's open by then. We can go out to my boat," he suggested. "I'm planning to take her over to Hong Kong. You can wire me the rest of the money." That made sense. No exit formalities and he could use his real passport or his Hong Kong ID at the other end, collecting the money in Hong Kong Dollars as he passed go. It was around 650 nautical miles and would take him three or four days in his motor yacht. It was a long enough journey to make alone so I suspected he had company. I wondered who that might be. Dickie had some other partners in his venture that I hadn't encountered yet.

"I can be there around lunchtime," I said.

"I'll call you when I'm on the way."

It wasn't until after two that he called. I got the bike out and rode down. The road was covered in fallen trees and the overall impression was as if a bomb had hit. Everyone I passed was cheerfully clearing up. If nobody in your family had been killed it was a blessing.

"You owe me a beer," I said to Goodyear as I came up the wooden staircase into the restaurant area of the Yacht Club. There were a dozen tables covered in red and white check table cloths. Dickie was perched on a stool at a teak bar which ran along one end of the room, staring at his mobile phone.

It was a pleasant wooden structure located on the Southern end of Muelle Bay. They had thirty or so guest moorings and the membership was mostly the great and the good from the expat community. Because it was located in the natural typhoon shelter of the bay it was now recognised as a hub for all cruising routes in and out of the West Pacific. They had reciprocal arrangements with other yacht clubs around the Asian region and beyond, including the Royal Hong Kong Yacht Club, which organised an annual race between the two ports. If you were cruising along and wanted to stop off for a few days, you'd contact the club on its VHF frequency, Marine Channel 68, and ask for a berth.

I slipped onto the stool next to Goodyear. His arm was in a sling and he favoured it as he turned, wincing as some pain shot through him. This man was sailing nowhere without some help.

"They patched you up okay then?"

He nodded. "The hospital were great. And you did great getting me there. I didn't know who else to trust. I haven't been shot since the time that PLA bastard opened up on us with his AK-47 in Sham Shui Po."

"That's right. You took a round, didn't you?"

"And BJ took his head off."

"Well deserved decapitation. Commissioner said so himself."

"Seems a long time ago, doesn't it, brother?"

"It was a long time ago," I said and took the San Miguel bottle from the barman, wiping the neck carefully as I always did.

"So I've got myself into a bit of trouble," Goodyear said.

"You have, with the nastiest of people."

"Fuck them." His face turned angry and ugly. "They are just small time gangsters. If I hadn't needed money in a hurry, I wouldn't have made the mistake of going into business with them."

"And why did you need the money?"

He looked as if he was debating whether to tell me, but in the end he simply said: "Women. 'Can't live without them, can't legally kill them' as a friend of mine was fond of saying."

"Lillibet's dead," I said.

"Who?"

"I found her in your house. She said she was your girlfriend."

"Fuck me," he said. "She was playing you. Sure, I screwed her from time to time. She hung around the Lapidas and turned tricks for them. Please tell me you didn't mention the hard drive to her?"

"I told her nothing, except where to get off," I said. He looked at me admiringly.

"You always were a good judge of women," he said.

"Hardly," I said, and I meant it. I was attracted to beautiful women who ended up, generally, trying to kill me or take me for a ride. There had been one who might have changed me, but she had ended up dead at the bottom of the South China Sea when her plane exploded.

"So which Lapida brother shot off part of your shoulder?"

"It was Alvin, the one who's half blind," he said, chuckling. "That's why he can't shoot. He was aiming for my foot."

I couldn't help but laugh at that one and Goodyear smiled ruefully.

"Yeah, fucking crazy, isn't it?"

"Were you selling them drugs?" I paused and I could see him hesitating, so I added: "You know I don't care. We're not coppers any more and we all have to earn our living in some way or other."

"Mikey Tomkins and I had plugged into a mainland guy in Hong Kong who offered us a great deal on regular shipments of MDMA. They were making them in Zhongshan or somewhere. Seemed too good an opportunity to pass up. We'd just been doing bootleg liquor and fags up to that point, but I had a temporary liquidity issue and this solved the problem."

"So you picked up somewhere in Hong Kong and then sailed over to here? Loaded the stuff onto your pickup truck in Batangas and motored back to Angeles?"

He laughed ruefully. "That's right. You could be a detective if you worked hard at it. We moored up at Hebe Haven Yacht Club and then we'd do the run over here. Once or twice a month."

"So where did it go wrong with the Lapida Brothers?"

"It's complicated. I guess they got greedy and we got sloppy. It happens in business." There was something else he wasn't telling me. You didn't have to be a detective to smell that the fish in this tale was mildly putrid.

"So just a falling out amongst business partners?" I wasn't going to push it if he wasn't prepared to tell me. Patience and persistence were good traits in a copper, even a former one.

"Yeah, that kind of thing. You want another beer?" I shook my head and he ordered himself another one. He was drinking the Light version which to my palate tasted like urine spiced up with too much saccharine.

"What's the plan now?" I asked him.

"Empty a couple of safety deposit boxes in Hong Kong then cut loose and take the boat down to Indonesia. Maybe further."

"That's a long way to sail by yourself," I observed.

"Maybe not by myself." He smiled, carnally.

"Well good luck. If you give me a bank account number I'll transfer the $50,000 over as soon as I get back to Manila."

Goodyear snapped his fingers at the barman and asked him for a pen and a slip of paper. Once he got them he wrote a string of numbers and letters on a piece of paper. "IBAN number. Bank is in Singapore." He passed it over to me. I recognised the code for LGT - the private bank owned by the princely House of Liechtenstein. They had a big operation in Singapore. Much of their work had originally been about shifting money out of Hong Kong, Jakarta and Manila, then lately - as the American tax authorities became more rabid - out of central Europe where wealthy Yanks and buccaneers like me had been parking their ill-gotten gains since Rockefeller's time.

"Will you take a ten percent commission?" he asked.

"I will do no such thing," I said. "Consider it a favour for a mate, do the same for me sometime." I reached down into my rucksack and extracted the canvas bag that contained the hard drive. He looked inside and nodded. I'd included an envelope containing $5,000 US which came from my safe at the *Casa Azul*.

He nodded in appreciation.

"That's the real loot isn't it, the hard drive?" I asked.

"Not just a pretty face, are you, Jedburgh?" he said.

"Not even that," I said. "What's so special about the contents? I took a quick look but the drive was password protected." For a brief moment he looked concerned that I'd cracked his password and knew what it contained, but then he reminded himself that it would take some serious computer knowledge to get into the data.

"It's my big pay day. You don't want to know the details, trust me. I'm going to sell the information on here for a shitload of cash and run for the hills."

"Blackmail?" I suggested, with one eyebrow raised. Two men had appeared at the top of the stairs and went to sit at the far corner table. I recognised one of them as the Commodore of the Yacht Club and the other was the Chief of Police, whose name was Atienza. The Commodore nodded at us in friendly recognition.

Goodyear snorted in derision. "I wouldn't call it blackmail. It's more like finders-keepers losers-weepers."

"I don't understand."

"It's simply some information that came into my possession from an individual who had come across it accidentally. I'm just selling it back to the owner who is very keen to have it returned."

"I see. So not blackmail. But presumably you will accidentally let it fall into the wrong hands unless he pays you a very large amount of money?"

He shook his good shoulder off-handedly. "He'd be well-advised to pay, given what is on here. I'm only asking for half a million."

"Pesos?"

"Real money. American dollars."

"That's half a million reasons for people to come after you. Watch your back and keep a round in the breech. You've got some guns on the boat?"

He nodded. "You're a good mate, Jedburgh."

"I tell you something," I said, meaning it. "If that hard drive is worth half a million dollars, I really don't want to know what's on it."

"It's way outside of our league," he admitted. "But this is my big pay day. I'm not asking for anything unreasonable. When he does the deal I'm full throttle on the boat out of the PI."

The barman brought us another round of San Miguel and the pisswater Goodyear was drinking. "Are you sure, Dickie," I said, "that's not the real reason the Lapida Brothers are gunning for you - they know you've got this information?"

He shifted uncomfortably on his stool and massaged his shoulder. "What makes you say that?"

I said, "My old copper's nose."

He laughed. "You were always a shit copper. The only thing you were good at was slotting people without batting an eyelid."

"I've no idea what you are talking about."

"That's what you should do for a living. Not farting about helping people with their health and safety policies." He suddenly warmed to the subject. "There's a guy out there somewhere, they call him the Reliable Man, he's one of the most successful professional hitmen in the world. You need someone taking out, you call up the Reliable Man and the next day, bang, bang, the job's done. They say he charges a quarter of a million US dollars a hit." He gave a gleeful laugh. "That's what you should be doing."

I shook my head gently "Nah, I'm doing okay. Don't need a career change."

Goodyear waggled a finger at me. "You should give it some serious consideration. You were always good at that. Fuck me, didn't you win a prize at Bisley when you were a youngster?"

"I did."

He gave another laugh and then we changed the subject and talked about some other people we'd known. We ate lunch and he paid for it.

"Thanks again for this," he said and held up the bag with his loot. I watched as he went down the stairs and took the tender out to his boat, which was a handsome sixty-footer moored nearby. He boarded his boat and gave me a cheerful wave then went downstairs. I was just turning back to finish my coffee when the boat exploded, throwing debris in all directions. The shockwave reached us at the club and my ears went pop. The Commodore and Chief of Police had hit the deck fearing there were more explosions to come, but there was just the one.

I came out of my crouch and watched the bow of Goodyear's yacht vanish beneath the waves to join the Spanish galleons that had found their final resting place there.

22

The Chief of Police knew me, so when a team of his men descended on the yacht club all I had to do was give a witness statement and within two hours I was on my way back home.

I told them that Dickie Goodyear had been having a business dispute with some people in Angeles City and they'd already tried to kill him once. Blowing up his boat, which was known to be moored in Puerto Galera, seemed a likely escalation of the feud. That made a lot of sense to the local coppers. They weren't looking at me as a suspect and in any case knew where to find me if they wanted to follow up their investigations.

There wasn't much to investigate. The yacht was in bits on the bottom of the ocean somewhere between 40 and 50 metres below. They were already on the phone to John Bennett asking him to put a team of divers together to bring up any evidence from the wreck. There wouldn't be anything of Goodyear left. The instructor in me realised that at that depth, Dickie's yacht might become a new attraction for deep diver training. The oxygen in compressed air becomes toxic at about 56 metres so if you liked pushing yourself, and were fit enough, you could dive to a depth of 50 metres on air, but you couldn't stay long without decompressing for hours at shallower depths. Ideally you dived that depth with mixed gases - you reduced the amount of oxygen in your tank by adding argon. That's what technical diving was all about.

I wasn't going to dive on that site. I had a pretty good idea that it was the Lapida Brothers who had arranged for a bomb to be fitted on Goodyear's yacht in case he turned up in PG planning to scarper. The Seagate hard drive would be in little fragments spread wide around Davy Jones Locker and the information that was on it slept with the fishes. You couldn't buy back what no longer existed. The Lapida Brothers would kill for a few thousand pesos and this was a much bigger craps game in which Goodyear had stepped up to roll his dice.

I saluted the old scoundrel, a silent farewell, wishing him success on the other side of the River Styx, then got on my bike and rode back to my mountain.

As I went past the third house in our development a tall, white-haired Scandinavian man in his sixties, waved to me. I slowed the Kawasaki down, pulling up next to him.

"Bill, I heard that you were here," Goran said. His English was perfect of course but each syllable informed you that this man was Swedish. He was a diplomat who had spent most of his career working in his country's embassies around Asia. His final posting had been as Deputy Ambassador in Manila. He'd built himself a house much more opulent than mine because he and his wife spent half the year here. She was German, so they spent the other half in an apartment overlooking the Alster Lake in Hamburg.

We exchanged pleasantries and he invited me over for dinner later that evening. I'd made up my mind that I wasn't going to dive tomorrow either. My head still ached from the concussion and a searing pain shot up my wrist whenever I twisted the throttle, so I'd decided to head back to Manila. Senator Guzman's granddaughter's wedding was planned for the weekend and I had promised to be there as a matter of courtesy and honour. I would come back to PG when I was in better shape.

Back on my veranda with a beer, I sat and pondered what had happened to Goodyear and what he'd told me. After a while I rang Larry and updated him on the unexpected developments. He didn't seem put out that the hard drive had exploded along with Dickie Goodyear. I assumed that was because SID had a backup of all the information on it.

Sometime later my second phone rang. It was Senator Guzman.

"Have you finished your diving for today?" he asked me. "Or is the weather still too bad?"

"I wasn't diving today but the typhoon has moved on."

"I am calling to remind you of our big celebration. Can you be in Manila tomorrow evening? I am having a select dinner party and I wish you to join us."

"It will be my pleasure," I said.

"I have booked you a room in the Manila Hotel on the Executive Floor."

It would have made me more comfortable to stay in a hotel of my own choosing but the way he said it the message was clear. He wanted me in the hotel, close at hand for whatever ulterior motives he might be harbouring. I assumed he wanted to introduce me to some of the other principals that I would be watching over during the big party.

I packed my stuff and arranged things around the house for the next hour, called Rannie and made the private *banca* arrangements for the next day. Then I got dressed for dinner. Slacks and a Polo shirt were all that was expected.

Goran and his wife were charming and the most gracious of hosts. Scandinavians fascinated me. How could the descendants of Vikings, who had criss-crossed the North Sea raping and pillaging, all turn out to be so utterly pleasant? Their womenfolk, also, were invariably competent, confident and elegant.

By 9 p.m. both Goran and I had drunk too much beer. To be fair we'd started off on Absolut vodka - I suspected he got it at discounted rates through his former colleagues at the embassy – followed by a dozen bottles of Tuborg beer that a Danish pilot friend of his had imported without a licence. These disappeared rapidly as Ilse, his wife, served us a thinly-sliced schnitzel of breaded pork with a lively salad and fried potatoes. For dessert she produced *Rote Grütze,* a Northern German delicacy cooked from red summer berries and served with milk and vanilla sauce. Then Goran brought out a bottle of O.P. Anderson aquavit.

"Well," he said in his sing-song accent, "you said you are not diving tomorrow. You can sleep in the car with a hangover."

I looked at his wife, who was sipping a cup of herbal tea as she watched her husband and me try to drink each other under the table. An enigmatic smile played around her lips.

"Ilse," I said, slurring my words slightly, "the food was marvellous as always."

"You don't eat properly," Goran said. "When you don't have a regular woman, then you never eat properly."

I laughed at that.

"Just one little glass more," he said and refilled them both with the aromatic liquor.

"So you have been invited to Senator Guzman's granddaughter's wedding?" he said, fixing me with an eye that was much clearer than mine felt at that moment. "Is she pretty?"

"I haven't met her," I said, passing the shot glass under my nose sniffing it like a cat does.

"You did some security work for the Senator, didn't you?" We were sitting at a long oak table next to his pool. His veranda was about twenty metres deep and they had a similar view to mine, although from a different angle.

"He's an interesting man," I said.

"You know what they are saying about him?" Goran asked. His manner was unassuming but I knew that a man did not become a Deputy Ambassador without being sharp as a whip. And that did not stop when you hung up the ceremonial sash and took up the state pension.

I shrugged. "What are they saying about him?"

"He is organising a military coup and it is happening soon. There are a lot of disgruntled senior politicians. They are not happy with the President and the way her husband has been carrying on." Goran watched me carefully. He was not simply making after-dinner conversation. He was curious what my reaction might be and if I had a role in this political drama as I had in Guzman's last attempt to become President. I drank the sharp alcohol in two quick flicks and it set my gullet on fire - in a pleasant way. I reached for a glass of water.

"I have no idea what Senator Guzman wants from me," I said, answering his unasked question. "I assumed he wanted someone competent and independent that he could trust in case something happened at the wedding." I gave a careless chuckle. "He hasn't asked me to help him with any military coup or to topple the government."

"You are trying to make light of this, Bill, my friend," the white-haired Swede said. He reached for the bottle of aquavit and I rolled my eyes. "Guzman is more dangerous than you imagine. You know this country as well as I do. It is a game of musical chairs. Everyone takes their turn. It is the same twenty-three families who make the music stop, jumping on the chairs, rewarding their circles of patronage with appointments and opportunities to further enrich themselves."

"The young are dreaming of change."

"The young also want to become rich. They see their path to wealth blocked by their elders. This group of plotters is exploiting that. They are calling themselves the new *Katipuneros*, a term that harks back to Spanish colonial times. Supreme and Venerable Association of the Children of the Nation."

"*Noli me tangere*," I quoted.

"You know your history," he nodded in approval. "The time of Jose Rizal, one of the great heroes of Philippine nationalism."

"You are exceedingly well informed," I said, "for a retired fellow who lives on a mountain in the provinces."

"It's not only the Singaporeans that have an intelligence service, Bill," he said. I looked at him open-mouthed. "I recognised your visitor yesterday. Part of my responsibilities at the embassy included working with KSI, our equivalent of the SID. Be careful of this Guzman, Bill. We are friends and I know you can take care of yourself. But all this could blow up in the next few weeks and bullets might fly again."

I nodded gravely and sipped from my glass of water. He'd be pushing another shot glass of aquavit on me. Nobody could outdrink a Swede except another Swede. Scandinavians made lovely drunks. They got mellower and mellower until they just subsided into unconsciousness. Unlike the Anglo-Saxons who became aggressive.

"They are mostly young army officers that are involved in this plot," he went on. "A few old disgruntled statesmen who want to be back in the limelight. But Senator Guzman is pulling all of their strings. He is hungry to become President and will use the idealism of the young to force change. To break the status quo."

"He's a clever man, I can vouch for that," I said. Ilse had gone off to supervise the maid in the kitchen and Goran was reaching for the bottle again. I waggled my finger at him. No more for me.

"If you like him," Goran said, "and if he likes you, perhaps you could find yourself working out of Malacanang Palace soon?" He'd framed it as a question.

I shook my head. "I have no ambitions in that direction. I'm terrible at working in hierarchical structures. If anyone asks you about me, you can tell them that."

Goran nodded. He understand what I was saying and I appreciated what he'd been telling me.

It took me about ten minutes to walk back to my house. It had taken less coming over because I'd been sober and it wasn't entirely dark yet at that time. I bumbled cautiously up Josef's fine tarmac road.

As I reached the turning to my pretty blue house - which was just a squat shadow in the nocturnal gloom - I could see torch light flickering through my living room.

23

The Lapida Brothers or one of their minions, was my first thought. I felt the adrenalin kick into my system and start to clear my head.

I walked delicately across my front lawn. It was all in shadow. Someone was definitely inside my house, flicking a torch around, searching for something. It felt clumsy. They should have closed the curtains or used a torch with a dim red light. Red Sox and Dodgers had not impressed me with their professionalism. If they had been the A team then it wasn't surprising. This was either the B team or a local contractor who'd been engaged to place the bomb on Dickie Goodyear's boat and perhaps take me out at the same time.

The back door led into the kitchen. It was made of steel but painted to look like wood. Behind me there was a hut in which the generator lived and gardening equipment was kept there as well. I toyed with the idea of getting a shovel as a weapon but decided to use the kitchen knives that were in a wooden stand just right of the door.

There might be more than one intruder and they could be armed but I'd have to face up to that. There was a handgun in a hidden safe in the guest bedroom but I was unlikely to be able to reach it without making my presence known. I made a mental note to stash some weapons outside the house in future.

I slotted the Yale key into the lock and turned it. I'd oiled the hinges on the back door before the arrival of the typhoon so it opened quietly. I let my right hand touch the kitchen counter, found the knife stand but no knives in it. I must have left them in the dishwasher.

There was nobody in the living room now. The torch light was flickering in my bedroom. I wondered how they'd managed to get in. To get to my gun safe, tap in the combination, turn the key and reach the Glock which I kept there would make too much noise, I concluded. I had to confront the intruder and rely on the element of surprise.

Before I could take any more steps towards the bedroom, a man came out from it. He was dressed in black clothes, holding a bag in one hand and a small torch in the other. The moment the light from his torch played across the Spanish-tiled floor and came to rest on me, he froze and dropped the bag at his feet. I couldn't see his face clearly, but his features were Asian.

"Shit," he said. Obviously he hadn't been expecting me back home. There was no other noise or movement from the bedrooms so it seemed that it was just him. The hand that had held the bag reached behind him and the black shape of a semi-automatic pistol jumped into his hand. I'd been expecting this and was on him by the time he pulled the gun from his waistband. The swipe from my left hand sent the gun flying towards the far corner of the room. My right fist connected with his face as my left hand drew back ready for the next punch.

But then he surprised me. He staggered back but recovered quickly. He fell into a fighting stance and dropped the torch which clattered on the floor and still cast some light on the proceedings.

I had a better idea. I stepped sideways and flicked the light switches by the bathroom door. The four lights hanging from the ceiling came instantly to life and the room was now bright as day.

The intruder blinked rapidly, trying to adjust to the sudden assault on his eyes. Now I could see his face. He was a Filipino in his forties. He was slight but appeared in good shape. He was a stranger to me. What impressed me was that he remained in a fighting stance: left leg forward, the right leg slightly bent, taking most of the weight, the left arm up protecting his face, the right arm pulled back. His hands were loosely curled, not bunched in fists.

There was something about the way his feet were positioned that told me he was a practitioner of the Filipino fighting style of *Suntukan*. I'd seen bouts on the local TV channels but never knowingly fought anyone using this style. I knew that it was a practical street fighting system that consisted of upper-body striking techniques such as punches, elbows and head-butts. It emphasised speed in striking, with the intent of overwhelming the adversary with a flurry of attacks which was not dissimilar to my own style of Kung Fu.

Could my *Wing Chun* stand up to what they called 'dirty boxing' in Tagalog? I didn't wait for him but launched a series of punches at his face and chest with my fists held vertically.

He was good.

He blocked all of my punches with his arms, shifting his body weight only slightly.

I was in horse stance. Next I tried finger jabs to his face. I managed to find a gap by pushing his right forearm aside and got close to his eyes but not close enough to wound. I switched suddenly to a palm strike but he ducked around that. I'd been on the offensive but now he came back at me.

What I couldn't understand was why he wasn't using any kicks. I was just testing him with my punches but now I flicked a low kick at his groin. He raised his leg and our shins collided. It was always painful when that happened which was why my *sifu* had made us kick and leg block until our legs were uniformly blue with bruises.

In the bright lights of my living room we fought each other for what felt like ten minutes. The intruder blocked my punches, all of my kicks. I managed to block all of his punches and he didn't kick. His style of street fighting didn't use legs. I assumed he could deploy elbows and arm traps but so far he hadn't. Then he caught me by surprise with a trip. It was very much like a *Ju Jutsu* technique, the reaping that swept your feet from under you. I nearly escaped with a skip but lost my balance.

I would have been done for if I hadn't let myself roll out of it, slapping the ground hard with the palm of my hand. When I came back to my feet he was closer to the kitchen door which I had not closed properly. He'd noticed it and I realised that he was planning to run.

I put up both my hands and shouted: "Stop, who sent you?"

My intruder simply grunted. He shook his head and bounded for the door, pulling it open and then disappearing into the night. I was out of breath from the fight, the adrenaline pounded around my system. My limbs ached from the brutal roll call of blows. I saw him silhouetted in the moonlight, his legs and arms pumping as he ran as fast as he could. I decided not to chase after him.

After recovering my breath for a few minutes, hands on thighs, I locked the kitchen door and went over to the bag he'd dropped. Inside were the usual tools of a burglar's trade: a bundle of picks, a hammer, a chisel, screwdrivers and black masking tape.

Whatever he'd been looking for, there was not much he had found. I kept a wad of pesos in the bedside drawer in case I entertained a young lady and she needed some taxi money to get home. He'd stolen that and I took it from the bag. He'd found the Rolex GMT-Master that I kept in the same bedside drawer when I was diving and wore my Suunto Dive Computer instead. Losing that would have upset me. I snapped the Swiss chronometer onto my right wrist.

"You're staying with me, baby," I whispered.

Had he been just an opportunistic burglar or had the man been sent to go through my belongings? I was fifty-fifty on that one. Either was possible.

Walking back into the living room I picked up the gun he'd dropped. It was a Beretta M9 semi-automatic, the standard service pistol of the United States Armed Forces since the early 1990s. It was black and although scuffed, seemed in reasonable condition. Some soldier would have been offered good money for this piece in a pawn shop. How could a common or garden burglar afford a weapon like this? But then, how come this burglar could fight so well? I was rarely bested in a *mano-mano* hand-to-hand fight.

I made sure all the windows and doors were secure, having come to the conclusion that he had entered through the same kitchen back door that he had used for his exit. I shot the heavy bolt on the inside, went to have a shower, scrubbed the irritation out of my hair, took some painkillers and fell into a deep, dreamless sleep with my new Beretta M9 lying on the bedside table. Finders-keepers, as my deceased friend Dickie Goodyear had told me only that morning.

24

We reached the city by late afternoon, having sat in traffic longer than expected. One of these days I was going to have to invest in a helicopter.

"This is a fancy one," Rannie commented as he pulled up in front of an ornate California mission-style edifice. The Manila Hotel commanded a fine view of Manila bay, the medieval fortress of Intramuros and the palm-lined promenades of Luneta Park. It had been officially opened in 1912. General MacArthur had made it his home at one point and Imelda Marcos regularly graced its halls. If she turned up at the wedding, I was not going to be surprised. This was the venue of choice for the great and the good of the capital. It was the only place that a man of Senator Guzman's ambition and flair for the dramatic would choose for a wedding.

My room was on the 15th Floor and was substantially more opulent than my regular hotel in Makati. I wandered downstairs in a fluffy monogrammed dressing gown and spent an hour in the pool. When I returned there was a note to meet Guzman in the Tap Room Bar. I dressed carefully for the meeting. Mr. Alan still made my custom suits in the New York atelier he had started when his grandfather's clothing store had finally gone bust just after the millennium. I kept two suits in PG in case I needed them for a job and had chosen a dark, single-breasted ultra-lightweight in Vitale Berberis Canonico cloth which fitted perfectly into the wood-panelled clubland-style atmosphere. Thankfully the air-con was on full blast. Guzman, in the company of several other Filipino men, all dressed in elegant and ornate *barong tagalog,* dominated a table at the far end.

"*Pare*, this my old English friend, Bill Jedburgh," he said, introducing me to the gathering. "You are looking smart, Bill, can I order you a drink?"

I chose fresh orange juice. The booze could wait for a while. I wanted to get a measure of the group first. Two of them were businessmen. Two were superannuated former ministers, one who had been, briefly, Vice President. The fifth man was Colonel Ricardo Fernandes who gave me a warm smile and directed me to the vacant armchair beside him.

"How was your scuba diving?" he asked me. "I understand there was an explosion at the Yacht Club."

"You're well informed," I said. "My trip started well, but ended badly. To top it off, I fell off my motorbike and experienced a mild concussion. Then the typhoon closed everything down."

"Is that why you are drinking orange juice?" he asked with a nod at my glass.

"I think the Senator wants me to be sharp and to listen carefully," I said and smiled at Guzman who was sitting on my left.

"But you are feeling fit?" Guzman asked with mild concern.

"No worries, I am fit enough for whatever you expect from me."

He gave a nod at that. "We want you to enjoy yourself at the wedding of my grand-daughter. It is an important occasion for us. Weddings are always special in the Filipino tradition. A joining of great families, the hope for more descendants to carry the family name. Many children are a blessing."

"Yes, but they can also be a burden," I said without any particular rancour, yet his face clouded up for instant, then it vanished.

"God blesses us with children and then he makes us suffer. They do not always lead their lives the way we wish them to."

"That's what I've heard."

"You don't have any children?" Guzman asked. The other men were speaking amongst themselves in Tagalog and only Ricardo was listening.

"I don't."

"That is strange for a man of your age. No ex-wives and previous marriages?"

"I've not met the right woman yet, I guess."

"You are handsome, you are probably quite rich. The girls must be throwing themselves at you, Bill."

"I do OK, sir. Just not met one that makes me want to put a ring on her finger."

"Oh, you will find her. She will find you. And then I think you will put a very large diamond ring on her finger."

I smiled politely. The conversation turned to other subjects. The stock market, local college basketball, American politics. One of the men commented on Nancy Pelosi the newly elected speaker of the House, the first woman in this role.

"Next they will have a black President, then a black woman President," said the former Minister. "What do you think, Bill?"

"I can't see the United States ever electing a black President," I said. "It's unthinkable for half of the population. The ones that live in the middle bit between New York and California."

"Have you been to the States?" the former Minister asked me.

"I go once or twice a year. They have some very good training academies for bodyguards. I like to keep my combat shooting skills sharp. In 1996 I spent nearly two months there during the Atlanta Olympics."

"What did you think of President Clinton?" Senator Guzman asked. "I remember you told me once that you met him?"

"I did, for about thirty seconds. He shook my hand, made me feel like the most important person in the room, told me a dirty joke and then it was the next guy in the line's turn."

"He had a lot of charisma, am I right?" Guzman asked.

"Oh, yes, he had an aura that was practically tangible. Some kind of magic pixie dust. If you spent too much time looking into his eyes you'd hand him your wallet and the keys of your Porsche if he asked for them."

"Do you think," the other old politician leant forward and fixed me with a rheumy eye, "our current President of the Philippines has that kind of charisma?" Of course it was a loaded question that demanded a side-step.

"I tell you who had charisma," I said, "and that was Charlie Santos."

The former Vice-President nodded in satisfaction. Obviously he was a friend of the old rogue's. "Have you met him?"

I laughed. "As a matter of fact he saved my life once in Manila." I briefly told them the story of Charlie leading a police raid like it was a scene from one of his movies. They all seemed impressed. This was the second part of a job interview that had started with a practical test at Camp Tecson and I was doing well so far. The board was liking what they were hearing. I had a good idea now what job I was being sounded out for.

We moved on to one of the private dining rooms where we demolished a fine meal of prime beef. One of the businessmen was interested in my views on China and Hong Kong. He was Filipino-Chinese and had invested a lot in property in Shanghai which was booming.

"In China you need to have the right connections, of course," he said in a tone that implied he did have them. Even if he didn't he would never admit that he'd mounted the wrong horse. "I am a very close friend of the Minister of Commerce," he boasted. "He is called Bo Xilai. Have you heard of him?"

"I haven't. Is he a rising star?"

"Oh, I hope so," said the old businessman with a smirk. He would have rubbed his hands like Ebenezer Scrooge if he hadn't been holding up his fork with a blood-red chunk of ribeye on it.

"Tell me, Bill," asked the other businessman, "what do you do with the money you earn in your line of work? How do you invest it?"

"I don't make that much money," I lied. After more than fifteen years of highly paid killing and the beneficial effect of compound investment on a diversified portfolio, not to mention some especially valuable artefacts I had acquired along the way, I reckoned my investment portfolio would probably equal either of theirs. But in my line of work it didn't do to tell people that. It made them wary of my independence. Or they tried to haggle. "I spend it mostly on property and what's left over I spend on loose women and cold beer."

"Don't you invest in shares?" The fellow raised his eyebrows.

"A little bit. Mostly funds. Nothing too adventurous."

"I'll give you a stock tip. Take it from me, Bill. There is a company called Amazon. They are an online bookstore. Buy their shares now. This company will make you rich." He blew his nose then added: "I've just bought 3 million US dollars of their shares, that's how much I like their business model."

"That's a lot of money to invest in one company," I said.

"When you invest, you have to invest big. Only fools buy little bundles of shares."

"I will seriously consider your advice, sir," I replied politely. I remembered the dot com bubble from a few years earlier and would stay clear of any online shop, however mundane its products.

As we stood up at the end of the meal Senator Guzman put his hand on my shoulder and said, "Ricardo and I would like to talk in private with you about something. Come upstairs to my suite."

I had imagined he would have chosen the Presidential Suite but perhaps he was superstitious. He had taken the MacArthur Suite instead. It was lavish but felt as if it was ready for refurbishment. The entire hotel exuded the smell of slightly faded grandeur, which made it no less impressive. It was like your ageing great-aunt who everyone agreed had once been a great beauty but these days used too much powder on her cheeks and wore her skirts in a style from an earlier age.

"Sit down, Bill," Senator Guzman said. "Cognac?"

"I'm fine."

"You're not a stupid man," he continued. "You understand what is going on, don't you?"

I shrugged because it's best not to speak at times, especially when there is the whiff of moral ambiguity in the air.

"There will be more than twenty men and women in the wedding party tomorrow who have been hired to provide discreet security. They will keep an eye out for any uninvited guests, any threat to me or my family."

I nodded and poured myself a glass of water from a crystal jug on the table that separated us.

"You," Guzman went on, "will be like my joker in the pack. I want you to keep close to me. Not too close to be obvious. Maybe five metres or so." He configured his features into an expression of great sadness, as if he could not contain his disappointment. "There are some people who hate me. Some people who would prefer to see me fail or even die before I have reached my destiny."

I nodded, keeping my own face studiously neutral.

"So that is the little favour to return the one I did for you in solving your misunderstanding with the police in Angeles." His sharp eyes watched me like the bird of prey that he embodied. "I also understand that I owe you a prize for your performance in the little competition which Ricardo arranged for me before you left for Puerto Galera. She is a very old friend. Very beautiful, very discreet. I think you will like her, and she will be your, how do they say, 'plus one' for the evening. What you get up to I will leave to the two of you."

"That is most kind," I said. And very cleverly done, you old dog.

"Ricardo and I have a much bigger favour to ask you. A favour for which we will pay…" He paused for a few seconds before he stated the number, "…half a million American dollars. Into any bank account of your choosing."

"Go on," I said.

"This is something that must not be done by a Filipino. Ricardo or any of his men are capable of doing this." He shrugged and appeared sad again. "This must be done by an unknown person."

"At the wedding?" I asked.

"No, precisely not at the wedding. She is not invited. I am not one of her friends. She is not a friend of my family."

"What is it you want me to do?"

"I can see from your eyes. Ricardo can see it also. You are a man who has killed before. You are able to kill people and still sleep peacefully at night."

A very mild shrug of my left shoulder was the only answer I dared give to this suggestion. I didn't want to lie. "I have been trained as a body-guard and I was a policeman."

"For half a million American dollars," Guzman said, his eyes staring calmly at mine, "We would like you to kill the President of the Philippines."

25

The wedding ceremony took place in Manila Cathedral which was only a mile from the hotel. There had been a Catholic church on the same spot since 1571 and the stolid, white, chunky edifice was the eighth iteration, the previous buildings having suffered destruction from earthquakes and war. Guarding the enormous, five-metre-high, front portal were six statues of Saints I did not recognise. Today they were augmented by soldiers in ceremonial dress, police officers in uniform and undercover security personnel including myself.

Inside the cathedral, under the high vaulted ceiling, the pillars and floor were fashioned from Italian marble. At the far end of the central nave, behind the ornately carved marble altar, draped in a blue cloak, stood a life-sized bronze statue of the Immaculate Conception of the Blessed Virgin Mary, to whom the church was dedicated. The smell I associated most with Catholic churches, incense, hung heavily in the air.

Two thousand people had been invited to watch the young couple exchange their vows and the presiding priest was the Cardinal himself. I was sitting about ten rows back at the end of the wooden bench so I could get out fast. On my left was a minor movie star in his sixties and his much younger wife. On my right was the chapel of St. Jude - the patron saint of lost causes. If I'd been a praying man, I would have said one there for Dickie Goodyear.

Ricardo had arranged for me to have a Glock 26 - a compact 9 mm with a 10-round double-stack magazine - which was sitting snugly in a nylon holster in the small of my back. I assumed that the Cardinal had given some special dispensation for security staff to carry weapons in the church but I hadn't asked the question. I was wearing a very loose fitting *barong tagalog* in a dark blue colour which disguised the contours of the weapon.

Everything went smoothly during the ceremony. Nobody ran down the aisle claiming they were already married to the bridegroom. Nobody fainted and more importantly, no bombs went off.

Unsurprisingly the first reading was the standard from Genesis, an invitation to 'Be fruitful and multiply'. What else would you expect for a marriage in the Philippines? For the second reading they'd gone for that perennial favourite from Corinthians: 'Love is patient; love is kind; love is not envious or boastful or arrogant or rude.' I liked women, but I didn't believe in love or pledging yourself to a lifetime with one of them. But these were still good rules to live by if you planned to. I'd been to a few weddings over the years, so I knew the drill. Not all of the marriages had lasted but that didn't stop the participants from trying a second or third time. The triumph of hope over experience. You went to weddings to show respect to your friends, to enjoy the booze and hopefully to meet a pretty bridesmaid or two.

One of the bridesmaids - there were four of them dressed in dark red dresses that evoked some biblical event perhaps - had caught my eye. She looked uncannily like Michelle Arupe, my new scuba diving pal. Of course, it was her. She couldn't see me in the crowd, but I enjoyed watching the flicker of emotions across her face as the celebrant went about his task and got the vows done and the rings sorted.

I slipped out before the end of the ceremony, just as the organist and the thirty-piece orchestra that was tucked in the front corner struck up the first chords of Mendelssohn's Wedding March. Outside, ducking behind one of the portal pillars I scanned the crowd for anything unusual. There was an area partitioned off for the press and paparazzi. There was a buzz of excitement as they heard the music and they began fiddling with their cameras. Limousines were already lined up to whisk the VIPs away to the hotel. Guzman's head of security - a white haired man who had once been a Chief Superintendent in the PNP - was talking into a handset. He nodded at me. We'd been introduced that morning.

I waited until the wedding party had left the building. The rest of the guests were being held back. Not all of the two thousand would be coming to the dinner and dance at the hotel. The Manila Ballroom could only accommodate 300 diners so they had been carefully selected, Guzman had explained to me, according to social merit and family connection.

An hour later, after the speeches and the first dance and a few courses of food had come and gone, I sidled up to Michelle Arupe and said: "Small world. Here you are again. Stalking me?"

She turned and gave a little gasp of surprise. "What are you doing here, Bill?" Her gaze travelled up and down me, her eyes telling me that she appreciated the silk embroidery on my traditional dress shirt. "You look very good in that."

"Better than in my Neoprene skin-tight wetsuit?" I said.

She laughed. "But really, how come you have been invited? This is a very exclusive wedding." Exclusive it was. Her immaculately stitched deep burgundy bridesmaid's dress looked like it had cost more than most wedding dresses and the diamond necklace she was wearing could have fed Lillibet's entire neighbourhood for a month.

"I'm an old acquaintance of Senator Guzman's," I said. "He asked me to come along and keep an eye on things. Remember I am in the security business."

"Are you undercover?" she asked, curiosity in her eyes.

"I am entirely above board. Can I get you another champagne?"

She shook her head then turned to the lady next to her. "Auntie, may I introduce Bill Jedburgh. He is from England. We have been scuba diving together recently."

I did my best to bow to the lady and resisted any temptation to ask how her shoe collection was holding up. Imelda Marcos was heavily made-up. She must have recently visited the best cosmetic surgeon in Los Angeles because she was nearly eighty and didn't look it. In her time she'd been a great beauty. For 21 years she'd been the First Lady of the Philippines and these days she might best be described as the Dowager Duchess of the province of Ilocos Norte.

"Do you know Noynoy, Bill?" Mrs. Marcos said, tugging on the sleeve of a man who had been standing next to her chatting to someone else. He was about my age and wore fashionable glasses and a tailored dinner jacket with a burgundy bow tie. Noynoy gave me a warm smile which reminded me somehow of an Asian Bill Clinton. Here was a man who had charisma.

"His mother is an old friend of mine," Mrs. Marcos giggled and I suspected there was a hint of irony in her words. "She was President of the Philippines after my husband. Are you familiar with our country and its history?"

"Not so much, ma'am," I said to give myself a bit of wiggle room in case I said anything foolish. Noynoy grasped my hand and shook it. He was the son of Cory Aquino which probably made him a congressman. With his talent and his lineage, he might do well in politics.

"And this is my son, Bongbong," Mrs. Marcos indicated the man who'd been in conversation with Noynoy. "He is the Governor of our province, Illocos Norte. That is in the north of Luzon."

We made small talk for ten minutes until Michelle rescued me by suggested we have a look at the presents which were arranged at the other end of the room.

"You are a dark horse, Bill," she said as she took my hand and fought through the crowds. "I took you for a simple ex-policeman. You're clearly much more than that."

She didn't lead me to the presents but instead to the dance floor where the famous Filipina songbird Kuh Ledesma had started crooning her classic 'I think I'm in love'.

Michelle put her arms around my waist and started swaying.

"Is that a gun you are wearing or are you just excited to see me again?" she teased, whispering into my ear. There was alcohol on her breath and flirtation on her mind.

"Not unless I keep my penis in the small of my back. But it's lovely to see you again," was my reply. "Have you sorted out your emotional challenges? The relationship that was giving you trouble?"

She snorted into my neck. "You should never start with one man before finishing with another. At least I've dealt with that. It's just the other bastard now that's giving me trouble."

"What makes that relationship so complicated?" I asked. By now her arms were around my neck and Kuh had moved into 'Till I met you'.

"His wife," Michelle said, with irritation in her voice, not at him but probably at herself.

"Is he here?"

"No, he left after church."

"I take it he's a little bit older than you?"

"You clever man. I have a weakness for older men." She was massaging my scalp with her fingers and it felt good.

"So, will he leave his wife for you?" I asked. It was a question, as my Latin master used to say, expecting the answer no.

"Of course not," she said and pushed me away then pulled me closer again for the next song.

"I know it's a stupid question," I said, "but why are you wasting your time with him?"

"It is a stupid question," she shouted in my ear over the music. "Don't you understand anything about women?"

"I understand very little about women even though I've been studying them for a good many years."

"We don't make it easy for ourselves. We fall in love with the bastards and we are bored with the nice guys."

I spun her around gently and she giggled at that. "I've noticed that bit about girls liking bastards," I said when we were face to face again. "I've occasionally taken advantage of that fact."

"Are you a bastard, Bill Jedburgh?"

"Very much so."

"I enjoyed scuba diving with you," she said, changing tack a bit which was clever. There was a glint of mischief in her eyes. I'd reminded her of the problem in her life and she wanted to think of other things.

"Do you see that man over there?" she said, pointing at a small, corpulent bloke in a policeman's dress uniform who was expounding to a group of younger men in dinner jackets gathered around him. "That is my godfather."

"A policeman?" I said.

"He's the Police Director General. Would you like me to introduce you?"

I shook my head. "I'd prefer to carry on dancing with you, my dear."

"That was the right answer. Can we go outside and smoke a cigarette?"

"Not good for your scuba diving, smoking."

"Screw you. I want a smoke."

"Let's go and have a smoke." And another glass of champagne, I thought as we walked past a waiter who was holding a tray aloft. He surrendered two flutes.

We sat on a low wall by the swimming pool and shared a Marlboro Light that she had produced from a clutch which had been slung over her shoulder.

"How is your work going?" I said, choosing a neutral subject.

She passed me the cigarette for a puff. I rolled the smoke around my mouth as if it were a cigar and didn't take it down into my lungs.

She freed the fag from my fingers and took a deep drag. After a while she let the smoke drift out through her nose. She said: "My boss is being transferred back to St. Louis so there might be a chance for a promotion."

"Do you like your work?"

She turned down the corners of her mouth. "It's okay. It pays the bills and keeps me busy."

"Do you have big bills to pay?" I said.

She turned her head and gave me a scathing look. "What kind of a question is that? I live in a four-bedroom condo which I bought and pay for myself. I send an allowance to my mother every month for food and the upkeep of our family estate."

"That's a beautiful necklace," I said, pointing to the one around her shapely neck, "for a woman with a lot of big bills". She put up her hand to it, protectively, or to feel the beauty of its workmanship. "Is it a family heirloom?"

"My family have very little left," she said. "Our loyalty to the Marcos family cost us everything. It killed my father and he lost his bank as a result. These diamonds were a present."

"I like diamonds myself," I said. "Beautiful, valuable and very portable."

"We are kindred spirits," she said, putting her hand on my sleeve. "See this tiny diamond here?" She showed me a small diamond in a simple gold mount on her right index finger. "My father gave it to me as he was dying. It is small but literally perfect. Only a quarter of a carat but finest white and flawless. He said that if I ever needed money, this would be my lifeline. So far, I have never needed it. But I have added to my collection."

"I have seen some pretty diamonds in my time," I said. "Have you heard of the Red Teardrop?" Her eyes glinted in delight. This was a lady who knew her gems.

"It's a legend, a cranberry coloured chimera. Supposedly found in Brazil and cut into over five carats of triangular brilliant. It was rumoured to be in Amsterdam a decade ago but hasn't been seen since."

"Suppose I told you I knew where it was?" I asked.

"Then I would make you a very happy man," she said, "even if you are a bastard."

"Well, let this bastard remind you that very few women in this country would be able to buy themselves a diamond, even if they worked hard for their entire lives."

She dropped the butt of the cigarette on the ground and crushed it to death with her high heeled slipper.

"I know I'm privileged. I know my life is better than 99.9% of Filipinos in my country. I do feel guilty about it, but it's not my fault. I didn't choose to be born into a family like mine."

"You don't have to feel guilty about anything," I said. "You Catholics are always ready to wrack yourself with guilt."

"I'm a terrible Catholic. I shouldn't be sleeping with a married man, committing adultery on a regular basis. Coveting wealth."

"You're not married, so half that sin is on his shoulders."

"One of the other great things about being a Catholic is redemption. Filipino men feel guilty but tell themselves they can't help giving in to temptation." She rolled her eyes. "And a pretty woman like me is always too much temptation for the men to resist."

"I've always felt that I can resist anything except the temptation of a pretty woman."

"Is that a clever thing to say?"

"It's perfectly phrased and absolutely true."

"You are a bastard," she said. "I am sure of that now."

"So does that mean you are ready to fall in love with me?" I asked.

She poked me in the chest and stood up. "I will have to think about that. And just because I've had a bottle of champagne doesn't mean I'll let you take advantage of me this evening." Her eyes flashed. "I'm not that sort of girl you know. It takes champagne and dinner and diamonds."

"That sounds like you're inviting me out on a date."

"Girls don't ask men out on dates," she said and took me by the hand to lead me back to the ballroom. As we entered the noisy, clammy interior we passed a group of five men who appeared grimly out of place. They were all wearing costly beige *barong tagalog* but their faces marked them as being from the rougher part of town. I whispered into Michelle's ear that I'd catch up with her a bit later, released my hand from hers, and turned to have a word with the Lapida Brothers.

26

I was staring at two men with three eyes and eighteen fingers. Alvin, the one who only had one eye spoke: "We didn't know you were a friend of Senator Guzman." He grinned, but there was a hint of nervousness in his bearing.

"You didn't know I was a friend of the Senator when you sent your two gunmen after me?" I reached across him to snare a waiter and relieve him of another glass of the French pop.

"That's right," Alvin said, after a moment of hesitation.

"You could have told us that you knew the Senator," said Marcial, the one who was missing two fingers.

"I told you I was a friend of Dickie Goodyear. Have you found him yet?"

There was flicker of confusion in Alvin's single eye and then he recovered and said: "No, he is still missing. Do you know where he is?"

"I do know where he is now," I said, managing to hide my anger.

Marcial leant forward. "Tell us where to find him. He owes us money. You remember don't you?"

"You won't be getting that money back from him. He's in bits at the bottom of the ocean. Someone blew up his boat."

Both of the gangsters looked first astonished and then unhappy. They were unable to dissemble. What played across their faces told me everything I wanted to know.

"Who killed him?" Alvin was the first to say it.

"I have no idea," I said and took a sip from my champagne while staring first at him and then his brother over the rim of my tall glass. "But I'm going to find out who did it. He wasn't a good man but he was a good friend."

Marcial said quickly: "I hope you can find out. He had a lot of enemies. He wasn't always straight in his way of business."

"I don't know about that. But Dickie didn't deserve to die like that."

"How do you know Senator Guzman?" Marcial now asked. They weren't comfortable with the subject of Goodyear and they were still trying to get the measure of me.

"I did some work for him a few years ago. And you?" I stared hard at both of them again. "Do you help the Senator sometimes?"

Alvin smiled oleaginously. "The Senator is a very important man in our province. We always like to help him when we can. It is good to have important friends. Is it not?"

"It helps knowing the right people. And the wrong people sometimes." I drained my champagne glass and placed it on a convenient side table along with other empties. "I'm sorry, guys, I'm going to go and talk to my new friend Bongbong Marcos. He was telling me about his new tobacco plantation."

I threw them one more hard stare and they gave as good as they got although I think I'd disconcerted them slightly. They hadn't asked me if I had seen their two minions Red Sox and Dodgers lately so perhaps they didn't suspect that I was involved in the gunmen's deaths.

My phone vibrated in my pocket as I came out of the men's room. It was Larry and he wanted to meet me in my hotel room for an urgent discussion.

"Now?" I said. "I'm in the middle of the wedding party."

"Yes," he insisted. "Nobody will notice if you're gone for half an hour."

"Fine, in five minutes," I said. My mind was still occupied with the conversation I'd had with the Lapida Brothers. A few pieces had clicked into place and I was now trying to work out what that meant.

Larry was waiting outside my room.

"What's so bloody urgent?" I asked. I let him in and got him a Coke from the minibar. I took a bottle of Perrier for myself. Best to ease off on the champagne for the moment. In a manner of speaking, I was still on duty. I went over to the window which looked down on to the swimming pool. The moon cast a romantic shadow across the water.

"How is the wedding going?" he asked.

"I've been to a few Filipino weddings but this one tops them all. The Cardinal of Manila stuffing wedding cake in his mouth as the former First Lady of the Philippines explains to him where to buy ermine slippers."

"Really?"

"That might be a slight exaggeration. But if you put a bomb into that ballroom downstairs now, you'd remove the entire upper echelon of society and only the poor and the middle classes would be left."

"You're starting to sound like a Socialist," Larry accused me with raised eyebrows.

"If I wanted to launch a military coup that's how I'd do it. Blow up all the aristocracy and then roll the tanks into town and throw bank notes into the streets. They'd be cheering me all the way to the palace."

"What a vivid imagination you've got, Bill," Larry said. "The more I start thinking about it, the less I want to go back downstairs again."

I shrugged. The fact was that security had been as tight as a kitten's arse and the guys I'd met all appeared competent. The chance of a bomb being snuck into the wedding was infinitely small. If I'd been tasked to take out half the political cadre of the Philippines I'd have done it with poison in the cake. My mind started wondering off on logistics on how that could best be done, when Larry called me back to the matter at hand.

"New instructions for you from the Brigadier," he said.

I nodded.

"Can I stand down from killing the Colonel? I quite like the guy."

"Yes, we no longer consider him to be an indispensable part of the coup. The Brigadier wants you to kill Senator Guzman instead. He is at the heart of the conspiracy. The only way to nip it in the bud is to remove him."

I turned from the window and glared at Larry Lim. "That's a Jacobean turn of phrase for a young Asian fellow like yourself."

"What's your problem?" he asked seeing my anger.

"I will not assassinate Senator Guzman."

"Why not? You never have a problem killing anybody, as a rule. I've known you for nearly fifteen years and there were only three times that you balked at a commission."

"Well, I'm damn well balking at this one. I have a debt of honour to the Senator. He's helped me out and he's treated me with respect."

Larry regarded me coldly for a long while. "He'd order you killed if he knew we were even having this conversation. He would discard you like a dirty pair of underpants the moment he no longer saw a use for you."

I moved my head from side to side slowly to show that I was considering his words carefully.

"You're probably right," I said. "He's asked me to kill the President." I explained briefly how that conversation had come about.

Larry snorted in victory. "If you did that, he'd set you up for a fall before you could say Sir Stamford Raffles."

"That thought had crossed my mind as well, which is why I'm not inclined to take up the job offer on that one."

"We want you to kill Senator Guzman," Larry repeated his missive.

"And I'm not going to take that one up either."

"The Brigadier will be very unhappy."

"Our arrangement has always been that I can say no, that I can refuse any job if I consider it too dangerous or inappropriate or damn well wrong. You know that your boss has less morals than I have. Which is a stunning achievement. You at least have a conscience and sometimes, in the wee small hours of the night, I know you feel guilty about some things the old Machiavelli makes you do."

A tight expression took hold of Larry's face, proving to me that I'd hit him in a soft spot.

"I will not kill Senator Guzman," I said, "because I am close to him and at the moment I like and respect him. If that situation should change, then you can put a gun in my hand."

"If Senator Guzman succeeds in toppling the government and Singapore Airlines loses the Philippines Airlines engineering deal, it will be a big problem."

"I'm on holiday here and it's a fucking business deal, Larry. Get real. The sun will still rise in the east the next morning." I gave an angry grunt. "And you know what, I might be in a position to put a kind word in for you and ask my friend, the new President, to still sign the deal."

Larry nodded, seeing the logic in that notion. "It's only a worst-case scenario," he said, backing off. "We don't believe the coup will be successful. They rarely are. They haven't enough support behind them. We just want to make sure, that's all."

"Brigadier Wee wants to make sure, you mean."

"And his bosses," Larry reminded me.

"I doubt any of them know what the old bastard is cooking up here. They leave the dirty work to him and would rather not know."

Larry laughed at that one. "So I'll go back and tell him you won't do it?"

"I'm not going to do it. But if it's that important to you there is new guy who calls himself Ozone. A former US Navy Seal, possibly of Filipino extraction. He's been doing jobs around Asia."

Larry frowned. "Yes, we've got a file on him."

"Do you know who he is?"

"No, he's just appeared on our radar."

"He's cheaper than I am, everybody keeps telling me."

"Do you have contact details for him?"

"No, but if you ask the right questions on the Dark Web somebody might know."

Larry chuckled. "Fine." He stood up and walked towards the door then turned. "Bill, I want to say that I respect you for your decision. I have always respected you. You have a unique sense of loyalty. Something about this makes me respect you even more."

"Fuck you too, Larry Lim," I said. "Let's just be clear about this. Even if the Brigadier offered me a million US dollars to slot you because you'd sold secrets to the North Koreans, I would turn him down. You can be sure of that. You're one of my best mates. Now, piss off and tell the old devil what I said. And if you do hire someone else for the job make sure he doesn't come anywhere near me."

For an instant I thought Larry was going to go all soft on me, then he got a grip, gave me the middle finger and left the room.

27

The rest of the wedding went smoothly and by three in the morning most of the guests had departed. I managed another twenty minutes of flirtatious conversation with Michelle before she was whisked off by the bride as part of their bedchamber duties.

Senator Guzman then pulled me aside. He asked me to have lunch with him the following day and then presented me with my prize from the target competition at Camp Tecson. I knew who she was. A famous Filipina actress and singer. She was well known, sang like an angel and screwed like a demented bunny. She owed her initial break to being an unacknowledged mistress of Senator Guzman and she owed him a debt of honour. I liked to think I made it an insignificant expense for her to repay it. As dawn flooded into my room she was singing one of her top ten hits while she bounced on top of me, her beautiful breasts wobbling in time to the song.

So at 1 p.m. I stood waiting in the lobby, feeling much better for having exercised twice that morning, once in my room and then followed up with an hour in the gym. If it's a good champagne there is rarely a hangover.

"You like Chinese food?" Guzman asked as he came up to me.

"I like all good food."

"I'm going to take you to 'Emerald Garden'. It's one of the oldest Chinese restaurants in Ermita."

Following a few steps behind him was one of his close protection guys. I nodded at him in recognition but struggled to recall his name. We all got into the silver S-Class Mercedes that had pulled up at the front.

It was only a five-minute drive. We walked up the steps into the restaurant. There was nothing fancy about it. It was functional with round tables covered in green tablecloths. The chairs were also green, as was the carpet. The manager ran over to us and led us to the corner table that must have been reserved. Guzman ordered shark fin soup with crab meat, fresh scallops with broccoli, the house fried noodles, abalone with oyster sauce and lobster with the chilli sauce.

"San Miguel or tea?" he asked me with a twinkle in his eye.

"Jasmine tea for now," I suggested.

His bodyguard was at another table, so it was just the two of us. I had my back to the wall as did Guzman. Most of the diners were ignoring us studiously but a few recognised him and cast the occasional curious glance in our direction. They would already have seen the wedding photos in that morning's papers.

"The Philippines is a beautiful country. Don't you agree?" he said. "We have everything that the heart can desire. The most beautiful beaches and the prettiest ladies."

"You should work on the traffic jams and improve the infrastructure," I challenged him.

"I will," he bristled mildly. "When I become President. That is what I will fix first. And I will bring factories back to this country and I will stop our young women going overseas to become domestic helpers and our young men from becoming sailors. There will be work for them all here in our own country."

It was too early in the day for a political discussion so I simply nodded. There was no need at this table for any of my finely-honed cynicism.

Guzman had asked me in the car if I'd enjoyed the wedding. I'd told him it had been one of the most fascinating events of my life. That had pleased him immensely. All had gone well and he was floating on a cloud of self-importance. His grand-daughter was now married to a handsome, wealthy man and his family name was currently on everyone's lips. Was there any better moment to make a grab for the highest office?

He slurped his hot tea from the tiny china cup, leant forward and whispered: "We will march on the city tomorrow. We have a thousand soldiers who are loyal to Ricardo and they will take control of various key locations then demand that the President resign."

"So soon?" was my reply.

"When the President appears in public, that is the moment I want you to assassinate her. Will you take this job, Bill?"

I shook my head and fixed him with a firm look. "I can't do that, Senator. It is not my kind of work."

"Is it about the money? I can pay you three quarters of a million US dollars."

"It's not about the money."

"Bill, you disappoint me. I thought you were my friend, that you were going to support me?" His hand gripped my forearm firmly. I could smell his after-shave, something musky with sandalwood.

I told him: "You have two choices. One is the best in the business today. The Reliable Man. He has been the most deadly assassin in the Far East for a very long time. He is very expensive but reputedly never misses, if he decides to take the assignment. Then there is a man they call Ozone. He's new. A Filipino who used to be in the US Marine Corps. A top sniper. One of these is the man you want for this job."

The Senator's eyes lit up. "How do you know these things?"

"In my business we need to know who the enemy might be. I have an email address for the Reliable Man. Some of my clients have used him in the past. But his price has been going up now for many years. They tell me he now charges nearly half a million US dollars. That's why people recently have been using this Ozone guy. He's supposed to be good. And I don't think you would need to pay him more than $200,000."

"Even for killing such an important person?" Guzman asked.

"From what I've heard, he'll see it as a matter of honour. It would be a feather in his cap. Great for business."

Guzman said, "Do you know how to contact him?"

"No, but I can make enquiries. But whether you use Ozone or the Reliable Man you cannot set up this kind of a job within a day. It takes time. A week at least."

He shook his head in irritation. "We can't wait that long, a few days delay, perhaps. The young soldiers are ready. They are charged up. They have been doing bloodletting ceremonies. It goes back to our old traditions. They call it *dinuguan*."

"I can try and get a contact for this guy Ozone as soon as we finish lunch. I'll email the Reliable Man as a back-up. I'm happy to do that for you. But I am not the person to do the shooting."

Guzman laughed grimly. "I know you can kill. I can smell it on you."

"I could kill if anyone attacked someone I cared about," I said, disingenuously.

"We could all kill in that situation. You on the other hand could kill coldly. Do not deny it."

He searched my eyes for acknowledgement, but I shrugged to change the subject. The food had arrived and we were making the chopsticks work. Having reached a conclusion on the most important piece of business, our conversation reverted to the wedding, the quality of the guests and their relative standing in society.

"I saw you talking a lot with Michelle Arupe," Guzman said with half a wink but there was a hint of warning in the tone of his voice. "Her father used to be a very powerful man. She was in high school with my granddaughter, of course, which is why she was a bridesmaid."

"She's a pretty girl," I said.

His face clouded over and there was a hint of command in his words. "If I can give you some advice. Stay away from that girl. From what I know, you would regret it."

"In what way?" I said evenly. He wasn't trying to insult me.

"Getting involved with her and her family could be troublesome for you and me, under the circumstances. There are so many other pretty girls in the Philippines."

I nodded to show agreement. "I was simply talking with her. We met in Puerto Galera scuba diving so she recognised me."

"Better stay away from her," he said, with a grim expression on his face. "She is involved in at least one very complicated relationship. She likes married men and she is very high maintenance."

"Then I'm safe." I laughed, trying to lighten the conversation now before it started annoying me. "I'm a carefree, foreign, bachelor with not a lot of cash."

"What do you think about this lobster? Does it need some more chilli?" the Senator asked. He had made his point.

It was nearly 3.30 p.m. by the time we stood up and left the restaurant. I was slightly behind Guzman while his bodyguard was five paces ahead, waving to the driver to start up the engine of the Senator's Mercedes. It was a busy main road and out of habit I checked the cars driving past. That's when I noticed the black Jeep Cherokee pull out from behind another car, accelerate and come to a sudden stop directly in front of us, at the bottom of the steps.

As the rear door opened, my hand was already on my Glock. I was trying to reach Guzman so I could shove him to the ground. The man who had leapt out from the black car wore a black balaclava and was holding a large revolver. My Glock snagged on the holster for a millisecond and that's when the man opened fire. The first shot went wild because I'd pushed the Senator hard from behind and he'd stumbled sideways across the steps. A broken collarbone healed faster than a bullet wound. Guzman was trying to catch his footing on the steps while I was trying to get a bead on the gunman.

I fired just as he fired.

His second shot hit the Senator and spun him around. My first shot grazed the gunman's thigh. I'd fired too early as my muzzle was still coming up.

The gunman hesitated, unsure whether to fire at me or to concentrate on his primary target. That was a mistake. My second shot hit him firmly in the chest which made him flinch and his third shot went wild. He'd staggered back a few feet from the impact but hadn't dropped. I realised he must be wearing a Kevlar vest underneath his baggy black shirt. He turned and aimed his big revolver at me just as the next round smacked him high in the chest. Two inches higher and I would have got him in the throat but the armour protected him again. This time he sprawled on the pavement. Another man appeared from inside the Jeep and dragged him back into the car. The door slammed shut and the car tore off with screeching rubber. I watched it for a while as it accelerated down the road.

Women and children were screaming and already there was the sound of a police siren in the distance. I got to Guzman with three quick steps and sank to my knees. A young Filipino man was already working on him.

"I am a doctor," he assured me. He was busy pressing on the wound which was low on the left side. There was a lot more blood than when Goodyear had come to my room.

"This is Senator Guzman, we have to get him to a hospital," I yelled superfluously.

"I know," the calm young man said. A young woman dropped to her knees beside us and said she was a nurse. "The General Hospital is just two streets away," she told me, as she ripped off part of her skirt to hand to the doctor. I got back to my feet. A tight crowd had gathered around us. I checked for other threats but found none, but waved them back with my gun nevertheless and they reluctantly complied. The bodyguard's face was ashen but he was already on the phone calling for support. I kept my Glock in my hand and watched, advancing on the crowd whenever they crept forward.

Guzman was breathing heavily. He was no longer a young man but he appeared fit. With a bullet wound you never knew what it had ripped apart as it entered and exited the body. I hoped he'd be OK.

For a second I had a flashback to a similar situation in Jakarta a few years earlier. I had to admit to myself that compared to my real work I was a lousy bodyguard. I just hoped that this time my employer would pull through.

28

After I'd watched Senator Guzman being rushed into the trauma room of the hospital and briefed his Head of Security, who'd met us there, I returned to the Manila Hotel and packed my stuff.

This was getting out of hand now. There had been a point about a decade ago when my assignments as Bill Jedburgh had got way too high profile for my alter ego as the Reliable Man. Since then I had consciously throttled back to ensure I lived a quiet life between assignments. This was déjà vu, all over again, and I didn't like it. I wanted to duck my head down and watch quietly from a dugout on the sidelines.

A shooting war between prominent, powerful Filipino families was not on my agenda. Whoever had come after Guzman wasn't worried about how influential he was. They'd been sent by someone even more influential and as that narrowed the available options, I had a pretty good idea who it might be.

I hadn't made up my mind yet where to go next. Rannie said he'd pick me up as soon as he could get through the traffic which might be an hour. Several choices presented themselves: I could head back South and hole up in Puerto Galera, or I could leave the Philippines entirely and return home to Singapore. If I decided to do that, I thought I should head north towards Angeles City again. It would be easier to get a flight out of Clark Airbase. Tiger Airways did a daily run to Singapore via Macau. It was a tiny airport with only four flights a day but using it would avoid the crowded mess that was Manila's Ninoy Aquino International Airport.

But I was wary of leaving the country immediately. If the police wanted to interview me then I should make myself available. Doing a runner gave a bad impression, however much I felt like shaking the dust from my desert boots and leaving the entire tangled web behind me.

Before I had made up my mind, one of my mobiles rang. It was Larry.

"He wants to see you," he said.

"I'm not in the mood." I was standing in the lobby, behind a pillar, waiting for Rannie to arrive. "Do you know what happened?"

"Of course, we've heard."

"Is this your doing?" I asked, an empty hole knitting itself in the centre of my gut. Larry paused for just a little too long.

"It's not, but we may have caused it indirectly."

"I'll be blaming you if he dies," I said.

"You told us to go and hire a guy called Ozone."

"I didn't think you'd take me up on that recommendation." I gave an angry grunt. "Not that quickly, in any case."

"We didn't, Bill. Just come on over to the Embassy or the Shangri-La Hotel. We can talk about it there."

"Damn you," I said.

The Singapore Embassy was due to move in the next year or so into a fancy new location in Taguig called

Bonifacio Global City. It was currently based in an office building on Ayala Avenue, a five minute walk from the Shangri-La. The hotel was a more discreet location so I chose that. An hour later I found myself back in the same suite the Brigadier Wee had occupied the last time we met.

"You don't seem to have lost any weight," he commented wryly.

"With one thing or another I haven't managed any serious diving yet."

"You've been leading a busy life," he said. This time he was wearing a charcoal suit with a military tie. Perhaps he was on his way to an important meeting later and had to convey the appropriate gravitas. The old bastard could turn up in his birthday suit and still exude gravitas. He possessed that rare sense of power common to the few men and women who truly pulled the strings of the world.

"Coffee?" he asked. I went to help myself.

"Have you heard anything from the hospital?" I said.

"He's still being operated on," Brigadier Wee said.

"Did you arrange for that joke of a gunman to take a pop at us?"

The Brigadier fixed me with a stare that would have done my old headmaster proud. I shrivelled to three-foot-nothing.

"Don't be ridiculous," he replied.

"So who did?"

"Did you get the car's number plate?" he asked with a sly smile.

I laughed. He was always five moves ahead of you and understood you better than even your own grandmother.

"You knew that I would," I conceded grudgingly.

"You are a smart man and it's the obvious thing to do."

I gave them the number plate that I'd memorised as the Cherokee was screeching away. Larry wrote it down and went into the other room to make a call.

"If it's any consolation to you," the Brigadier said in order to mollify me, "I told Larry that you would turn down the job. And I told him not to push you too hard."

"So it was a test?"

He shrugged. "No, it was an operational decision. We decided that we wanted him dead. The obvious person was you, our own contracted assassin. But I realised the dynamic was complicated. It was nevertheless worth asking the question." He moved his face into a shape intended to be a paternal smile. It came across mirthless and contrived but I knew it was genuine. He hitched up his trousers and checked with his thumb for a speck on his polished black brogues that wasn't there. "I wasn't surprised when you refused. There was an outside chance that he'd annoyed you with something that he'd said or done and that you might take the job."

I made a sound that was close to a growl. "You're starting to persuade me that it wasn't you."

"What we did, which is why we are partly responsible," Wee said, "is we passed the relevant information from the hard drive to our connections in Malacanang Palace."

"Right, I can see how that would have put everyone's noses out of joint including the President's. Did you have to do that?"

"As Larry told you in Puerto Galera, it contained lists of all the conspirators, MP3 recordings of their conversations and digital photos of them together. That was pretty damning evidence. It's why we thought it was best to remove Guzman. Once we had the full list and could see to what level each person was committed, how much money they had donated, it became pretty clear that he was the one key person, the vital central cog of the conspiracy."

The Brigadier managed to smile and look sad at the same time now. He rubbed the bridge of his nose. I suspected that he might be tired and would rather have been in his office block in Singapore getting ready to walk across the parade ground to his bungalow for an early evening meal.

"Sometimes we have to do things for our nation that are messy and might even be harmful to people of other nations. The greater good of the people of Singapore is the only thing that informs my decision making. SQ wants this contract with PAL and we want a stable government in the Philippines. My assessment is that means we want to keep the current administration in power."

I frowned at him. In chess there is a move called a fork which is when a single piece - a knight perhaps - makes two or more simultaneous attacks. Whatever action the defender chooses he will end up losing a piece or a strategic position. Brigadier Wee lived his life playing forks. I was convinced that there was much more to the Singapore Airlines story. But it was unlikely that he would explain more than I needed to know.

Larry came back into the room waving his piece of paper. "Licence plate is registered to the PSG, the Presidential Security Group. It's one of their pool cars."

I had to chuckle. "That obvious?"

Larry shrugged. "Maybe they weren't expecting anyone to be as eagle-eyed as you."

"Maybe they were feeling cocky?" I suggested. "It's the Philippines after all. If you work for the most powerful person in the land you might be a bit careless about covering up your tracks."

Larry nodded and didn't say anything.

"Or perhaps someone is trying to frame the PSG and in turn point the finger at the President for ordering the assassination of a prominent Senator and opponent?" I continued. That felt a bit more devious to me. Was it likely? I looked at both of the men and neither of their faces revealed anything.

I gave a snort. "Maybe I just don't care. I'm going to get away from Manila and sit this one out for the next few rounds." I raised my eyebrows and stared at the Brigadier then added firmly: "I hope you have no objection to that?"

"You are released of your obligations for now, Bill," the old chess-master said. "I'd like you to stay in the Philippines in case things get complicated and we need your expert talents after all. Why don't you go and get on with your scuba diving?"

I stared at him for ten seconds or more. "That's exactly what I'm going to do. And I'll turn my phone off."

"If your phone is off, then I'll send Larry down to tell you when we require you to switch it on. Please make yourself available."

My marching orders were loud and clear. Larry walked me out of the suite and towards the lifts.

"I checked out Michelle Arupe like you asked," Larry said while we waited. "Pretty girl."

"You jealous?" I asked.

"Happily married, as I keep telling you," he said, waving his wedding ring finger at me. "She's not your usual type, Bill. Bright, diligent at work. Supports an elderly mother. Seems to have had a lot of rich boyfriends. Likes older men, who can support her lifestyle. So you might stand a chance."

"Sounds like the marrying kind," I said.

"Not yet, she hasn't," Larry said, looking thoughtful. "Nor have you of course."

"There you go," I said to him as the lift arrived and I waved him a cheerful goodbye. "Maybe Michelle and I are more alike than you think."

29

Rannie was downstairs with his Toyota and I told him to head for Angeles City. Once I'd calmed myself down from the irritation of dealing with my old pals from Singapore, I called Michelle Arupe's number. I hadn't been surprised to find a napkin with her contact details on it in my pocket when I'd retrieved my trousers from the floor after I'd finished romping with the Filipina singer.

After five rings the phone went to voicemail. "*Hey, I'm just totally busy at the moment, so why not send me a text and I'll get back to you,*" was her cheerful message. I didn't leave a voicemail but sent a text asking her to call me urgently. There was no particular reason for me to speak with her other than a desire to hear her voice. Ostensibly I planned to warn her to keep her head down and avoid talking politics or being seen in public. Manila had experienced plenty of protests, some of them peaceful others less so. It was a volatile city full of passionate people and when men and women fought each other for power, bystanders often got hurt.

My next call was to Guzman's Chief of Security to find out how his boss was doing. I was told he was still in a coma. I informed him that I'd be going out of town for a few days but he should call me when Guzman came out of the coma and was well enough to receive visitors. He thanked me again for saving his boss's life. Everyone agreed that if I hadn't been there with the Glock in my hand the assassination attempt would have been successful.

"Tell him I'll come and see him as soon as he is awake," I repeated. There was a piece of personal business that I wanted to pursue first. I wanted to satisfy my curiosity. I wanted to understand the causes of things. Mostly I wanted to vent my frustrations and wreak vengeance on the deserving.

We were somewhere around San Fernando when my phone started vibrating. I wasn't Michelle but Colonel Ricardo Fernandes.

"Everyone tells me you saved the life of my brother-in-law," he got straight to the point.

"I did what I could. If I'd been faster on the draw he wouldn't have been hit at all."

"You did your best," he said. "We are all very grateful to you."

"How is he? Last I heard, he was still in a coma."

"He is still unconscious, but the doctors say it is looking good. The bullet didn't do as much damage as they first thought."

"It was a heavy calibre revolver."

"The round passed through him," he said, "and it didn't disintegrate."

"Very odd for a walk up hit like that not to use a hollow point bullet," I commented. That was an interesting slice of information to file away.

"Thank God they were not professionals," was the Colonel's comment. He couldn't be more wrong. They were professionals but they didn't want to kill him. If I'd been tasked with the job I would have used Winchester Black Talon ammunition. At close range it would shred the target's thorax.

I said, "Is the special project you have been working on, now cancelled?"

There was a long pause at the other end as he mulled over how to answer my question. It was obvious enough what I was referring to and if anyone was monitoring his phone they wouldn't be fooled by my circumlocution.

"We haven't decided yet," was his answer. "Can you come to see me in my barracks? I want to discuss Senator Guzman's situation with you. You are one of the few outsiders we trust."

What I really wanted to tell him was that I was at the airport and leaving the country for a very long time. I was curious though. Surely they would abandon their whole crazy mutiny idea now and wait for another opportunity? Perhaps I could help by explaining to them that it was already a lost cause. I now knew they were being watched and taking even one step forward would be foolish and most likely fatal.

So I arrogantly agreed to come over and see Ricardo once I had finished what I was working on. I told him I'd be over the following morning. I couldn't manage it any earlier.

This time I got Rannie to drop me off outside the Oasis Hotel. I told him some friends from Hong Kong were staying there. The Oasis was a run-down musty resort hotel from the sixties that had seen better times and needed a serious make-over. It had lots of bedrooms and a big lobby so was more anonymous than any of the hotels around Walking Street. Most importantly, it was on the Clark Perimeter Road and not far from the 'Happy Days' diner.

Before leaving Manila, we'd stopped off at the Coconut Planters Bank and I'd spent ten minutes retrieving some items from my safe deposit box there.

This was the first time I'd stayed in the Oasis Hotel, which was good because I used a passport with a different name in it. It was Belgian and the photo showed my face with long hair that fell over my forehead and with a three o'clock shadow. The room they gave me was out past the swimming pool and I could come and go without walking through the lobby. Everything felt sombre and musty. I wasn't intending on spending much time there. All I needed was warm running water and a bed.

I lay down and slept for an hour, then made my preparations. By this time it was shortly after midnight. I was counting on the fact that the Lapida Brothers would be at their place of work until the early hours, having meetings, receiving payments, handing out instructions and conducting their illicit commerce.

The diner was as it had been on my last visit. Two chubby Americans in Hawaiian shirts sat at the counter discussing politics while they worked their way through burgers and fries. There were several couples dotted around the room: older white men accompanied by much younger Filipinas. In the corner by the door was a skinny Filipino man who had fallen asleep, his head resting on his arms which were folded on the table. I studied him quickly but carefully in case he was the door guard, then I slid onto a red-cushioned stool at the bar counter. The two Americans glanced my way and we exchanged friendly nods. I was sitting four stools away from them so it was clear I wasn't intent on making conversation.

Glancing up at the mirror in the far corner of the ceiling I could tell that Alvin and Marcial Lapida were open for business, sitting at their usual table with a gang of cronies. There were five of them at the table. They were playing cards and drinking beer while a college basketball game was in progress on the television set hanging above their heads. By the door that led into the back of the restaurant, where the toilets and storage area were located, sat a heavy bruiser on a wooden chair. Across his knees was a shotgun. It looked like a Remington 870, the serious gangster's pump-action shotgun of choice. It appeared that Mr. Remington was the replacement for Red Sox and Dodgers.

The Lapida Brothers, looking up at that same mirror, would have noticed me entering the diner but I didn't think they'd have seen through my disguise. Across my right cheek and down my neck was a skin discolouration which drew the eye. It could have been a birthmark or skin disease. People would remember that and not much else. I had a grey-haired wig on my head and skin-coloured latex gloves that the waitress would have to stare carefully at my hands to notice. Even then she wouldn't comment. Filipinos are polite to strangers. She might assume that I wore gloves because the skin disease on my face also spread across my hands.

I ordered a Balibago burger, a vanilla milkshake and a mug of coffee. The other TV screen on the wall behind the counter was showing an episode of 'Friends'. I think it was called 'The One Where No One's Ready'. My food arrived and I ate it slowly, keeping an eye on the other end of the room.

Shortly after I finished my French fries one of the waitresses woke the sleeping Filipino man. He turned out to be drunk and staggered out into the night. That made my job easier: no door guard, just Mr. Remington to deal with. He sat quietly watching the door and the diner, occasionally checking the progress of the basketball on the TV.

Just as I got to the bottom of my milkshake - slurping the last dregs up through the straw - a man entered and walked through to where the Lapida Brothers were holding court. He was in his thirties and dressed in shorts, T-shirt and flip-flops. Mr. Remington nodded at him and he stood at the end of the table explaining something to Alvin Lapida. Afterwards he handed over a brown paper bag, was given a fistful of pesos and left the diner. I could see all this in the mirror.

It was shortly after one by now. In Angeles City the night still felt very young. Some bars didn't close until dawn. I ordered another coffee and made up my mind.

What I was keen to do was to interrogate one or both of the brothers and find out who had hired them to come after Goodyear. I suspected it might be Senator Guzman but I had no proof. Both they and the Senator had indicated at the wedding that there was a link between them. I suspected that it was a matter of traditional patronage. They gave the Senator respect and he knew they were available to him. He was the big animal in this park and they were the hyenas that hunted in his shadow.

Perhaps Dickie Goodyear had tried to sell the external hard drive and the sensitive information it contained back to the Senator. Guzman had asked the Lapida Brothers to help him retrieve it without having to pay Goodyear's price. Somebody had then decided that Goodyear's boat should be rigged with explosives. What confused me though was my conversation at the wedding with Alvin and Marcial Lapida. They weren't great actors and they had been genuinely surprised about Dickie's death. However I still reckoned they were the catalysts for the explosion and might even have ordered it. I wanted to confirm that, but had come to the conclusion that I wasn't going to be able to kidnap them and drag them away from the rest of their gang. Not with Mr. Remington there, and not in public. I sorely wanted to take at least one of the brothers to a dark, quiet place and beat him until the bones in his arms and legs were shattered.

But it wasn't going to happen tonight.

The other critical piece of information that I still needed was how Goodyear had come into possession of the information in the first place. Who had given or sold him the names and photos of the conspirators? Who had been close enough to the conspiracy to copy a spreadsheet that showed the conspirators' financial contributions and level of commitment to the cause. In some ways it was a foolish document for Guzman and Fernandes to have kept. But there was a logic to it. They needed a formula that allowed them to calculate the odds of the coup being successful. In a column next to every supporter's name, they had ranked their commitment, from a pulldown menu:

1 - Will come out and support us in public if victory is certain
2 - Maybe will come out and support us in public
3 - Will support us in public unless they are influenced otherwise
4 - Will support us in public from the start
5 - Will be seen in public as a leader and commits full loyalty

In the adjacent column was the amount of money that had been donated or promised. Some men had donated large sums - up to a million pesos - despite only being allocated a factor of 1 for commitment. This much Larry had shared with me after they'd unlocked the files.

Who had given this information to Goodyear so that he could enrich himself? I felt there might be the hand of a woman in all of this. There was a whiff of jealousy that might engender that level of treachery. It had been occupying my thoughts for some time but I'd been unable to formulate a neat conclusion.

I didn't think there would be a neat conclusion this evening. The diner was too full and Mr. Remington too attentive. I'd have to forgo eliciting any answers on that one from the Lapida Brothers this evening so I shrugged and resigned myself to switching to Plan B.

I finished my coffee and paid my bill. Then I stood up and walked slowly, unsteadily in the direction of Mr. Remington. The two stout Americans had long gone and there were only two couples left in the diner.

I pointed at the far door and asked in a loud voice if that was where the bathrooms were. The big man with the big shotgun nodded and pointed with his thumb over his right shoulder. That was when his hand was farthest from his weapon.

The Beretta M9 that I'd acquired from my burglar had a 15 round magazine. It fired 9 mm rounds and was accurate up to 50 metres. I was no more than two metres from my target and I had loaded the Beretta with Hydra Shok expanding hollow-point rounds from my stash in Manila. Half of Mr. Remington's head vanished when my first round struck him in the eye.

Taking your targets in the right order was one of the most important aspects in planning a walk-up hit. You had to be sure no bodyguards would interfere as you drew a bead on the primary target. It was never easy to get this perfectly right. My stakeout had concluded that the other men at the table, although they might still be armed, were most likely to be drinking pals. Everyone had been relying on the big shotgun for protection. If any of the three men produced weapons I would shoot them. If they simply froze, they might get out of this alive.

I shot Alvin first, aiming for his milky eye. My next round found Marcial just under the nose. Both of them were dead by the time my muzzle had shifted to the other men. One of them had produced a small revolver from his waistband so I took his head off as well. The last two had their hands so high up they were practically touching the ceiling.

"Don't fucking move or you're dead too," I barked in what I hoped sounded like an American accent. Then I changed my mind and decided to eliminate the witnesses as well. If it was going to look like gang warfare, then best to remove all the pawns from the board. I shot them both in the throat below the Adam's Apple, turned and ran through the diner.

Sometimes you walk away calmly. This time it was best to run for the hills. The waitresses had dropped behind the counter, the other customers were flat on the floor. I burst out through the front door and disappeared into the sweltering night.

30

I'd booked a car and driver for 5.30 a.m. from the hotel, so I'd managed a few hours of kip. My dreams were troubled only by images of naked dancing girls. At my age that was as close as I got to a wet dream. It told me that my body was in need of female companionship.

I found myself back at Camp Tecson shortly before 9 a.m. This time Lieutenant Obregon showed me into Ricardo Fernandes' office. It was long and narrow, with a desk at one end and a briefing table at the other. There was a map of Central Manila on a cork board resting on an easel in front of it. I could see arrows and orders of battle drawn on it with chinagraph pencils. It looked as if an O Group had just concluded. Around it were the same officers I had met previously. This time the mood was less one of suppressed excitement and more an eve-of-battle apprehension. They realised they were about to embark on a risky venture. Some of them, perhaps, were entertaining doubts whether they would truly be serving their country and the people by marching on Manila. If they had doubts, the military structure would not permit them to back out. It was what had kept soldiers going over the top at Passchendaele and helped Julius Caesar keep his men tight under the most vicious barbarian onslaughts.

"So, Colonel Fernandes," I asked. "Have you decided whether to launch the coup or are you still debating?"

"*Alea iacta est,* as the Roman General said when he crossed the Rubicon. The die is cast. We leave camp in an hour." He spoke firmly and went to sit down at the briefing table. I sat in the metal chair next to him. He gave a command in Tagalog and his officers began to file out of the room, leaving only the two of us. The smell of boot polish and gun oil lingered in the air.

I said: "Do you think this is wise with Senator Guzman in hospital? Do you really know how many supporters you still have?"

"Our cause is just," he assured me and toyed with the black beret that was on the table in front of him, lying on top of blueprints of a building that they had been studying before I arrived.

"Will you kill the President for us?" Fernandes asked me.

"No, I can't do that. That is not my kind of work," I lied. "I made that clear to the Senator over lunch just before he was shot."

"You are not supporting us then?" His face clouded over with a mixture of concern and anger.

"I am not a Filipino. This is not my fight. I told the Senator before he was shot that he needed a professional assassin. I gave him two names. The most cost-effective solution is a man they call Ozone. A former Navy Seal, the rumour goes, and most likely originally from the Philippines."

"Where can we find this man? This must happen quickly."

"I don't mean to be flippant, but professional assassins are not in the telephone book," I told him. "It will take a few days for me to ask around, make contact and set up this type of a job."

"We don't have a few days. Did you not look around you when you drove through the camp? Did you not see the armoured personnel carriers standing by, and the lorries? We are ready to strike. And when the First Scout Ranger Regiment strikes…"

"It's strikes hard," I interrupted him. "But Colonel, the important thing is that you strike successfully. This is not the right moment. Put it on hold, Colonel. As you know I used to be in the British Army and that is my military advice. If you launch the coup while the Senator is in hospital, and before you have hired an assassin, you will not be successful."

He sat back in his chair and it creaked. He folded his arms and gave me a harsh look. "Do you think we are cowards? That we will shirk our responsibility?"

"Let me tell you something." I leaned forward into his space and lowered my voice, giving it more depth to make sure my point got across. "The man who tried to kill Senator Guzman was most likely from the Presidential Security Group. I recognised the car. I also suspect that they were not trying to kill him. They didn't use the right ammunition. This was a warning shot across your bows." I tapped him on the knee and he flinched at the overly familiar contact. "Malacanang Palace knows all about your plan. They have been watching you."

He stood up and his face was now full of anger. "Are you the traitor? Have you betrayed us?"

I shook my head. "Of course not. I'm telling you what I suspect. Go ahead. Storm Manila. Do your best, but men will get killed or at the very least their careers will be ruined."

"We must do what is right for our people," he barked at me.

"Every commander knows that when you take on a mission there must be at least a good chance of victory."

"And you think we won't be successful?" he demanded of me. "Half of the old families are behind us. Over thirty influential businessmen. They will come out against the President."

"Talk is cheap, Ricardo," I said. "Your young men are the ones putting their bodies on the firing line."

"I will lead from the front," he said.

"You will, I know that. But, for now, the rich billionaires are just hedging their bets. They will sit back and watch what happens on television. They won't come out of their guarded compounds to stand on the street shoulder to shoulder with you unless they think you are guaranteed to win."

"You don't understand the Philippines," he snapped.

"I don't," I admitted.

"I believe you are a coward," he said.

"I believe in staying alive by planning to succeed, not to fail. I'm not the one leading my men into the jaws of certain destruction. That's not courage, it's foolhardiness. Please, Colonel, reconsider this operation. Take a few days. Explain today's activities away as a training exercise. Wait for further instructions from the Senator when he comes out of his coma."

"If someone killed the President, our cause would be stronger," he said, fitting his beret on his head and smoothing out the creases.

"I disagree," I said. "If the President is killed you will be seen as the bad guys not patriots. It's entirely the wrong move. You have to play this the right way if you hope to be successful. Go back and study how Marcos was deposed. That was true People Power not just an army regiment riding into town in armoured vehicles."

He shook his head angrily, then got to his feet. He was an imposing figure and I could see how the men would follow him into the breach. But this was a mission doomed to failure. Why couldn't the man see that?

"What exactly is your plan when you get into town?" I asked.

"I can't tell you that if you are not with us," he said tersely.

"You're going to storm some of the radio and television stations and lock them down? You'll barricade the police and army barracks in town and stop them from being able to get out? You will seize control of the airport?"

He nodded slowly.

"Have you heard of a man called Edward Luttwak who wrote a book called *Coup d'Etat: A Practical Handbook*?"

He snorted in disdain. "Everybody has to read Luttwak at our Staff College," he said.

"Right, so everybody knows the blueprint of what you are about to do. And you also studied Sun Tzu. And what does he say about confusing the enemy?"

"We should never be predictable?" he asked, a note of doubt creeping into his voice.

"Yes, but the Sun Tzu axiom that particularly springs to mind from my time at Sandhurst is: 'He will win who knows when to fight and when not to fight'." I stared him down. "Where are you going to base yourself?" I asked.

"One of the hotels in Makati," he said.

"That's straight out of Luttwak. So how are you confusing the enemy? They think you will take over the Oakwood Hotel but instead you'll take over the Mandarin?"

He gave me a sad smile. "Everything you say, Bill, makes much sense but you can't change my mind. And now that you know what our plan is I can't permit you to go free. You must come along with us."

"That's not going to happen."

"I have no choice," he said and his hand touched the holster that was on his belt. "I do not wish you to come as our prisoner. As our foreign observer perhaps."

"Having a foreigner along sounds suspiciously like bringing a hostage to make sure your colleagues on the other side don't open fire indiscriminately."

He laughed grimly. "That hadn't crossed my mind. But it's not a bad idea." Fernandes took a step closer to me. "I respect you, Bill Jedburgh, but if you are not fighting for our cause then we must make sure you don't create any problems for us. You will come with us."

I wanted to kick myself for not having got on a plane the day before. What business of mine was it, getting involved in an ill-fated coup? This was something you watched on CNN or the BBC with a cold beer in your hand and popcorn in your mouth.

31

Which was how I found myself - eight hours later - ensconced in the Rizal Ballroom on the second floor of the Peninsula Manila Hotel. The ballroom had become the de facto command centre of the insurrection. Most of the tourists who'd been staying in the hotel had been sent away. Snipers were positioned on the roof and Fernandes' men had set up barricades and claymore anti-personnel mines around the perimeter. We were currently in a stand-off.

The strangest aspect of this operation was that the ballroom was half full of journalists. Thirty or forty of them scurried around the rooms and corridors trying to persuade anyone they could to talk to them. Their cameras followed every move of the military commanders and I was having a tough time ducking away in corners to keep my face out of sight.

A particularly irritating woman from TV5 had spotted me earlier on and kept trying to pin me down.

"Who are you, sir? Are you a Filipino?" she said, poking a tape recorder at my nose.

I gently pushed the device aside. "I am nobody. You should not concern yourself with me."

"Are you a CIA agent?" she wanted to know.

"Do I sound like an American?" I countered, holding in the snigger brewing inside me at this strange assumption.

"You are Australian then?" She was an attractive woman but about twenty pounds overweight, dressed in a beige trouser suit that was tight over all her curves.

"I'm not Australian," I said and tried to walk away, but she grabbed me by the sleeve. Someone at journalism college had taught her that being pushy and aggressive was the only way to get on.

"What are you doing here, sir?" she asked again.

"I was staying in the hotel and somehow I've got caught up in this... excitement."

She stared at me with disbelieving eyes. "Are you sure you are a hotel guest? Are you not a foreign advisor to the mutineers? Is this coup being financed by a foreign power?" She didn't seem inclined to give up, so I tried a different tack.

"I am a senior business executive working for the Peninsula Group, based in Hong Kong. You can ask the hotel manager and he will confirm that I was visiting from the head office on a routine audit."

That seemed to work for a moment but then she asked: "Why do you have two soldiers from the Scout Ranger Regiment following you around? Are they guarding you?"

I smiled and shook my head slowly. "They are keeping an eye on me because that's what is meant by being a hostage. I suspect Colonel Fernandes wants some of us hotel employees available as human shields in case the marines outside storm the hotel."

"You are a human shield?" That got her excited.

"I didn't say I was. I suggested it may be a reason that these two men are following me around. Now will you excuse me, I need to go into the men's room."

That was the best tactic for the moment. She might get bored of waiting for me outside the door. She might begin to worry that she was missing out on the excitement back in the ballroom.

The two Rangers came into the opulent room with me. The floor was marble and there were five booths and six urinals. A lemon fragrance hung in the air.

"Do you guys smoke?" I asked them. They were both holding their M4 assault rifles in their hands with the stock in their shoulder. It was the favoured weapon of American Special Forces with a shorter barrel for Close Quarters Battle and fired the standard 5.56 mm NATO round.

One of the men, who told me his name was Alberto, produced a pack of Lucky Strike and we had a leisurely smoke. They were good kids and I didn't want to frighten them. Ricardo had instructed his troops that I should be treated as a guest but not allowed to leave the building. He'd taken all my phones off me so I couldn't communicate with anyone on the outside. I explained to them that I had done some work body-guarding Senator Guzman. That gave them some framework for reference. They'd all read about the assassination attempt so in their minds I must be a good guy. At least that's what I was trying to convey.

"Fucking journalists," I said and lit another cigarette from the packet that lay next to the marble wash basin. "Why does your boss need so many of them in the hotel?"

"We must let the world know why we are doing this," Alberto said. "If they know we are against corruption and our cause is just, then the people of Manila will come out into the streets and support us."

I let the smoke trickle out through my nose. I hadn't smoked cigarettes for a very long time but at moments like this a man has to have something to keep him busy.

"I sincerely hope for your sakes that this will work out as planned," I said. It was more of a rhetorical statement because I could feel things already going to shit. Surrounding the hotel, we'd been told, were three thousand marines and the vaunted Special Action Force of the National Philippines Police.

"What's their motto?" I'd asked Alberto when I heard.

"By skill and virtue, we triumph," he'd replied.

Everybody seemed to have a bloody gung-ho motto in this operation. My motto was: 'Frankly I don't give a damn'. I just wanted to leave so I could get on with my holiday, scuba diving and shagging.

"Do you think that bitch has moved on yet?" I asked. We decided to risk it and thankfully exited without being accosted. As we crossed the corridor a bishop in full regalia appeared.

"Who's that?" I asked my companions.

"I think he's the bishop from Quezon," said Alberto. "He's acting as a go-between."

We wandered off and eventually found a bar, imaginatively named 'The Bar', which was empty and quiet. I helped myself to a San Miguel, but my two guards declined the offer. The television was on. From the news broadcasts we could see armoured personnel carriers blocking all the access roads and a small tank pointing its barrel at the front entrance of the hotel. It looked as if the commanders of the forces on the outside were being bugged by journalists as much as those on the inside.

Nobody came to look for us for hours so I kept drinking until a woman in a chef's uniform appeared and asked if we wanted some food. The hotel's kitchen was providing everyone in the building with something to eat to reduce tensions and keep everyone calm. That sounded like a fine idea.

The lads opted for pizza while I asked for steak. Half an hour later I was tucking into a medium-rare chunk of sirloin with a sweet orange-coloured baked potato on the side. I had a feeling that very few military coups were as well provisioned as this one.

Ricardo found us eventually. He appeared tired and drawn. On television nothing much had changed. There was much to-ing and fro-ing. Important people came and conferred with other important people in uniform, their shoulders heavy with insignia. There was no sign of the President. The PSG probably had her locked down tight in the palace.

"How are we doing?" I asked Ricardo as he sat down next to me in a plush leather armchair. He ran his hands across his face, then ordered his two men to wait outside in the corridor.

"We were not successful in capturing the airport. They were waiting for us on all the main roads."

"Bad luck. According to Luttwak the airport is always key."

He gave me an irritable look and went behind the bar and fetched himself a glass that he'd filled three inches deep with Glenmorangie. He sniffed it with appreciation then took a measured sip.

"Bonnie Prince Charlie would have had a few of those before the Battle of Culloden kicked off."

"You believe there will be bloodshed?" Ricardo asked.

"I have no idea what is going on. I can't tell."

"We are negotiating to make a public statement condemning the corruption of the President and her government."

"Do you think they will allow that?"

He shrugged.

"Who has come out in support of you on the outside?" I asked.

"Not enough influential men and women," he confirmed.

"Time to surrender?" I suggested mildly.

He gave an angry growl. He wasn't ready yet to concede defeat. Perhaps there had to be more posturing or even some bloodshed before he would pull the plug on this ill-fated expedition.

"I must talk to you about something personal," Ricardo said.

"Fire away."

"When I confiscated your mobile phones, I found the phone number of Michelle Arupe on one of them. You made a phone call to her yesterday."

"I did," I admitted.

"What is your business with Miss Arupe?" he said sharply.

A little voice in my head told me to tread carefully. "I met her scuba diving recently in Puerto Galera, then at the Senator's granddaughter's wedding. She was a bridesmaid, as you know." I watched his reactions carefully. "I warned her that things might get messy in Manila and to get out of town for a few days. I didn't speak with her. I left her a voicemail."

"That is the truth?" he said, his eyebrows high on his forehead, his eyes wide open, trying to dig into my soul.

"She's an attractive lady. Not really my type," I said. That was a lie of course, the second part of that statement, but I felt it might be expedient. He confirmed that my caution was well-founded.

"I am in love with Michelle Arupe," he said, colouring with emotion.

"She is not your wife." It was a statement of the bleeding obvious, but I needed some high ground in this conversation.

"A man cannot help himself if he falls in love with a woman who is not his wife," he declared. He was writing some sort of novel in his head in which he was the tragic hero. I wasn't sure that augured well for the outcome of the coup.

"That's certainly true," I admitted. "You are a few years older than Michelle. Is she in love with you?"

"Of course," he snapped.

"Where is she?" I asked.

"I sent her away to Baguio. My family has a holiday home there. She will be safe."

"Is it commonly known that you are having an affair with her?"

He shook his head sharply and took a long drink from his single malt.

"There is nothing between me and Michelle Arupe," I said. "You do not need to trouble yourself on that account."

"You must stay away from her," he said and his eyes narrowed in threat.

"That's what the Senator told me. I will follow both of your advice. There are plenty of pretty girls in the Philippines. You are a very lucky man to have a woman like that who loves you."

"It has not always been easy," he commented.

"When are they ever easy?" I said. "Will you permit me to make one phone call to a friend of mine to let him know that I'm all right and that I'm here? You may listen in to my call."

He thought about that for a while and then nodded in assent. He handed me one of my phones and watched as I punched up the number that I had for Larry Lim.

"Where are you?" my Singaporean friend said, dispensing with any formalities.

"Thank you, I'm very well. I'm stuck in the Peninsula Manila Hotel with my military mates. It's a complicated story. Just tell anyone who wants to know that I am fine and being treated well."

Larry asked: "Are you with Colonel Ricardo Fernandes?"

"That is correct," I said smiling innocently at Ricardo who was watching me like a bird of prey. "I'm having a very civilised whisky with Colonel Fernandes as we speak."

"You must kill him, the Brigadier says. That will solve a lot of problems for a lot of people." Larry sounded serious. I told him that I was looking forward to seeing him again soon and I would consider his advice on healthy eating very seriously.

32

It was getting late so I gave the assistant manager a thousand pesos for his passkey and found myself a comfortable bedroom on the third floor well away from the tank. My two Ranger guards opted to stay outside in the corridor. They would take turns napping. I had a vast double-bed with crisp clean sheets and after a scorching hot, twenty-minute shower I fell quickly into a deep slumber.

When I woke up at six in the morning and turned on the news channels, they were discussing a statement that had just been made by the rebels - as they were being called.

Surrounded by a gaggle of journalists Colonel Fernandes, looking tired and drawn, read out what was intended to be a rousing speech. It rambled on for a while about the plotters' grievances with the current administration and the endemic corruption that was damaging to the economy and the future of the nation. It ended by calling for the resignation of the President and a 'unilateral declaration of their withdrawal of support from the chain of command'.

I fluffed up my pillows and sat up straighter in bed. I wondered if room service might be available. Slipping into the shaggy hotel bathrobe I went to open the door.

Alberto and his oppo had been replaced by two other young soldiers. I wished them good morning and they nodded and smiled. This was a big adventure and, however it ended, would be something they'd be telling their grandchildren about. That is, unless they died in a gun battle before they could write their memoirs.

There had been a previous military coup in the 80s - I couldn't remember which one - where the rebels all marched back peacefully to their base. Their leaders were court-martialled but the soldiers were pardoned. Gaius Marius, the man who had reformed the Roman Army, would have used decimation - that strange process where every tenth man was stoned by his nine other comrades - to deal with a mutiny like this.

Showered and dressed, I wandered downstairs and located the kitchens. A few cooks were sitting about smoking, gossiping and watching the latest developments on the television screen. One of them rustled me up an excellent Spanish omelette and a big mug of coffee.

I took my plate to 'The Bar' which was as convenient a location to hang around in as any. Close enough to the action but out of the way.

Nothing much happened over the next few hours. The President had declared a 'State of Rebellion' but instructed her troops to use reasonable force, and pay due regard to constitutional rights, in putting down the rebellion. She gave the plotters a deadline of 5 p.m. to surrender.

Around ten, there was a squawk over my escort's radio summoning me to the Rizal Ballroom. I wandered upstairs and found myself in the middle of the usual tumult and confusion. Everyone was talking at each other loudly and the same journalists, who by now all looked tired and unwashed after a long night, were still chasing around for gossip and soundbites.

Ricardo was surrounded by a small group of his senior officers. They were in the middle of a heated discussion. He summoned me over and I went to stand by his side. He hadn't shaved since the morning we set out from Camp Tecson. My chin was as smooth as Hong Kong Airport's primary runway 7R/25L. My pilot friends told me it was one of the best asphalt-concrete surfaces in the world.

"My men are telling me we have achieved as much as we can hope and it is time to surrender," Ricardo said to me.

"How can I help?" I asked.

"We want your professional opinion. As a former British Army officer."

"I was in the Intelligence Corps. Strategy was never my area of expertise."

"You are an outsider," Ricardo said. "You are not affected by the same emotion we feel. You can give us your opinion." I could tell he was playing to the audience. He wanted my support, because there was obviously dissent in the ranks.

"I gave you my advice before we set out from Camp Tecson. You didn't like it."

"We will respect your opinion," one of the majors said.

"First of all, get rid of these vulture journalists. Tell them to wait in the lobby downstairs. We can't have a decent O-Group with civilians trying to film us or even lip read what we are discussing."

Ricardo nodded. He gave the order and the soldiers began clearing the media correspondents out. They were not happy, but they sensed something was about to happen, and expectation filled the room even as the soldiers were shoo-ing them through the ballroom doors. They were like a dog pricking up its ears at the sound of an intruder. When the doors were closed the big room fell strangely silent. The soldiers sat cross-legged at the far end and their officers and I pulled up our chairs around a table at the other end.

"What is your plan now?" I asked them and stared around the circle of men. With the exception of Fernandes, not one was older than thirty. Most of them had experienced firefights and death in the southern Philippines dealing with Muslim insurgents. They were hardened in battle but in matters of state they were babes in arms.

"Some of these men are asking me to call an end to our operation," Ricardo said. I couldn't tell exactly which of the commanders he meant but a few of them nodded at his words.

I said: "Have you achieved your objective?"

Ricardo shrugged. Some of the officers shook their heads.

"What was your objective?" I asked.

"To force the resignation of the President and her government," Ricardo said.

"Is that likely now? You were counting on the streets being filled with anti-government protesters. That hasn't happened, has it?"

"The people will come out when they see our continued resolve," he said. I could tell from most of the faces around me that they were doubtful this would happen.

"It might have worked if Senator Guzman was outside making speeches," I pointed out. "But you and your men were only half of the equation."

Ricardo stared at me fiercely but didn't contradict me. He'd asked for my opinion. There was no point in getting angry if I spoke my mind.

"What do you suggest we do, Mr. Bill?" said the man I thought was Major Gerardo.

"Everything in war is very simple. But the simplest thing is difficult," I said cryptically.

They stared at me with confusion in their eyes. "Negotiate an honourable truce now, while you still can. You've said your piece. You've shown your resolve, but you can't win this battle."

I looked Major Gerardo in the eye and pointed at him. He felt like the weakest link in this group, a breach that could be exploited. I wasn't a coward, but I knew that if troops loyal to the President stormed the hotel there was a reasonable chance I'd be injured or die in the crossfire. I needed to convince them to surrender peacefully, or find a way of getting out of the hotel before the shit hit the fan. My best bet would be to disarm my guards and take my chances at finding an exit with an M4 in my hand.

"Frankly," I said, "you can go out and die heroes if you choose. But nobody will remember you in five years' time. If you live to fight another day, you might get another chance. You can become politicians and attack the system from the inside. A famous German general once said: 'courage which goes against military expediency is stupidity, or, if it is insisted upon by a commander, irresponsibility.' I think this battle is over."

Half of the officers were nodding now. I'd taken my eyes off Ricardo to watch the reactions of the others. Turning back, I found myself staring down the barrel of his stainless-steel officer-issue Beretta M9.

"We will not surrender," he said firmly.

I suspected that he'd pulled the gun not to point at me but to make sure his officers got the message that he wouldn't permit them to break ranks at this point. This was his unit and although he'd opened the door to a discussion, he was now using his executive power to veto any decision that went against his own will.

I shrugged. "You asked for my opinion. You may ignore it, if you so wish."

The muzzle of the Beretta had moved and was pointing at Major Gerardo. Ricardo repeated: "We will not surrender. We will die with honour."

I took stock of the faces sitting around me and made my own executive decision. In Ju Jutsu there is a move called *Chikama No Tanju* which is a gun disarming technique. You have to be close up and it involves twisting the hand at the wrist so the weapon is released.

Ricardo was busy staring down his recalcitrant men. I turned, twisted the Beretta out of his grip and kicked him out of his chair. He fell and rolled over on the floor. I stepped back, holding the gun muzzle down, my left hand up, palm outwards, telling him to stop and calm down. He bounded to his feet, his face gripped by fury.

The officers were all standing now but they were confused, unsure of what was happening.

"Guys, everyone calm down," I yelled, getting their attention. "We don't need to be pointing weapons at each other. Let's do this in a democratic way. Who wants to surrender now? Put your hands in the air? No bloodshed. An honourable surrender."

All of the officers but three raised their hands. Ricardo was hopping from one foot to the other, spitting like a rabid cat. But I had the gun and he wasn't prepared to come at me.

"How about everyone who wants to leave, leaves? Then the rest of you can carry on until the commandos from the Special Action Force storm the building this evening," I said. That sobered them up suddenly. One of the three holdouts put his hand in the air.

"Ricardo, your men want to stop this nonsense now," I advised him. "Why not call it a day?"

"This is The Army, not a democracy," he snarled and came at me. I didn't know if he had a round in the chamber but I flicked the safety catch on his M9 and pulled the trigger.

33

The bullet hit Fernandes low in the shin, exactly where I'd been aiming, and he went crashing to the plush carpet. His left leg was whipped out from under him by the impact.

There was an eerie silence after the crack of the shot. Then a low murmuring began from the troops in the room. This was the time to grip the situation before I lost control and was lynched.

"Major Gerardo, calm the men down," I ordered, using my best Sandhurst officer's voice. "You, Captain, get a field dressing on the Colonel's leg. Stop the bleeding."

I'd slipped the safety back on Ricardo's Beretta and stuffed it down the back of my trousers so I could hold both my hands up. Body language was important in volatile situations.

"Officers of the First Scout Ranger Regiment. You have decided to surrender. Now Colonel Fernandes is incapacitated, who is the ranking officer?"

There was confusion in their faces but also relief. None of them had shot their commander. But someone had to stop him or the whole sorry business would drag on and end badly. I'd taken the decision out of their hands.

"I am," said a short, broad-shouldered major with a broken nose. I noticed that, like me, Major Somera had found the opportunity to shave at some point.

"Major, you are in command," I said.

He nodded grimly and turning to the other officers, fired off a volley of orders in Tagalog at them. Their training took over, they saluted and went to talk to their men at the other end of the room.

It took another three hours for Major Somera to negotiate a truce with the Government's Chief Negotiator, a recently retired four-star General and former Chief of Staff. Everyone wanted this to be over. Fernandes, whose lower leg was swaddled in field dressings, had been rushed off to hospital. I went back to The Bar. My two guards were still with me since nobody had told them to stand down, so I used them to keep the journalists away from me.

Eventually the soldiers started filing out through the lobby and into the flashing lights of the cameramen outside. They had been ordered to lay down their weapons, which were piled up in untidy stacks under the watchful eye of a platoon of black-clad, armed policemen. Once outside the Scout Rangers would board buses and be taken back to their barracks at Camp Tecson. The officers would be taken to another location and debriefed by the PNP. It later emerged that several of them, including the two captains who had not wanted to surrender, managed to slip out of the back of the hotel through the laundry rooms and vanish into the crowd. I found myself identified as a 'person of interest' and bundled into a police van that headed off in the direction of Taguig, in the South of Metro Manila.

We arrived at Camp Babong Diwa, the headquarters of the National Capital Region Police, as it was starting to get dark. Sitting opposite me in the van were two of the journalists who had been in the hotel for the last two days. That put a smile on my face. They had tried to explain who they were, but the police got it into their heads that they were plotters who'd disguised themselves by getting hold of press credentials and civvies.

For the second time in ten days I found myself sitting in a police cell. This time not for murder but for sedition. The police were at a loss to explain who I was and I didn't try to enlighten them. Common consensus was that I must be working for the CIA but nobody could explain why I had an English accent. I'd made a quick call to Larry Lim before I was scooped up, so he knew what was happening and hopefully would try and get me released.

I was given a bottle of mineral water and some chicken adobo with rice, which wasn't bad. Not up to the standard of the Peninsula Manila Hotel but it was edible. They'd taken my watch away so I could not tell what time it was but it felt like a few hours later when I was taken to an interrogation room.

Four armed police officers in the black SWAT style uniform of the Special Action Force stood on either side of the door. They carried Heckler & Koch UMP45s slung across their chests. The UMP - German for Universal Submachine Gun - was the successor to the classic MP5 that we'd used in the Hong Kong Police. The four men stared fixedly into the space above my head so I decided not to make small talk. There was a time and a season for everything.

Eventually a policeman in dress uniform appeared, accompanied by a young woman holding a notebook and pencil. He was short and corpulent but his face was familiar. It took me a while to remember where I'd seen him before.

"I am Police Director General Alvarez," the man said by way of introduction. "This is my secretary. She will take notes."

"Pleased to meet you, sir. I believe I saw you at Senator Guzman's granddaughter's wedding." His brow furrowed for a moment and then he also recognised me.

"Yes, yes," he said, "you were doing some security for the Senator. Now I understand."

"Happy the man who understands the causes of things," I said.

"What is that? What does that mean?" Alvarez asked. His secretary made a few marks on the pad with her pencil, then stared at me silently. She was disturbingly pretty as well as a dab hand at shorthand.

"It's an old saying one of my teachers in the Army liked to use."

Alvarez frowned and made an 'umm' noise. I was confusing him.

"You were in the Army?" he asked.

"The British Army, and in the Royal Hong Kong Police. That is how I came to undertake security and body-guarding work for the Senator. We have known each other for a few years."

"Do you live in the Philippines?" he asked.

"I visit Puerto Galera regularly to scuba dive but mostly I live in Singapore."

I was starting to get the feeling that he was uncomfortable with this conversation, which was odd until a possible explanation came to mind.

He said: "What were you doing with the mutineers in the Peninsula Manila Hotel?"

"I was abducted by Colonel Fernandes. He asked me to come to Camp Tecson to give him an update on Senator Guzman's health. When I arrived I was told that I could no longer leave and had to join them."

"That is true?" he asked and leant back in the metal chair. He made a whistling noise inhaling through his pursed lips.

"Yes, sir."

He pointed his index finger at me and said, "We have reports that you are the one who shot Colonel Fernandes in the leg and persuaded the mutineers to surrender."

I shrugged modestly. "You'd have to ask the other witnesses to corroborate that. They were pretty much ready to give up but the Colonel wanted to drag it out. I thought he was angling for a hero's death, which would have caused considerable bloodshed."

"A traitor's death, most likely," the Police Director General said with a grunt that would have done Mr. Grimwig proud.

"Colonel Fernandes was under the impression that there would be support from the people," I said, "and leading members of the establishment for the coup d'état. He was sadly mistaken in that assumption."

There was a twitch under Alvarez's right eye that confirmed my suspicions. He had been at the wedding and his name was most likely on the list of supporters. I'd never seen the full list but if I got the chance I'd ask Larry to confirm it. I decided to change tack slightly because I'd remembered something else.

"You are Michelle Arupe's godfather, I believe, sir?"

That confused him for a moment. "I am, do you know her? Yes, you were dancing with her at the wedding. For a long time."

"We met last week, scuba diving. She is a nice lady." I paused and watched him carefully before I added the next sentence. "Do you know that she is involved romantically with Colonel Fernandes?"

His face clouded over. Of course he knew but he wasn't going to get into that conversation with five junior police officers in the room.

"Is that true?" was his response.

I shrugged apologetically. "It might just be a rumour. I understand Michelle went out of town and so she was not involved in this whole business."

"My goddaughter is a good girl. She has had a difficult life. Her father's bankruptcy left her penniless and forced her to make her own way in the world. Perhaps, in such circumstances, one is forced to rely on the comfort of strangers. But she understands that politics is complicated and loyalty to the constitution is paramount."

I wasn't entirely sure what he meant by that monologue but it sounded like that was as much as he was prepared to say about Michelle Arupe and my gentle attempt at blackmailing him into letting me go. So I tried again.

"In this matter of the mutiny, I am an innocent bystander who happened to be in the wrong place at the wrong time. I hope you will come to that conclusion and I can be released when you have finished your investigations."

He stared at me without any emotion for a long while, as his brain ticked over and analysed what he knew about me.

"Some of the journalists are saying that you must be an American spy and that you instigated this coup to destabilise our nation."

"General Alvarez, I am British and have no possible motive for wanting to influence Filipino politics. I do confess that I have done some security work for Senator Guzman, who is currently in a coma because somebody ordered their men to shoot him. I was standing next to him when the attempt was made on his life. I think you know very well that the notion of me being a spy of any kind is ridiculous."

He nodded grimly but then finally cracked me a small smile.

"How does your saying go again? Happy is the man who knows the causes of things?"

"Yes, it's a quote from Virgil."

His smile broadened. "I think we all know the causes of things, Mr. Bill Jedburgh. I will go and discuss this matter with the President. And we will try to corroborate your story with some of the other plotters." He stood up and extended his hand so I could shake it. "If it is true that you shot Colonel Fernandes and brought the mutiny to an end peacefully, then we must be grateful to you. The President made it clear from the start that there should be no bloodshed if possible. We do not like shedding the blood of our countrymen."

"Colonel Fernandes only lost a little bit of blood. He'll be running marathons again in a few months."

Police Director General Alvarez gave me a long lingering stare, then turned and left the interrogation room.

But it wasn't until the next morning that Larry Lim turned up and I was released on my own recognisance into his tender care. Despite the hardness of the mattress and the noise of wailing from other prisoners I had slept the sleep of the just.

34

My dive bag had come to the Peninsula Manila with me when we left Camp Tecson. Larry took me back there and after some discussion we managed to persuade the police guards to let us in and I retrieved my bag from the room I'd been using.

Larry had booked me a room in the Shangri-La on a different floor from the Brigadier's suite. I thanked him and told him that I had a few errands to run so I'd catch up with him later. When I'd been released by the PNP they'd also returned my mobile phones. I sent a couple of text messages.

Carla texted back to say she was fine. 'The Tighter Pussy' had been taken over by one of the other shareholders and it was business as usual. I texted back to say it might be a few weeks before I would return to Angeles. I was tied up with a big project at work. I got a reply to my second text, saying I could see Senator Guzman at 3 p.m.

Then I hit the gym. I spent two hours lifting weights and running on the machine to get the kinks out of my muscles. Insurrections took it out of you physically. Mentally too, and I needed a clear head to process what I had learned. The rhythm of the exercise provided that.

The coup had been doomed from the start. The Brigadier's leak of information had meant the PSG had been ahead of the game all along. Their foresight in removing Guzman, the plotter's most valuable piece from the chessboard had left Fernandes, a lone knight, trying to defeat his opponent with a motley collection of pawns while all the White Queen's pieces were still intact.

History is written by the victors, and in a place like the Philippines, where coups were as common as typhoons, most people waited for victory before writing themselves into the storybooks. I suspected that many of those on Guzman's list, when approached by the PSG, would explain away their presence as the Senator's wishful thinking or with further cash donations to the other side. Most likely they'd been hedging their bets this way already.

However hard I bench-pressed I couldn't help coming back to the fact that whoever had stolen the list and given it to Dickie Goodyear was responsible for this entire snafu, the death of my colleague and the interruption of my holiday. I still wasn't certain who it was, but I knew it was somebody close to the Senator and I now had my suspicions.

The Manila Doctors Hospital, which is where they'd moved Senator Guzman, was about 10 miles from the hotel through the snarly traffic. It was one of the finest private hospitals in the city.

They showed me to his room which was on a high floor. Two of his usual guards were outside the door. Flowers and get-well-soon cards covered most of the surface space around Guzman's bed. He was tired and drawn but sitting up in bed barking down a mobile phone at someone in Tagalog. Guzman waved me to a vacant chair and held up his fingers to show that he'd be a few more minutes. One of his daughters sat in a chair by the window reading a romance novel. She was in her late thirties and heavy set. Her husband ran an energy company in their home province. I waited patiently and made small talk with her. She told me her father was getting stronger and the doctors were happy with his progress.

When Guzman finished the call he asked his daughter to step out and leave us for half an hour. He waited until the door snicked shut, then sighed and said: "So it is all over, our dream. I saw the end on the news."

"The dream was dead from the moment you hit the sidewalk with a bullet in you, sir. Fernandes was a fool to go ahead while you were in a coma. I told him as much in Camp Tecson but he wouldn't listen. Then he dragged me along to Manila."

"I should have made you my General, Bill," he said, shaking his head bitterly. "You are a man not only of action, but of strategy and tactics as well. Ricardo is a man of honour, but a blunt instrument. That woman knew that if she had me shot it would stop us from being successful."

"It was a smart move. They didn't want to kill you."

"She wanted to kill me."

"I don't think so. It was a warning shot."

He tapped his abdomen which was still covered in a heavy dressing and said, "That didn't feel like a warning shot."

"It was a through and through, missed all your vital organs."

He glared at me because it didn't sound as heroic as he wanted to appear. Then he relented in face of the facts. "I am eternally grateful to you for saving my life."

"It was my job. If I'd been a bit faster and a bit better prepared, you would not have been hit at all. I didn't expect them to be wearing body armour."

His eyes narrowed at that. "Who were they?"

"A hit team from the PSG. I'm sure of that."

He nodded. "I believe that."

"Will you make your peace with her?" I asked.

He nodded ruefully. "Someone has already been in touch to open a discussion."

"I spent the night in Camp Bagong Diwa being interrogated by your friend Police Director General Alvarez."

"That traitor," Senator Guzman snapped. "He promised to come out in support of us with the entire PNP. If he had done what Ping Lacson did in 2001 we would have been successful. What did you tell him?"

"Not much. The truth. I told him I was providing close protection for you and that Ricardo had dragged me along unwillingly. How is he, by the way?"

"Under house arrest. I was talking to him on the phone earlier. He is angry with you."

"Ricardo was going to get his men killed. The mission had failed. It was the right time to surrender peacefully. That's what most of his officers wanted. But he was all fired up."

"And that is why you shot him?" Guzman wanted to know.

"I was outside his chain of command, so I had the freedom to act that was denied to his subordinates. He came at me and I had his gun in my hand. I could have handled it better but…" I shrugged.

"They want to charge him with treason and put him in prison for twenty years."

I smiled maliciously. "If they locked up all the officers in the Philippines Army who have contemplated taking part in a coup, you wouldn't have many left. You'll get him reinstated within a year and promoted to Brigadier. Then they can send him to Mindanao for a tour of duty, where he will redeem his honour and win a few medals."

Guzman thought for a while, then replied: "Yes, that's what I intend to arrange. We still have many friends high up in the Army."

"Will you try again to oust her from office?" I asked.

He gave me a sly smile. "Of course. But I have a new plan. We will accuse her of electoral sabotage and vote rigging. If that doesn't work we'll allege economic plunder."

"You are a tenacious opponent, Senator."

He shrugged off my sarcasm as if it was a compliment.

"Maybe I will put my resources at the disposal of Noynoy Aquino," Guzman said. "He has indicated that he would like to run for President. He has an honest face and a strong family name. The people of the Philippines like that."

"A strong economy is what the people should like best. Lots of jobs and full bellies. More social and financial equality."

Senator Guzman stared at me and started to laugh. That was painful for him, so he stopped.

"What will you do now, my friend Bill?" he said. There was still an elephant in the room that had not been acknowledged.

I leant forward in my chair and came as close to his face as I could. I lowered my voice to a whisper. "One thing I will not do is tell anyone, ever, that you asked me to assassinate the President."

I sat back and watched his face and his expression told me that the question had been niggling at him and he liked what I'd said.

"Do you need money?" he asked quietly.

"No, I have enough for my needs," I said. "What I really want to do is get back to my holiday. I just ask for your friendship and your support, and for you to watch my back if I ever need your help."

He nodded with satisfaction. "That is a deal." He held out his hand and we shook on it. Because he was a politician but also a Catholic I reached out and took the Bible from the bedside drawer and put it in his hand. "It's a deal on the Holy Scriptures."

His face told me that he took my words seriously. He repeated what he'd just said, holding up the Bible. It wasn't a cast-iron guarantee, but I didn't want to be looking over my shoulder every time I came into town wondering if Senator Guzman had decided my knowledge was a liability. On balance, I suspected the risk was low. Within a few years this sorry episode would be forgotten and there'd be a new President ruling the roost.

"There is something else I want to understand," I said. "My old Hong Kong police buddy Dickie Goodyear was blackmailing you with confidential information that he'd obtained, wasn't he?"

Guzman thought about that one for a while then gave a short, sharp nod.

"But he was asking for too much money?"

Guzman nodded again, this time more slowly, wondering where my questions were heading.

I said firmly: "He was a drug dealer as well as a blackmailer. He was an old colleague and I liked him, but it was clear his moral compass was wavering all over the place. If you live by the sword there is always a risk you will die by the sword."

Guzman gave me a wary smile and nodded slowly one more time.

"I gave him $50,000 to keep him quiet, but he wanted five hundred thousand US dollars more. I would have paid half that, perhaps, but he started to get aggressive," the Senator said. "He said he had obligations to his partners. So I asked some friends to speak with him and to get the information back for me. I told them they could keep the $50,000 if they were successful."

I was right, it was the Senator who had put the Lapida Brothers in motion. I wondered whether he had heard that they had been killed in a gang war, but that was neither here nor there. Nobody except Rannie knew that I'd been in Angeles City at the time of their deaths.

"How did Goodyear obtain that confidential information in the first place? Someone you trust must have given it to him." I watched his eyes carefully and could see his discomfort. "Am I right? Do you know who it was?"

He gave a long sigh which could have covered up a possible lie. "I do not know who betrayed me, but when I find out, then you and I will deal with it. Is that acceptable? I will pay you whatever is needed." I cursed inwardly. I had meant to let sleeping dogs lie. I stood up and poured him a glass of water, putting it into his hand.

"Dickie Goodyear is dead. The rebellion is over. You have new plans. You are alive, Ricardo is alive. It's probably best just to sweep it all under the carpet."

He took a sip from the glass and placed it on the tray in front of him. For a few seconds I watched his eyes as he speculated and weighed up what we were discussing.

"Go, enjoy your scuba diving. But you will work for me again when I need you?" he said by way of conclusion.

"Of course, Senator. I am always at your service."

He smiled happily at that and it concluded our interview.

35

Michelle Arupe had finally replied to my texts. We arranged to meet for dinner at the 'Hard Rock Makati' which was located in the Glorietta mall opposite the Shangri-La Hotel.

I arrived on time but she was twenty minutes late. I watched as she made her way between the wooden tables, her fine legs and rear sheathed in a tight pair of black Armani jeans with a strappy turquoise blouse from Dolce & Gabbana. She wore a simple diamond pendant, another beautiful stone, and smelled of Anais Anais by Cacherel. I recognised the fragrance from a brief dalliance I'd had in Hong Kong the previous year with an Indonesian investment banker.

"You missed all the excitement," I said once she was seated. It was too early for the band, but Bon Jovi serenaded us from the speakers. We sat at a table beneath some rock star's old guitar but I didn't make the effort to read the sign that would have told me which one.

Michelle's eyes narrowed for a moment. "You mean the Peninsula Manila siege?"

"That's the one. Did you follow it on television?"

She hesitated for longer than was necessary. Then she admitted it. "Of course. The whole country was nervous."

"How was Baguio City?" I asked and waved over the waitress so Michelle could order a glass of Chablis.

"How did you know I was in Baguio?"

"Ricardo Fernandes told me he'd sent you there before it all kicked off."

"You know Ricardo?" she said cautiously.

"I spent two days in the Peninsula Manila with the Colonel, as his guest."

That shut her up for half a minute. She stared at me in confusion unsure what to expect from me. "You were with him during the siege?" she finally said.

"I was. He dragged me along unwillingly. He's somewhat angry with me. I shot him in the leg."

She stared at me again, lost for words. "You shot him?"

I shrugged. "It's a long story but it's all over now. Senator Guzman will pull some strings. Hopefully he won't come out of it too badly." I fell silent and waited for her to tell me something about Ricardo.

Her wine arrived and she tasted it, found it sour and sent it back. I think she was trying to buy herself time to process what she'd just learned.

"So you know that I've been having an affair with Ricardo?" she ventured.

"It came up in conversation. He was jealous that I had your number. I explained to him that we were just dive buddies." I cracked a big jolly smile and reached for my glass of San Miguel.

"Is that what we are? Dive buddies?" Her eyes were very brown and they were burrowing into mine. Her lipstick was very red and I felt colour rising in my cheeks. Her fingernails were very pink. A frisson of excitement crept across my chest.

"We are better friends than that, I hope?" The words came out more smoothly than the emotions inside me. I definitely hadn't expected this.

"I hardly know you," she teased. The waitress brought a Jim Beam & Coke which was more to Michelle's liking.

"Are you in love with Ricardo Fernandes?" I asked.

"Not any more," she said, staring down at a cracked fingernail on her index finger and at the small, flawless, diamond solitaire further up. She rubbed over it with the thumb.

"Apparently," I said, attempting the moral high ground, "he has a wife and she wants him back."

"Don't be mean, Bill," Michelle said. "That's not fair. We can't help ourselves sometimes. One doesn't always fall in love with the right person."

"He is a very impressive man," I commented.

"He is too old-fashioned for me. Too controlling. And not free. I am not some cheap mistress he can play with and set up in an apartment in Oakwood." There was fire in her eyes as her passion flared.

"Ricardo told me he was madly in love with you."

"He is deceiving himself. He was in love with the fact that a young woman like me found him attractive. But he was very attentive. That diamond necklace you saw me wearing, he gave it to me." I understood a little more. It must have cost a good $30,000 US at least. A lot for an ordinary Colonel but a bagatelle for a Filipino of Fernandes' rank in society. That would create a lot of obligation in her mind and was an indication of

Fernandes' passion for her. I wondered what she would look like wearing only that necklace. She was a gal who loved her diamonds. As did I. Perhaps for similar reasons.

I sighed. "It all sounds very complicated. Would you prefer if we don't talk about this anymore?"

She was relieved. We consulted the menus and I ordered the Cobb salad - which I always had in every Hard Rock I visited in the world - while she had the half slab of ribs. For dessert she had the hot fudge brownie and I had the New York cheesecake.

We'd avoided the subject of politics but spent some time talking about the future of rice farming in the Philippines and how genetically modified crops were not as awful as everyone made them out to be. Her employer was hoping to make big bucks selling agro-chemicals that would improve the yield for farmers.

"My family owned a lot of land," she said. "We grew a lot of rice. I've seen first-hand what works and what doesn't. The Philippines is the ninth largest rice producer in the world. But we also import more rice than any other country in the world. Which is a bit crazy. We shouldn't have to import anything."

"You used to have the largest garment industry in Asia in the 1980s. The communist unions killed that off and it ended up in China and Bangladesh."

She shook her head sadly. "We are our own worst enemy sometimes."

It was when the coffees arrived that I circled back to the topic of the failed military coup.

"Is there anyone who hated Ricardo and was close to Senator Guzman who would want the rebellion to fail?

Someone betrayed them by sending confidential documents to the authorities."

Michelle had become mellow after three more bourbons and Coke. Now she sat up with a start and stared at me.

"What do you mean?"

"Someone got hold of a list of all the plotters, as well as photos and recordings of their conversations. Someone who wanted to cause Senator Guzman a problem, directly or indirectly."

She thought about it for a while then suggested: "His youngest son hates his father," Michelle said pointedly.

"Is that Sonny?"

"Yes. Sonny has had a crush on me for a long time. When Sonny found out that I was dating Ricardo he was furious. He sent me hundreds of texts. Real nasty ones. Jealous ones." Michelle wrinkled her nose in distaste. "I slapped him off and told him to leave it out."

"He sounds like a slime ball."

"Actually, he's kind of sweet. He's just one of those Filipino kids from the richest families who are packed off to school in America and learn all the wrong things while they are there. He didn't study and use his time there wisely like I did, Plus, he's been addicted to drink and drugs on and off since he was fifteen."

"What sort of drugs is Sonny into?"

"What's he not into? He drinks expensive imported whisky like a fish. But he has a real weakness for *shabu*."

"Did he ever say anything about his dealer when you talked to him? Where was he buying the stuff?"

She shook her head. She dropped two sugar cubes into her coffee and stirred slowly with her spoon. "Now that

I think about it, we met at a party in 'Euphoria' a few weeks ago and he was boasting about getting a big bag of gear from a British supplier which would last him six months."

"That's very interesting. This British supplier was in Manila, do you think?"

She shrugged. "I have no idea. It was a typically Sonny comment. He was sitting at a VIP table with a gang of his guys and girls and he waved me over and wanted me to join their after-hours party."

I fell silent for a while and thought it through. There could be a connection. Sonny knew Dickie Goodyear from Angeles City. He probably bought drugs from the Lapida Brothers. Maybe he didn't have any money and couldn't get any more credit. So he offered Goodyear something else that could be converted into cash through blackmail. Sonny records some of the meetings his father is having with his cronies, takes some pictures and gives it to Goodyear in exchange for a big bag of drugs.

"Did Ricardo ever tell you who the other men were that he and Senator Guzman were plotting with?"

"Me, why would I want to know? Sure, we'd meet up somewhere and he'd be telling me about this man or that man who wanted to help out. But I never really listened. It's always the same bunch of people. It's like musical chairs. They take turns in plundering the people." She glared at me because they were her people.

"So when are we going to go scuba diving together again?" I asked.

She smiled happily. "Whenever you invite me."

"I'm inviting you now. I'm leaving Manila tomorrow. I'm sick and tired of all this political bullshit and I just want to hang out with the fishes for a while."

"And with me?"

"Yes," I said, surprising myself with just how good that idea felt. Not just because I wanted to feel her lithe young body naked beneath me, but because she seemed like a kindred spirit, and perhaps what passed for my soul was in need of that as well.

"Will you come and stay with me? How about this weekend? Or take a few days off?"

"I've taken far too many days off already," she said, and the spark inside me sputtered as she poured cold water on my fantasy. "In America they'd have fired me by now but here they can't touch me because of who my family is."

"Don't knock nepotism. It's relatively better than other forms of crony capitalism."

"Ha ha." She tilted her head to one side and stared at me speculatively. "I should stay away from older men. And I'm not really into foreign guys."

"That's hurtful," I said, but the part of my psyche that knew opening up too far to a woman was mad, bad and dangerous, reasserted itself on hearing her words.

"I need to go and visit Ricardo," she said, "wherever they are detaining him. I have to tell him it's truly over now."

"Once you've done that, will you come and stay with me in Puerto Galera?"

She nodded cagily. "I'll think about it. You're a nice guy but maybe I should stay single for a while." Her phone buzzed and she looked at it briefly then added:

"Maybe I should become a lesbian. I dated a girl in college once. It was fun. Not as complicated as guys."

"There are certain things a woman can't do to another woman without artificial assistance," I said, "and I don't mean getting them pregnant. I've never had any complaints in that department."

"You are disgusting," she said. But I could tell she was mulling over my offer.

"Maybe on my next visit to PG we could discuss the Red Teardrop and your own diamond collection?" she continued eventually. "Or maybe some other hard substance known to man." Now we were getting somewhere.

"I can contribute a lot to both discussions," I said. "Diamonds and men should both be a girl's best friend." But unlike men, the diamonds lingered.

I got the bill shortly after that and we left the Hard Rock. I walked her over to the taxi stand and waved her off. When I turned to head back to my hotel, two hard looking Filipino men in dark suits, white shirts and black ties blocked my way.

"Mr. Jedburgh, please come with us," said the man on the right. He was wearing mirrored sunglasses even though dusk was already on us. His hair was closely cropped.

"Who are you?" I said and debated whether I had the energy for a scrap. They were both tall, younger than me and muscular. They were wearing earpieces and I guessed they'd have Glock 17s under their suit jackets.

"Presidential Security Group, sir," the same guy said and produced a wallet with a badge and some kind of ID that I couldn't read from three metres away.

"Guys, I've just been released by the Philippine National Police. I really don't think you're interested in me. I'm just an innocent bystander."

He cracked a smile at this and there was a hint of warmth in it. "You are wrong. We are very interested in you, Mr. Jedburgh."

"Where do you want to take me?" I asked, still weighing up if this was a time for fight, flight or surrender.

"The President wants to meet you, sir," the man said deferentially. "Her Excellency is at the Malacanang Palace."

36

She was small in stature and her face reminded me of a cute chipmunk. When she spoke there was a tiny lisp in her voice. We were in a meeting room in the Presidential palace. Five chairs had been arranged in a semi-circle. She sat in a chair which was high-backed and ornate, a pretender aspiring to the status of a small throne. My armchair, opposite her, was less ornate but the cushion was plush. It wasn't quite an audience with the Sun King but there was some pomp and ceremony to the proceedings.

Standing by the door was 'Ding Dong' Marquez, who'd introduced himself as the commander of the PSG as he led me down a long marbled corridor to my audience. Sitting on my left was a thin, sallow, man in a suit who held a pen and notebook in his hands.

The President of the Philippines wore an elegant dark blue outfit and black patent shoes with three-inch heels. She smiled warmly and said: "I have heard many things about you, Bill, so I wanted to meet you in person. You don't mind if I call you Bill?"

"Of course not, Madam President. It is a great honour to meet you."

"I have been told that I owe you thanks for your services in two regards."

Her accent was strongly upper-class Manila while her English was grammatically perfect and her speech punctilious. She too came from one of the great Filipino political dynasties. Her father had been a President. I knew she had studied at the oldest Jesuit university in America and then became a Professor at Manila's finest university, also established by the Society of Jesus, the Pope's shock troops of the Reformation. Their concept of casuistry – the belief that you could deceive in the pursuit of the greater good – would be hard-wired into her. Although she came across as a friendly academic, I had no doubt she was a razor-sharp politician and would play ruthless with the best of them.

"You are a very handsome man," she flattered me. "Are you married?"

"No, ma'am, I'm still single."

"You must find yourself a good woman. Every man needs one to keep him in check."

I smiled politely. "That's why I've been avoiding marriage. It would cramp my style."

She nodded in understanding. "What exactly is your profession, Bill?"

"I am a security consultant. I advise corporations on risk. Sometimes I work as a bodyguard. That is how I came to know Senator Guzman. I am sure you've been informed of that."

"You worked for him for several months when he was running for President a few years ago?"

"That is correct, ma'am."

"And you also know Charlie Santos, I believe?"

"I had some work dealings with him in the mid-90s."

"He wasn't suited to be President. He enjoyed drinking and womanising too much. Would you agree with me, Bill?" She smiled pleasantly again but was watching me with the predatory attention of a panther.

"I truly can't comment on that. I'm a foreigner and it is not appropriate for me to have an opinion on these matters."

"Well said. Everyone likes Charlie but he didn't do our country much good." She said something rapidly in Tagalog and the sallow amanuensis got up and exited the room. He left his notebook and pen behind on the chair.

"You know, a very dear friend of mine from college is also called Bill," the President went on.

I smiled. "I think I know the man. I met him once in 1996 at a fundraising dinner after the Atlanta Olympics."

"There is a man who was a great politician. At school all the girls loved him and he couldn't keep his hands to himself or his trousers zipped up. He could have been one of the greatest statesmen of the 20th Century if he had been able to control his urges." She shook her head and there was a wistful look in her eyes.

"Cigars are best used for smoking," I said. "And one should always inhale."

She laughed at that. "Some of my men tell me that you are in fact a spy. Maybe working for the Americans, maybe for the British or even for the Singaporeans. What is the truth?"

"The truth is that I am not, nor ever was, an American or a British spy," I replied precisely. "I was in the Intelligence Corps in the Army but they kicked me out. Sort of."

"What about the Singaporeans?" she asked, her head tilted slightly. She knew the answer of course and was testing me.

"Sometimes I have had dealings with the SID. They've asked me to help out in the past as a security consultant and to work VIP Protection. That's why I was in America at the Olympics."

"I know that you provided information on the names of all the plotters to a man called Brigadier Wee, who passed this information to us. Did you betray the trust of Senator Guzman in obtaining this information?" She was watching me again with a raptorial smile. I took a long deep breath. How best to explain this complex chain of events? Life is always more incredible than fiction will permit.

"The information was on an encrypted hard drive," I said, "which accidentally came into my possession. I passed it on to Brigadier Wee because I thought his people might be able to decrypt the information on it. If I'd known that it related to a client, I might have been more circumspect." She considered what I said for a while and I worried this reply wasn't to her liking.

"A commercial relationship must be respected," she said finally, "otherwise no-one can safely do business. However, it was a great and good thing that you did by passing this information on to our mutual friend the Brigadier. It helped us to anticipate the mutiny and make sure it would fail. That is why I am personally grateful to you."

I nodded, maintained an earnest expression on my face and kept my mouth shut.

The President said: "We have spoken to enough witnesses now to understand why you were at the Peninsula Manila. We have concluded that you were not in league with the mutineers but being held there involuntarily. Is that true?"

"Yes, ma'am. I was taken at gunpoint to the hotel by Colonel Fernandes and he would not let me leave."

She nodded gravely. "It was you who shot Colonel Fernandes in the leg and persuaded the other officers to surrender and avoid any further bloodshed?"

I shrugged stoically at her description.

"The Filipino people, and this administration, are grateful to you for such a great act of courage."

"It was all a bit silly. The fight was lost before they even left Camp Tecson. I told the Colonel he was an idiot but he wouldn't listen. He was a romantic."

The President stared at me quietly. She was wondering. There was much she knew and understood but she wasn't quite happy with all of the facts. I wondered how long this interview would go on for and where it was heading.

She answered my unspoken question: "This matter must remain secret and we will ask you to sign an undertaking to that effect."

"Of course, ma'am."

"As compensation for this, it is my pleasure to award you, for meritorious service in defence affairs," she said, "the Philippine Legion of Honour in the rank of Legionnaire." She wiggled her finger at Ding Dong Marquez who stepped forward and produced a black case. He snapped it open and revealed an eight-pointed gold decoration with the emblem of a sea lion sitting up and holding a short sword. The ribbon was red, white and blue.

"Kneel," the President commanded. The amanuensis, who had returned, bustled over with a kneeler and I did as I was told. The small, fierce woman stood up, took out the medal from the case that Ding Dong was still holding open and placed the ribbon around my neck.

"Only twenty-three foreigners have been awarded this honour. Carry it with dignity," she said quietly. She indicated that I should stand up and once I was back on my feet, she shook my hand.

"You would do well to ponder on the significance of this honour the next time the Senator, or anyone else, suggests you should get involved in Philippines politics," she said. "On a personal note, my family recognise that we owe you a debt that you can seek to call on when you need it."

Then she left the room. I had been rewarded, warned off and offered a carrot, in as neat a fashion as you could have wished. Ding Dong grinned. He was a man in his fifties and had scars across his cheeks that suggested he was a combat veteran.

"You better take it off now and put it back in its box. If I catch you trying to sell it, I'll send some of my men to hunt you down." He laughed to show me that he was joking but I didn't intend to take his words lightly.

"No hard feelings?" I asked. "I think I shot at one of your men when I was protecting Senator Guzman."

Ding Dong grunted and shook his head. "He was wearing Level 4 body armour. Only bruises. He'll forget it."

"Only doing my job."

Ding Dong grinned again and slapped me on the back as he led me out into the corridor. "We are the foot soldiers. Men like you and me. We shoot and get shot at. In the service of our masters."

"*Molon labe*," I said, echoing the words of a Spartan warrior.

The boss of the PSG gave me a quizzical look. "What does that mean?"

"'Come and take my weapons, if you can'," I explained. "It's what the King of Sparta shouted to his enemy before battle."

"That is a good one. I will teach you some Tagalog phrases. We are going to the mess for a drink now and you can meet the man you shot."

37

They were a good bunch of lads, the men from the Presidential Security Group. We spent a few hours in their bar drinking tequila shots and San Miguel while swapping war stories. I told them about the biggest VIP protection operation I'd ever witnessed, which was the handover of Hong Kong in 1997. Forty-five foreign ministers and hundreds of dignitaries had descended onto the territory and it had taken the police years to prepare for the event. Nobody had got killed during the proceedings except for one man. Two actually, but the second death had been certified as natural causes when his body had washed up several days later on Stanley beach. I didn't mention that I'd killed them both nor why they had to die. That was a story buried deep in the files. It had only been ten years ago. It felt like an eternity. I had come a long way since then and there had been many adventures in the intervening years.

Ding Dong Marquez told me he'd been in Hong Kong regularly protecting the President at the time, but he'd missed the handover. "He had three girlfriends in Hong Kong so he was always flying over to visit them."

"How many did he have back home in Manila?" I asked.

Ding Dong frowned and began counting the fingers on both of his hands. "Four girlfriends and five mistresses, twelve illegitimate children," he concluded.

"A busy man. When did he have time to run the country?"

"Other smart men did that for him," the commander of the PSG replied with a sly grin. "He just collected the women and the money."

I was introduced to Romeo, the man I'd shot. He took off his shirt and showed me his bruise. It was a livid-blue bloody blotch that covered all four of his pectoral muscles. I could see the outline of a dressing beneath his trousers where I had winged him on the thigh. But he barely limped.

"Have you been shot before?" I asked him. He was a gaunt fellow in his late thirties and looked as if he'd been in the wars. I noticed a slight twitch under his left eye as I addressed him.

By way of reply he took off the rest of his shirt and showed me machete scars on his arms and a bullet scar on his back.

"Romeo comes from Davao City and used to work for Mayor Duterte," Ding Dong said. "They have an informal policy of summarily executing criminals, so there are often gun battles in the street. It's the safest city in the Philippines." Both men laughed at this as if it were a private joke.

"Why didn't you use hollow point ammunition when you were coming after Senator Guzman?" I asked Romeo. He and I both knew the answer, but he looked at his boss for instructions before confirming it.

"We didn't want to kill him. Those were the orders. We were told to wound him, to incapacitate him," Ding Dong explained. "We didn't know he'd have someone like you with him. We had bribed his own guy to hang back and not to fire."

I nodded. Now it made sense. "That's what I thought. It was just a warning. A shot across the bows."

The PSG men smiled knowingly.

I held out my hand to Romeo and we shook. "I'm sorry. I could have killed you. I usually fire at the throat but something upset my aim."

"Divine providence," Ding Dong said, ever the Filipino Catholic. "We must drink to it."

A tray of shot glasses materialised. I suspected that most of them had been watered down, but not the glass I was given. They'd be trying to drink me under the table. The sport of all fighting men who survived to live another day and sing of arms and the man.

Shortly after two in the morning I was dropped off at the Shangri-La Hotel. I could just about walk but not in a straight line. I waved at Ding Dong and Romeo as they stood by the car door grinning. For sure the bastards had been lacing my drinks.

It wasn't until after lunch that I surfaced and checked my phone. Larry had left me five messages to get in touch. An hour later when I felt capable of intelligible speech, I called him back.

"He wants to see you," Larry said tersely.

"Where is he?" I asked.

"In his suite five floors above you," was the answer.

"Can you ask him to order Eggs Benedict and a pint of freshly squeezed orange juice. I was drinking with the PSG boys at Malacanang Palace last night."

"I'll see what I can do," my Chinese friend said.

I dragged myself into the lift ten minutes later and Larry opened the door. Brigadier Wee was standing by the window. His hands clasped behind his back. He was studying the stationary traffic on the junction of Ayala and Makati Avenues. He turned and waved me to sit in my usual chair. His eyes travelled up and down and found me wanting. I had put on a pair of shorts and a T shirt that was clean but crumpled. On my feet were the hotel slippers made from cardboard.

"I will never understand this country," he said. He wasn't wearing a suit but simply an open necked white shirt. His cufflinks and brogues gleamed. I felt like a bad penny in the presence of a gold sovereign.

"None of us do," I commented. Larry handed me a mug of coffee which I accepted gratefully.

"A little bird tells me that you were awarded the highest military honour this country bestows on foreign civilians?" the Brigadier said fixing me with his sharp gaze.

"It's supposed to be a secret. I promised not to tell anyone."

"Nothing is a secret in a country like this." He smiled. "The President's secretary told us as a matter of courtesy. As she must have explained to you, she is very happy with you and by association she is very happy with the Singapore government."

"So your airline deal is safe and going ahead?"

"It is in good shape and we will fix their airplanes and make their airline profitable again."

"I'm pleased. They have very pretty stewardesses. Much prettier than the ones they now have on Cathay Pacific. Since the handover they are just hiring ugly, flat chested Chinese girls with shrill voices."

I could tell from Wee's frown that he wasn't interested in my comparative analysis of the pulchritude of Asian airlines' cabin crew. His view was firmly that someone who travelled on any airline other than SQ deserved what they got.

"Are you going to pay me for any of my work?" I asked.

"Have you not been richly rewarded with the Philippines Legion of Honour?" he suggested.

"Medals and baubles won't pay the hospital bills when I'm old," I said pointedly.

"Your *ang-mo* friend," the Brigadier said, speaking to Larry, "remains forever the unrelenting mercenary. All he truly cares about is money and the pleasures of the flesh."

"A man should be paid for his labours," I said. "I was supposed to be on holiday."

There was a knock on the door and room service rolled in a trolley with my brunch. The Brigadier allowed me to eat while he continued his lecture. Usually I stood to attention like a recalcitrant subaltern in front of his commanding officer. For once I was too hung over and too hungry to bother.

"We asked you to kill Senator Guzman and you refused. We told you to kill Colonel Fernandes and all you did was shoot him in the leg."

"It solved the problem," I said, buttering a piece of white toast then applying a heavy layer of thick-cut marmalade.

"We will accept that it solved the problem and in the words of the bard, 'All's well that ends well'." Wee said, giving me one of his snarky smiles. "But you didn't do the work we asked you to do."

"I found alternative solutions," was my petulant reply. "In my old age I am developing a conscience. And the President did not want Senator Guzman killed, so that would have been a mistake." I chewed on my toast for a while then added: "And you still owe me for that job last year, the Mongolian woman in Kuala Lumpur."

"We've paid you for that," Wee bristled. "Larry will check our records."

"No, you haven't. Only for the job in Pakistan. You're the only client of mine that gets credit. For the rest of them, a bullet in the head is the only statement they receive."

The Brigadier grunted irritably and then relented. "We will give you a bonus. A good performance bonus, how about that? Early Christmas present. How about 50,000 US dollars?"

I frowned as if I had to consider it, then said: "I'm happy with that. I want to buy myself one of the new Accuracy International AS50s. It's just come on the market. And they're not cheap."

Brigadier Wee smirked. "Toys for the boys."

"Tools for the professional," I said, wiping my hands carefully on the napkin, now that I'd finished eating. "It fires the .50 BMG round and can engage a target up to 1500 metres."

Both of the men laughed at my sudden enthusiasm. A man has to have a passion in life. Mine were precision weapons of selective destruction, scuba diving and beautiful Asian women.

"By the way, where do you keep your collection of sniper rifles?" Larry asked. It wasn't an idle question. I'd never told him and he was forever bugging me about it. In truth my large collection was artfully distributed around the Pacific Rim. The growth of the drugs trade meant that customs and coastguard patrols were becoming more of a nuisance in my profession. I used a resourceful and amoral courier service owned by Harry Bolt if I needed a particular weapon delivered discreetly, but you couldn't always tell when or where you would need a weapon in a hurry. On balance I wasn't inclined to tell Larry or anyone, because a secret shared is no longer a secret. When I died perhaps, I'd mention him in my will and he could inherit the guns.

I shook my head. "Confidential trade secret."

The Brigadier cleared his throat and said: "Are there any other loose ends?"

For a moment I considered not telling them. It was my little secret and my loose end. Then I did tell them. "Not confirmed yet but I suspect that the traitor who sold the information about the plotters was Senator Guzman's youngest son. He's called Sonny and he traded it with Dickie Goodyear for a massive bag of methamphetamine."

"Who told you that?" Wee wanted to know.

"Nobody, but it makes sense. I'm going to go and ask the man and see what he says."

Larry sat forward in his chair and asked sharply: "You're just going to go and ask him and you think he'll admit it?"

I shrugged. "I'm going to ask him nicely but in a particularly aggressive manner which might involve extreme pain."

38

Michelle came out of the spare bedroom wearing a shimmering, silk nightgown that stopped just above her knees. Around her neck she was sporting the diamond necklace that she'd worn at the wedding. I was sitting on the veranda watching the night and looked up at her.

She said: "I'm sorry, Bill, don't be angry with me but I shouldn't sleep with you. Not tonight, not yet." She put a warm hand on my shoulder and slid into the steamer chair next to me.

I'd been diving all day, so my body was feeling the effects of the nitrogen. Part of me was relieved that she wasn't expecting anything physical. But perhaps what she was saying wasn't what she meant? That happened sometimes with women.

"I had no expectations," I replied, choosing gallantry over petulance until I knew where the conversation was going. "Would you like a Tanduay Sprite?"

"That would be nice."

The girl smelt fresh from her shower and it played havoc with my loins. I pretended to ignore it and fixed her drink. She'd arrived on a late private *banca* before the sun went down. I'd been busy the last few days and the following night would see the big 70th birthday party that Paul, William and James were throwing for their

Indian friend Rohan, who owned the nightclub 'Squirt'. The mountain would be busy and noisy tomorrow evening, but tonight it was peaceful. From my iPod, connected to a small set of speakers, Carly Simon's 'Best of' album was playing gently in the background.

"This is an amazing view," Michelle commented with a contented sigh. She took a sip from the sweet drink I'd mixed her. The night air was warm, but there was a cooling breeze coming off the ocean. "How long have you had this place?"

"Just a few years," I said. "I sort of bought it by accident."

"How much did you pay for it?" she asked.

"Land and house altogether cost me just over 3 million pesos." It sounded a lot but for $80,000 US you'd not get much of a sea view in any other premier dive resort around the world.

"How much is your beach house in Thailand worth?" she asked. On one level they were casual questions, small talk even, but the woman was doing what women had done since the stone age: checking out the robustness of a potential mate.

"About a hundred times the price of this one, although it didn't cost me that. That's what a developer offered me last year. He wanted to put a new resort hotel on my slice of land."

"Did you consider it?" She turned in her chair, her knees now pulled up to her chin. She watched me over the rim of the glass of yellow rum she was holding to her lips.

"Not really. I've owned my house and my beach for over a quarter of a century. It's special to me. It's what I call home."

"Isn't Singapore home?"

I laughed. "Home is wherever you lay your hat, young lady. But Thailand is special to me. It's where I went to escape when I first left the Hong Kong Police."

She studied me for a minute. "Is it true what they say about Thai women?"

I chuckled. "What is it that they say about Thai women?"

"That they can shoot darts from their pussies and burst balloons?"

"That's a nasty comment," I said sharply.

"I know," she replied and laughed. We sat in silence and listened to Carly warbling 'Nobody does it better'.

"You understand why I can't sleep with you tonight, don't you?" Michelle said, when the next song had come on.

"Not entirely," I said, deciding to make her work for it. "Unless it's because, as Carly says, I'm so vain. Explain."

"Everything is over now with Ricardo. He understands that. But I'm not ready to commit to another relationship so soon. I'm not that kind of girl."

"No, you are not that kind of girl." I stretched my legs and massaged the right thigh just above the knees. There was a muscular pain lingering there. I'd put some *Naman Wooi* - a traditional embrocation used by Thai boxers - on it earlier but it hadn't taken effect yet.

"Do you think you could be serious about me?" Michelle asked. It was starting to sound more and more like an interview. "I am a very demanding woman."

I considered her question for a while. "You are a fascinating woman, I have to confess. You are not like most of the girls I've dated in the past."

She gave a low, naughty laugh. "You are not like any man I've ever dated before. You are made of smoke. Behind the good looks and the banter, it is hard for me to get a grasp of who you are. It makes me nervous. It scares me. But it also attracts me."

I shrugged. "I want to answer your question honestly. I have no idea if I could be serious about you. There are not many girls with whom I have been serious." I held up my hand, the fingers spread out. "Less than five in my life."

"How many girls have you dated in your life?" she asked.

"Too many," I replied cryptically, "but not enough."

"Bastard," she said mildly.

"We established that in Manila," I said, smiling. "Some girls like bastards. It was you who told me that."

She shook her head sadly. "I don't know what sort of man I really want. But I need to be taken seriously." She gave me a long, challenging look. "I want to be wooed properly by a man who can take care of me financially. I am the sole bread-winner for my family but we are used to an expensive lifestyle. We have to maintain our position in society." I considered this. Senator Guzman was right, she would be high maintenance. I certainly had the cash to do so if I chose, but I had never seriously considered sharing my life with a woman like that. I was the man who kicked women out of bed so that I could get a good night's sleep. I wasn't sure I could change.

"So that is how it is?"

Michelle said, "I just wanted to make things clear. I'm not some casual little fuck that you can throw over or visit every few months when you are horny." She gave me a warm smile to take the edge off the words.

"Oh, I understand that."

"You don't have to make a decision now," she said quietly. "Did you not say you wanted to show me your collection of diamonds sometime?" she provided me with an appropriate hint.

"I keep my nicest diamonds in a vault in Hong Kong. Why don't we fly there for a fun weekend sometime?"

"Will we stay in the Peninsula Hotel?" she said. "That is my favourite."

"We certainly can. We could take a suite. We can have dinner at 'Felix'. I've had some fun times there in the past."

She laughed louder this time, pleasure twinkled in her eyes and in the diamond necklace in the light from the candles that I'd placed on the low table between us. "You see, you are getting the hang of it, Bill Jedburgh. How to woo a woman of my class."

"It is an entirely new experience for me," I said. "Normally I just go to a bar, hold up a few balloons and whoever manages to shoot them out of my hand gets to come home with me for the night."

"You really are a bastard," she said firmly, "but a funny one." She laughed as she stood up and the silk negligee shifted over her body but revealed nothing she didn't intend to reveal. "I'm going to bed now. We need a good night's sleep if we are going to attempt that crazy drift dive you are proposing."

"The Kilima Drift will be fun," I said.

"I will be locking my bedroom door," she said tempering it with a coquettish smile. "Don't come knocking on it at three in the morning."

"The bedroom doors in my house don't have locks on them."

"Behave. Good things come to those who wait," she admonished me. I had stood up and went to kiss her chastely on the cheek. Her scent was intoxicating and it made me think of another girl whose name had been Desdemona. She slyly turned her head and let her lips briefly brush against mine. Then she was gone.

Within half an hour I'd fallen into a deep, dreamless, nitrogen enhanced sleep.

The following morning she woke me up with a cup of tea and a cheery poke between the ribs.

"How is the mattress in the spare room?" I asked.

"It's hard," she replied.

"It doesn't get used much," I said.

"We will see about that," she joked cheerily. She was already showered and dressed in a designer T-shirt and shorts. It was 7 a.m. We had a few pieces of toast then she climbed onto the back of the Kawasaki, putting her arms around my waist, and we rode down to Sabang Beach.

Roscoe was in his usual place behind the counter. He was like a captain on his bridge: sturdy, dependable, surveying his domain. His eyebrows twitched marginally as he registered our arrival. As Michelle turned her back to say hello to the boat-boy, the old Kiwi shook his head at me in warning. I grinned at him and shrugged my shoulders.

"The tide is ebbing," Roscoe said, "the current could be up to 10 knots on the Kilima Drift."

"The girl craves excitement."

"That's what you'll get in spades on this dive."

"Anyone else planning to join us?"

"No, the two German lads want to do the Canyons." He pointed with his pencil at the front of the shop where two men had appeared. One was a tall, lean German called Matthias. He was a bean-counter for the oil company Shell and based in Hong Kong. His buddy, Tony, looked like a slimmed down version of Schwarzenegger, although more handsome. I'd met them a many times before, dived with them, drunk with them and enjoyed their company.

Matthias shook my hand in greeting and asked me how I'd been. We exchanged some small talk. When I was in Hong Kong I sometimes met him for dinner and practised my German that had become rusty over the years. I'd grown up as an army brat when my father served in the British Army on the Rhine.

"You pussies too scared to dive the Kilima Drift with us this morning?"

"*Du kannst mich mal am Arsch lecken*," Tony said pleasantly, quoting Goethe's profanity, as he began setting up his regulator. He had his own trading company sourcing cosmetics in China for big name brands like L'Oreal and Revlon. He was understated and worth a small fortune. He had been separated from his Korean wife for many years but had no inclination to get divorced or remarry. Like me, he spent a lot of time traveling for work and pleasure.

"Are you guys free this evening?" I asked. "Why not come along to the biggest party Puerto Galera has seen since the Spanish left in eighteen hundred and ninety eight?"

"Sounds like fun," Tony said. He turned the first stage open on his tank and checked the pressure and that the regulator was working properly. Then he turned it off again, released the pressure from the hose by squeezing the regulator demand valve and laid the tank and its BCD down on the ground so it couldn't be knocked over by accident.

"Might be a hundred people there," I said. "Roscoe will arrange transportation from Sabang Beach. Be there at seven, German time not Filipino time. No need to bring anything except your libido. There will be plenty of food, drink and other entertainment."

"We will be there," Tony assured me.

"They are posting me to Shanghai," Matthias said to me in German.

"Is that good or bad?" I asked as we all continued preparing our dive gear.

"It is neutral. I will have a car and a driver and other luxuries but my boss will be a mainland Chinese."

"That will be strange."

"It is the way of the world now. China is taking over. If you have an office in China it can no longer be run just by some expat." He shrugged. "Anyway, they are more highly qualified but cost less in salary and benefits." Matthias was about my age. His own role would be localised and the cushy expat perks that had existed for decades would disappear. The same thing had happened to my old colleagues in the Hong Kong Police. I clapped him on the back and went to check on how Michelle was getting on.

"Have you got a spare mask in case yours gets torn off your face by the current?" I asked the girl, running an appraising eye over her gear. She was diving with top of the range Scubapro kit. I checked how she had fastened her alternative air source – known as an Octopus – because if I had a problem, that was for me. I'd grab the yellow regulator from her and stuff it into my mouth.

Michelle tapped one of her pockets to prove she had a spare mask. In advanced scuba diving everything was about redundancy. You had a spare set of everything that mattered. I bent down to pick up her fins. They were long, sleek Mares Avanti Quattros in a hot pink colour. I checked the straps and tugged at them to ensure they were in good working condition. Losing a fin on a fast drift dive where you often had to manoeuvre against the current could be a disaster. Sometimes there was an effect called 'the washing machine' where currents would tug divers up and down, making them lose orientation. Suddenly bubbles that were supposed to ascend to the surface were being forced in the other direction.

Apart from the exhilaration of flying along at high speeds, the fish life to be seen feeding in the currents was fascinating. The last time I'd done the Kilima Drift we'd seen a shoal of monster turtles, like a squadron of Luftwaffe bombers on their way to London.

"You look good enough to eat," I whispered into Michelle's ear. Today her full body wetsuit matched the neon pink of her fins. It sat firmly on every contour of her delicious figure.

"Catch me if you can," she replied and turned to defog her mask.

39

The Ascott Makati was a luxury development of serviced residences located in the Ayala Centre, close to the Shangri-La Hotel. Larry, through the wonder of electronic surveillance that was at the disposal of most modern intelligence services, had determined that, when he was in Manila, Sonny Guzman lived in a three-bedroom penthouse suite there paid for by his father.

The GSM locator on his cell phone confirmed that he'd been in town for the last few days and its last ping showed him in residence. I selected eight o'clock in the morning as a convenient time for a visit. Going on the assumption that he was a man who stayed up late enjoying the trendy nightclubs in that area, I wanted him to be at home in bed, and feeling worse for wear, when I came to call.

The building was split into two towers, with a lobby joining them. I approached the concierge behind his desk and told him that I'd been sent by Senator Guzman to drop off some papers for his son. I was a foreigner and wearing a suit, so he felt obliged to permit me to pass through to the lifts. He had tried to call up to the apartment but there had been no answer. Neither of us was surprised about that. It was very early in the morning for Sonny to be conducting business.

The concierge pressed the top button, slid his card into the lift and wished me a good day. The lift whisked me up to the 30th floor and I went to ring the bell on one of the four doors. It took five minutes of pressure before some grumbling could be heard on the other side.

"Who is it?" a man's voice said.

"This is Bill Jedburgh. I've been sent by your father with some papers for you."

"Jedburgh?"

"Yes," I said putting a note of impatience into my voice.

There was the rattling of a chain and Sonny's face peeked out. He looked tired, jaded and confused to see me. "What time is it?" he asked.

I held up the bulky brown A4 envelope and waved it at him. He stepped back and opened the door.

"It's early," I told him. He was wearing a silk dressing gown which revealed a hairy chest and bare feet.

"Why didn't you call first?" he said.

"You didn't answer. Your cell phone is off."

"Out of load," he said, leading me across the vast living room to the open plan kitchen area. "Have you been to visit my father already this morning?"

"Yes," I said and gave the place a quick inspection. There was a short corridor that led to the bedrooms. All the doors were closed at the moment which meant Sonny was probably not alone. I counted on perhaps one or two female companions in the master bedroom. But they'd stay quiet if they were even awake. I was surprised there was no bodyguard and that Sonny had opened the door himself.

"Don't you have any close protection?" I asked him, sounding like a concerned professional.

He was busying himself with the coffee machine, slotting a capsule into the device.

"They only come later, if I want to go out in town. My father doesn't like it but I don't want strangers hanging around me and selling my secrets to the gossip magazines." His black hair was a mess and he was scratching his scalp as he spoke.

"Where did you go last night?" I asked, standing by the picture windows which presented a panoramic view of the Manila skyline. Across from us they were constructing a taller building which was going to be another set of luxury condominiums owned by Ayala Land, the company run by Jaime Zobel de Ayala y Pfitz, currently the patriarch of the second richest family in the Philippines.

"Different places. We hung out in 'Giraffe', then we went to check out a new club called 'White Bird'." He gave me an inquiring look. 'Giraffe' was popular with the gilded youth of the capital and had been around for a long time. I'd never heard of 'White Bird'. It must be new.

"How is my father?" he asked, a note of concern in his voice.

"He's getting stronger. At his age, getting shot is not something to be taken lightly."

Sonny stared at me blankly as if his mind was somewhere else. He walked over and threw himself onto one of the beige sofas. The furniture and decorations were bland. Despite the money that had been spent on it by the corporate designers, it was a functional apartment with very little character.

I placed the brown envelope on the long, glass coffee table in front of me and sat down opposite him.

"We need to have a serious chat, Sonny," I said, getting down to business. "I need you to answer some questions for me."

His sleepy eyes looked confused and he began to frown. "What do you mean?"

"I need to understand your involvement in recent events."

He appeared bewildered for an instant, then sat up and bristled: "I don't have anything to do with politics. What my father and Ricardo were doing, that was all just bullshit."

"You are lying to me, Sonny," I said severely. "Aren't you?"

"What the fuck…" was his reply.

I held up my hand to calm him down. "Let's start with your drug habit. You enjoy partying, you enjoy using *shabu*, don't you?"

"So what, everybody does. Old guys like you drink beer. We take drugs."

I nodded and pulled the envelope towards me, standing it up and reaching inside between the newspaper I had stuffed in it. "That makes sense. Where do you buy your drugs?"

"None of your business, cop," he sneered.

"I was a cop once, but no more." I said in a matter-of-fact way. "These days I occasionally cross over to the dark side in the course of my work. As you are about to find out."

From the envelope I produced a rectangular device made of black plastic. It was ten centimetres longer than an electric shaver, but of similar shape. At its end were two tiny electrodes placed one centimetre apart. He stared at the tool as I held it up for him to see.

"This is a Sabre Tactical Stun Gun," I explained. "It delivers a charge of 1.17 microcoulombs. According to a study I read, any charge over 1 microcoulomb causes unbearable pain." I paused to wave the sleek device in front of his face. "Not that I've tested it on myself, but it seemed to work that way when I've interrogated reluctant witnesses."

"You are fucking joking, aren't you?" he said with a mixture of bravado and fear. "When I tell my father that you threatened me, he'll have you thrown in prison for the rest of your life."

"Sonny-boy, I'm not threatening you. I'm telling you that I am going to use this device on your testicles."

He must have seen something in my eyes to make him realise that my intentions were deadly serious. Suddenly he scrambled to his feet, slipped with his bare feet on the smooth, elegant carpet, tumbled and fell on his face. I was wearing shoes and had no such problems. I moved on top of him, crunching my knees into his shoulder blades, holding him down so I could touch the two electrodes to his neck and whisper into his ear:

"Be very careful, my boy, do not move. I've had a twitchy finger ever since someone broke it for me. Answer my questions and I will try to keep it under control."

On the side of the Sabre was a red switch. When you flicked it from 0 to 1 with your thumb it activated the charge. He lay very still, breathing heavily.

"Question number one is: Did you know Dickie Goodyear? Yes and No answers for now."

"Yes," he managed to say into the carpet, as I pressed down hard on the back of his head. He stank of sweat and cigarettes. As well as urine.

"Did you buy your drugs from Goodyear?"

"Yes, but only once," he said, speaking a bit louder now as he calmed down. To ensure he didn't forget who was calling the shots, I dug the electrodes into the fine hairs and skin on the back of his neck.

"Did you sell Dickie Goodyear the names and photographs of the conspirators your father was plotting with?"

"No fucking way," he said, almost shouting. There was genuine surprise and revulsion in his voice.

"I'll ask again," I said, lowering the tone of my voice so I sounded as threatening as I could. "Did Dickie sell you a big bag of drugs in exchange for the confidential information about the planned mutiny?"

"No," he said, more forcefully and emotionally. "How could I betray my father that way? It is none of my business but he's still my family."

"Somebody told me you hated your father?" It was framed as a question.

"Who said that? I don't particularly like my father. Lots of sons don't like their domineering fathers. But I wouldn't betray him." He tried to push himself back up so he could look me in the eye but I held him down firmly. "Are you crazy? Who's been telling you this bullshit?"

"Did you instruct the Lapida Brothers to kill Goodyear?"

"No," he said. A petulant, even aggrieved note, had now snuck into his attitude. A part of me was starting to believe his story. "I stopped taking drugs months ago. I had a bad trip and someone persuaded me it was stupid."

"That's convenient," I said. My mind was kicking around the variables and I tried to work out what to ask him next. This was not turning out exactly as I'd expected. Unless Sonny was an award-winning actor in the making, it was beginning to look as if I'd taken a wrong turn.

"Who told you that I sold my father's secrets for a bag of drugs?" he demanded. By now I'd let him turn his head so we were looking at each other. The Sabre S1001 was still on his neck, but my pressure had loosened.

"Michelle Arupe told me that you'd boasted of getting a bag of *shabu* that would last you for months."

"That bitch," he said, spitting the words out. "You can't believe a word she says. She sells herself to whoever will buy her the largest diamond. Look at Ricardo. She fucked him over completely. He handed over all of his family jewellery to her. Bought her properties overseas and all along she was still seeing another guy."

"I see," I said. But in fact I didn't see it yet.

"He's telling the truth," a man's voice said. It was a familiar voice, but not one that I had expected to hear in this apartment.

40

It was only Michelle and me doing the Kilima Drift. First we were going to drop off Matthias, Tony and Rico so they could do their dive. We all waded out to the *banca* and the boat-boy pulled up our gear. Then we hauled ourselves over the gunwale and, after donning our BCDs again, sat facing each other. The boat-boy would then take us around the corner to Sinandigan Wall where we'd start our dive.

The German lads and their Divemaster gave us a cheery wave and rolled back into the water at West Escarceo. To get to the Canyons they would drop in on top of the reef, catch the current for about a mile and then descend to 30 metres. The *banca* started to move again and ten minutes further on we reached our own drop off point.

"Remember to stay close to me," I reminded the girl.

"Yes, boss," she said with mild sarcasm.

"If at any point you don't feel comfortable or feel you are losing control give me the ascend signal and we'll pull out."

"I've logged over 800 hundred dives, Mr. Staff Instructor."

"I know you're good. Let's just be safe," I said, giving her a stern look. "We'll drop straight down the wall to

30 metres, so roll in with a deflated BCD. If you have any problems equalising your ears, pause and let me know by pointing to your ear."

She nodded as she tightened the straps on her mask, getting the fit just right. I checked the Suunto on my left wrist and my compass on the other. We did a quick buddy check. Rico had once rolled into the water and found out at 30 metres that he was diving with an empty tank that had been left over from his previous dive. Luckily one of his customers had been close by and a few fin kicks had brought him to the diver's Octopus. 30 metres would have been a long way to swim up on only half a breath of air.

I gave Michelle the OK sign and she gave it back to me. The boat-boy was holding the *banca* steady, watching us carefully. The BCD is basically a sack that holds air. With a press of a button you can pump air into it from the tank and create more buoyancy; press the deflator button and air escapes. I held up the hose and using my elbows squeezed out every last bit of air from the bladder. Michelle was doing the same thing.

"Ready?" I asked.

She'd popped her regulator in her mouth already, so simply nodded. I gave the sign and we both rolled backwards into the brisk, tropical water. The temperature was about 27 degrees Celsius. Refreshing. We'd warm up pretty soon from the adrenalin and the amount of finning we'd have to do to maintain control.

When you first hit the water you feel disorientated because you might have done a backwards somersault by the time the water around you cleared. With no air in our BCDs and the weights on our belts we were pulled down swiftly. At three metres I did the Valsalva manoeuvre - swallowing to clear the pressure differential in my eustachian tubes. I watched as the girl did the same. Then I kicked hard with my fins, put my head down and descended even faster, keeping her pink wetsuit in my peripheral vision.

At 30 metres the dive tables only allow you twenty minutes of bottom time before you start hitting a decompression ceiling. We'd agreed that at the end of the dive we'd do a ten minutes safety stop - pausing at 5 metres to let the body metabolise nitrogen - to avoid any risk of decompression sickness caused by nitrogen bubbles.

You could dive the Kilima Drift shallow or deep. We were going to go deep which was where the current was fastest. The problem with going deep was that if you missed the turning at Shark Cave and hit the wrong current you could be dragged out into the depths of the Batangas Channel. If you did, you had to kick hard against it to escape. Sometimes it dragged you down, sometimes it dragged you up, and however hard your fins worked, the outcome was potentially deadly.

It took us a minute to hit the sea bed. My dive computer had turned on as soon as it touched the water and was telling me the depth, the elapsed time and how many more minutes we could dive before we exceeded the safety margins.

Michelle and I exchanged OK signs. We were already in the grip of the strong tides. We started accelerating. I kept an eye on the needle on my compass. I checked the air on my pressure gauge. We'd started with 200 bar in the tank. I was on 195 bar. The first stage at the top of my tank made a reassuring 'clunk' and 'chunk' whenever I inhaled and exhaled. I concentrated on getting my breathing deep and slow. Out of habit I checked that all my kit was hanging where it should be. My dive reel was clipped to a carabiner at the bottom of my BCD. The signal tube which I would use at the end of the dive was safely stashed in the right pocket. My dive knife was strapped to my right calf.

Michelle was gliding beside me, two metres to my right. She had her arms crossed over her chest and was showing excellent form. She kicked left or right to correct herself as we began picking up even more speed. I did the same.

Visibility was poor. On good days you could see up to 20 metres. We had less than 5 metres today. But we were skimming along over the bottom of the sea bed and at least we could see that. The atmosphere was grey and chilly. It felt ominous. There was more than a simple frisson of excitement. This was not a dive for the faint-hearted.

We shot along for another five minutes. I checked my pressure gauge, which was moving down steadily. Once you hit 50 bar, the training insisted, you ended your dive. That left a decent safety margin for a nice steady, controlled ascent, a short decompression stop and plenty of spare air in case someone else needed to share yours.

Michelle was looking at me. I could just see her eyes behind the big lenses on her pink mask. We exchanged OK signs, then were hit by a massive up-current that pushed us back to 25 metres. I lost sight of the sea bed. Then another current tugged us left and right. We kicked hard to correct and keep control.

Not far to go before we came to the turn. The current we were riding seemed to pick up even more speed.

'This is wild, hasn't been this wild for a long time,' was the thought that crossed my mind.

More aquatic turbulence, and this time it was the full washing machine effect. We tumbled in the grey waters, trying to orientate ourselves. I could feel my breathing picking up rapidly as my legs worked hard to gain control. You don't use your arms. You keep them tucked in close to your body. Mine were not crossed like Michelle's but it was my habit to hold my right wrist in my left hand making it easy for me to see both of my displays. The pressure gauge was strapped across my chest. I was down to 100 bar.

For a moment I lost sight of the girl. Then she appeared again in a swirl of bubbles. She was flapping her arms to get control.

I checked the compass. I checked the time and I checked our depth.

The dive computer said we had four minutes left at this depth. This was the moment I'd been anticipating. This was the tricky part.

We carried on riding the waves at breakneck speed. I manoeuvred myself closer to Michelle. Visibility was about 10 metres now and I recognised the landmarks I'd selected.

With several more fin kicks I got myself just above her. She moved her head, looking over her shoulder, wondering what I was doing.

Moving purposefully, I grabbed hold of the lower skirt of her BCD and with my right hand tugged off first one of her fins, then the other. I had to get my fingers under the strap and it took a few fiddly seconds. She suddenly understood what I was doing and started struggling. But I'd been too quick for her. The fins disappeared into the grey water behind us.

She was panicking now. I'd expected this. But without the fins she had no more leverage in the water. I was squatting on her back, turning the valve at the top of her tank. 'Righty tighty, lefty loosey' - was the rule. I turned it four times to the right until it would go no further, then I tugged hard on the hose and dragged the regulator out of her mouth.

Her immediate reaction would be to grab for her yellow octopus. But with the air turned off from her tank there was perhaps only one decent breath left in the hoses.

We rode along in the wild current. She struggled for her life while I squatted on her back. I waited another minute - but it could have been longer - until she stopped flapping. Then I pushed her hard in the direction of the Batangas Channel while I kicked firmly to move the other way, back towards the big old Spanish anchor that marked the end of the Canyons dive and our pick up point.

It took me ten minutes to get control and escape the death grip of the current. I started to panic but forced it back down, letting my experience take control. I had no desire to join Michelle in Poseidon's deathly embraces. Eventually I began to ascend, using only my depth gauge as reference. All around me there was only blue water. No point of reference.

When I reached eight metres I deployed my orange signalling sausage by blowing air into it from my octopus. The sausage, attached to the reel I held in my hand, shot up to the surface as the air inside it expanded. By that time I was at five metres depth. I dumped some air through my deflator in order to become negatively buoyant. Then I bobbed around for ten minutes, hanging from the bottom of my sausage. The surface shimmered up above me. There were no other divers around me, so I had no idea exactly where I had ended up. But the boat-boy would recognise my signalling tube and bring the *banca* over, waiting to pick me up.

Michelle would have lost consciousness by the time I'd released her. Within a few minutes she would have drowned. Even if she'd miraculously managed to turn her air back on by reaching behind and opening the valve, without fins she had no chance of fighting the current. Within twenty minutes she'd be three miles out in the channel. Her body might surface in a few days, although the channel was a mile deep in parts and predators hunted at that depth. The year before two Koreans had got lost on the Kilima Drift and when they turned up there was not much left to identify.

I checked my pressure gauge and found I was down to 20 bar. My breathing was slow and steady. The first stage made its comforting noise telling me all was well. Gently I began spooling in the reel as I allowed myself to ascend to the surface. The slower you went the more efficiently the residual nitrogen was released from your tissues.

My head broke the surface and I pumped up my BCD at a touch of the button making me fully buoyant. I rolled up my signalling sausage as the *banca* came closer. Rico and the German lads were smiling.

As the *banca* bobbed closer to me I yelled out in my best anguished voice. "I lost her. The current took her. I couldn't reach her."

The smiles on their faces turned to horror. The boat-boy made the sign of the cross.

I shucked out of my BCD and swam next to it allowing Tony to pull it up on the boat.

"What happened, man?" Rico shouted.

"The current was crazy. I've never seen it that fast." The German lads stared at me in consternation.

"Fuck," I said, and then repeated the harsh, ugly, word a few times. Finally I grabbed the gunwale, kicked hard, pulled myself up and rolled over into the *banca*.

41

It was Lieutenant Obregon who had come out from Sonny's bedroom two days earlier.

I stared at him trying to make sense of it.

"He is telling the truth, Mr Jedburgh, sir. Sonny has been off the *shabu* for a few months now. I asked him to stop it and get a grip on his life."

Obregon was wearing a pair of long basket-ball shorts and nothing else. His chest was hairless, obviously waxed, and his pectorals indicated long hours with heavy weights in the gym. I eased the pressure slightly on Sonny and removed the Stun Gun from his neck. Obregon seemed embarrassed, apologetic even, pleading for me to believe them. He was not spoiling for a fight.

"Are there any girls in the bedroom?" I asked.

"No," Obregon said, making it sound like an insult.

"Is there anyone else in the apartment?"

"No, sir."

I got off Sonny's back and stood up. If he decided to take advantage of the situation in any way, a quick lunge forward would floor him again with a hundred thousand volts.

"Let me get my head around this," I said. "'White Bird' is a gay club, isn't it?"

"It's a club for men who like men," Obregon confirmed and gave me a challenging look.

"You are Sonny's boyfriend?"

"Yes," he said and appeared to relax a bit.

"I have no issue with anyone who is *bakla*. That's cool with me. I have a number of gay friends."

"The Army doesn't see it that way," Sonny said, petulantly, as he massaged the back of his neck. Obregon nodded grimly in agreement.

"Fuck the Army," I said to make my point. "We're living in the twenty-first century. Everyone should be more tolerant."

"It's nice that you say that, Bill," Obregon commented and a small smile appeared at the side of his mouth.

I waved at them both and told them to sit down on the sofa opposite me. "Let's have a more civilised conversation then. Sonny, I'm sorry if we got off on the wrong foot here. Someone killed my old colleague Dickie Goodyear and I want to know who and why."

"It had nothing to do with Sonny," the Ranger Lieutenant said firmly.

"Tell me about Michelle Arupe," I asked them both, looking from one to the other.

"She's a gold digger," Sonny said, his face suffused, all of a sudden, with anger. "She tried to date me because of my father's money, until she realised her charms didn't work on me."

"She likes diamonds more than gold," Obregon added wryly.

Sonny sneered. "Her family lost all of their money after Marcos was deposed. She told me once it was her ambition to get it all back even if she had to sleep with a hundred rich men to do so."

If this was really true, the lady was good. She'd totally pulled the wool over my eyes. She came across all sweetness and light. Butter would not melt in her perfect mouth. Was I so mistaken in my judgement of her or were these two men trying to sell me a bum steer? I bit my lip and thought about what I had been told about her and what she herself had told me. My reason told me the facts fitted, but my emotion wasn't ready to accept it.

"So what happened between her and Colonel Fernandes?" I asked, searching for flaws in their evidence.

"She set her sights on him," Obregon explained, "because he came from old money and is married. We do not have divorce in the Philippines. It costs a lot of money to pay the church for an annulment and since the Colonel already has children it would be nearly impossible anyway. Michelle knew that he could only keep her as a mistress, so she made the price a heavy one."

"That sort of thing happens," I said cynically.

Sonny said: "Two years ago, rumour has it, she was dating a man in his fifties. A judge. He was found dead in a love hotel. They said it was a heart attack but all his bank accounts had been emptied."

"Was there any evidence it might have been Michelle?"

"Not really. But everyone talked about it." There was a sharp edge to his voice as he said it.

Obregon said: "Colonel Fernandes discovered she was dating an Englishman. She told him he was an older man and was bringing back diamonds for her every time he visited Hong Kong. So he gave her family heirlooms. He thought it might be you at one point. That upset him very much, because he likes you."

The facts pointed to Dickie Goodyear being the Englishman. He'd seemed pretty well-off when I'd seen him on previous trips to Angeles City. His need to smuggle goods. His mysterious partner, often inferred but never visible. Dickie who could not resist women with a fraction of the allure of Michelle Arupe. I could understand how he might abase himself in his pursuit of her.

The two men sat close, next to each other on the sofa and there was a tangible chemistry between them. There was a warmth and friendliness in their relationship which felt honest and true, even if it had to be concealed from public view. I believed their story, or at least I believed that they believed it.

"Could Michelle have had access to Colonel Fernandes' confidential papers? Maybe he brought them along in a briefcase when he was spending the night with her?" I said, testing the theory.

Both of the men nodded. I looked at Sonny and asked: "Was Michelle present when your father and Fernandes had meetings with other conspirators?"

He thought about it then nodded. "Yes, three of four times she was there in the house. I wasn't always there, unless Francisco accompanied him, but she would often come and go with Ricardo. Our country estate was a convenient place for them to meet away from his wife."

"So she could have even made some of the recordings and taken the pictures herself ..." I said to myself.

"Knavery's plain face is never seen till used." I frowned at the Ranger Lieutenant. "How come you are here and not locked up in Camp Tecson?"

He smiled. "I'm only a junior officer. We were all allowed to go free. There will be a court martial, but it is a formality. Only the senior officers will be formally charged."

"It's a strange land, you live in," I said with a shake of my head. Ten minutes later, after some more questions and answers that lent more credibility to my new theory, I left them.

Larry Lim was still at the Shangri-La. The Brigadier was accompanying the CEO of Singapore Airlines to the formal signing of the PAL servicing contract.

"I need your computer whizz-kids' help to check something out. I need to see if Dickie Goodyear ever visited Michelle Arupe's house in Makati. I've got the address."

"Of course you do," Larry said disapprovingly. "Jealousy of the dead is unbecoming. Does that justify putting our resources at your disposal again?

"The last time worked out pretty well," I said, putting my feet up on the desk he was using."

"That's true," he admitted.

"And it's not in aid of my love life. I think she was Dickie Goodyear's mole in Guzman's camp. She was Ricardo Fernandes' mistress, so she had means, motive and opportunity."

"It's like an episode of Colombo with you, Jedburgh. You'll be telling me she blew him up next."

"I can't prove it, but she was in PG at the time it happened with a childhood friend who, according to

Sonny Guzman, works for the largest explosives manufacturer in the country. And another who used to work in IT suspiciously close to GCHQ."

Larry was still hesitating. I suspected he was hoping the Brigadier would return and absolve him of the need to take the decision, but I didn't have a lot of time.

"Look Larry," I said impatiently, if you don't help me with your fancy IT systems I will tell my new friend Ding Dong of the PSG that you are planning to place electronic listening devices into the First Class seats of the Philippines Airlines planes you will be servicing."

He stared at me in horror. "That's a lie."

"No, it's not. You have them on all the SQ planes. I know that for a fact. Jane Tan told me that after she resigned to go and marry her millionaire." I bent a paper clip that I'd taken from his desk out of shape. "Lots of VIPs and billionaires flying First Class on PAL," I said with a smirk.

"If you ever mention that to anyone, I will have you killed."

"Who by?"

"We've made contact with your guy Ozone," he said. "Now let's get you some stuff on this bitch of a woman." He'd picked up the phone and a scrawny Chinese boy had appeared five minutes later to take instruction. A few hours later I was looking at security footage showing Dickie Goodyear visiting Michelle on numerous occasions at her condo in Makati. Judging by the hours he turned up at, they were more than social calls and the furtive expression on his face was all the confirmation I needed.

So the case for the prosecution was simple: Michelle had met Goodyear somehow, somewhere. They had become lovers and he had showered her with diamonds until he had to become a drug runner to pay for them. They had cooked up a scheme to extort a larger sum of money - half a million US dollars or more - from Senator Guzman. Then they planned to run away together. But instead of that, Michelle had placed a bomb on his boat. Then she'd looked round for her next rich mark and her eyes had alighted on Bill Jedburgh, who had foolishly boasted of owning a diamond fit for a queen.

Senator Guzman was delighted when I rang him in hospital and told him that I knew who had betrayed the coup. When I told him who, he agreed that my theory was more than plausible. He also reminded me that he had warned me about her so I only had myself to blame.

I had debated whether to tell him about Sonny and Lieutenant Obregon, but when I did he surprised me by confirming that he knew his son was gay.

"I am an old-fashioned man, Bill," he said, his voice thick with emotion. "I am sad that Sonny will never have children, but I am delighted to tell you that my granddaughter is already pregnant with her first child. They have promised me it will be a boy and if it is they will call him Antonio."

"That is indeed happy news, sir," I said.

"I am proud of Sonny. He was a wild boy, perhaps because he was not allowed to admit his nature to me or the world in general. I hope in his lifetime that will change, but for now his life is healthier and our relationship is good. If you had told me you suspected him, I could not have believed he would betray me."

"I can only apologise for my failure to spot it was this woman earlier," I said. "Now that we know, are you happy for me to deal with the matter in my own way? There will be no charge."

"Thank you, Bill," he said, and terminated the call.

It was time to assume my role as the Lord High Executioner. I took no pleasure in what I did to her on the Kilima Drift. But it was a righteous act. She'd killed my crooked old rogue of a colleague after bleeding him dry and that had to be revenged. Worse, she had nearly persuaded me to let her into my life and potentially my secrets. If she was guilty of other crimes, they were none of my business.

42

"Where the hell have you been, you tosser? You're late," Paul said and handed me a bottle of San Miguel.

It was just after 8 p.m. and the pounding of the bass on the four foot high speakers that were arranged all around the swimming pool had been shaking my house for two hours already. William's second band was getting ready to launch into their first set soon, busying themselves plugging guitars into amps and warming up.

"Had some problems down on the beach," I said.

The Englishman gave me an appraising look, then nodded. He obviously hadn't heard. "We've got most of the girls from 'Rogues' and half of 'Dimples' here. Did you say you could put up five or six of them in your spare rooms?"

"Stack 'em, pack 'em and rack 'em. I can probably manage about ten on the floor of the *sala*. No house guests at my place anymore."

We walked through the airy living room and out onto the pool side. There must have been at least 120 people at the party. Most of the other owners from the mountain had been invited, as well as Josef, the Mayor, and a selection of the great and good of the area. Or at least those who didn't object to scantily clad ladies flaunting their washboard stomachs, making whoopee and getting drunk on free tequila.

"Let me introduce you to my old mate Roger," Paul said. "He used to work for Argos as a Quality Manager." I shook hands with a tall, dashing man in his late fifties who had a moustache like Douglas Fairbanks Junior. He was wearing dark Wayfarer sunglasses and a bright yellow Hawaiian shirt on top of burgundy shorts.

"Hell of a party," Roger said by way of small talk.

"Do you know Rohan, the owner of 'Squirt'?" I asked.

"No, I'm here doing a Rescue Diver course and Paul invited me. We knew each other in the old days when I worked in Hong Kong."

"What do you do now?"

"I'm retired, back in Nottingham. Mostly babysitting my grandchildren."

"Do you miss Asia?"

He gave me a little sad shrug that answered my question. "I come back once or twice a year for the Rugby Sevens and a bit of scuba diving out here."

We stood and watched as an Indian man - wearing Speedo swimming trunks with a physique that belied the fact that he was now a septuagenarian - catapulted off the diving board while trying not to spill his glass of pink gin.

"Did you hear what happened at Rohan's place the other evening?" Paul asked.

"Did it involve half a dozen naked women, the Bishop of Batangas and a large radish?" I asked. "Because otherwise I'm not interested."

Roger laughed and choked on his beer.

"You know there's been this spate of burglaries?" Paul continued regardless.

"I'd heard."

"Well the guy made the mistake of trying to break into Rohan's place and the security guard took his head off with a shotgun. Turns out that he was a divemaster from the Ranger school. He'd been supplementing his income from the Army for years. Saving up to buy a dive shop apparently."

So the final loose end had resolved itself. Nothing to do with Dickie, or the Lapida Brothers or even Michelle Arupe. It did explain why the man had been so fit, and how he had come by an M9 Beretta.

Goran appeared beside us and I introduced him to Roger. "Nice to see you in one piece," the urbane Swede said. He turned to Roger. "Bill here was accidentally-on-purpose dragged into the Peninsula Manila siege."

Roger appeared impressed.

Goran said: "I also heard you had a terrible diving accident this morning?"

I nodded laconically. Goran's eyebrows shot up waiting for me to say more. When I didn't he gave me a searching stare. "We will talk about it when you are drunk. Then you will bare your soul to me." He began walking off, stopped and turned. "I brought a new bottle of aquavit to the party."

"I will come and find you," I told him.

Roger and I wandered over to the buffet. Five chefs were hard at work on a smorgasbord of culinary delight. I grabbed a handful of beef satay and put them on a plate, dousing them with peanut sauce.

"What was that about a diving accident?" Roger asked once he'd heaped slices of roast suckling pig onto his plate.

"We lost one of our divers. It was a terrible tragedy."

"What happened to him?"

"Her. She got caught in one of the worst currents I've experienced for a long time and lost control." I gave him the official version of events and he nodded gravely.

"You'll need a few aquavits to stop yourself from having nightmares," he said.

My face looked suitably pensive, but it wasn't Aquavit I needed to dull the pain. It was female company. As if to rub it in, James chose that moment to wander over. He had two young ladies wearing lime-green bikinis, one tucked under each arm. They giggled and struggled to stand up straight.

"Thought you weren't coming, you Pommie bastard." He turned his head from left to right. "This here is Dolores and this is Lolita. They say they're sisters but I think they're bullshitting me."

The two ladies giggled. James excused himself to escort them upstairs so that he could explain to them the significance of the early aboriginal cave drawings on his bedroom walls.

"You don't have parties like this in Nottingham, do you?" I said to Roger.

"Not since I sang in a folk group," he replied, "and wore beads around my neck."

We ate in silence for a while watching the antics of the other revellers. Rohan was keen to perfect his swallow dive so kept getting back up on the diving board. A semi-circle of admiring young ladies - including a pretty lady-boy with large, perfect breasts and a protruding Adam's apple - clapped him whenever he hit the water with a heavy splash.

I spotted Matthias and Tony sitting on the first floor veranda so brought Roger along to introduce him to the German lads.

"Hey, Bill. How are you feeling?" said Tony in his Bavarian accent.

"As well as can be expected," I said and shrugged. "Enjoying the party?"

"It's hard to enjoy, after such a terrible morning."

"Yeah," I said noncommittally and tried to look sad. After they'd pulled me into the boat we'd circled around for two hours, accompanied by other dive boats looking for any evidence that Michelle might have surfaced. But eventually we'd given up. Everyone who knew the currents and the dive sites agreed that if she hadn't surfaced by now she was not coming back. We rode the *banca* several miles out into the channel but no signalling sausage was to be seen.

Roscoe was grim when we returned. He'd been given the news by the other dive boats we'd alerted. A policeman was at the dive shop and he took statements from all of us.

But the fact was that this had happened before. Every one or two years some divers drowned or disappeared. Sometimes because they were cocky and overconfident, sometimes because they panicked on a simple dive and forgot their training. It wasn't a sport without its dangers.

I had done my best to look distraught all morning but finally left the beach and returned home in the early afternoon. I'd showered, eaten an omelette and taken a long nap. Afterwards I had packed up Michelle's things so the guest room was free. In a false bottom in her suitcase I found a hard drive identical to Dickie's. After ten minutes with a hammer, I had ridden back down to the Yacht Club and chucked the mangled pieces on top of Dickie's watery grave. The large bag of diamonds and jewellery that had nestled beside it was now in my safe in *Casa Azul*.

"You don't have much luck with women," Matthias said. His eyes had already taken on the first glaze of inebriation.

"That's true," I replied. Below us the party frolicked. The Mayor, a fleshy man wearing a *barong tagalog* and a permanently unctuous smile, was deep in discussion with Josef, probably about the upcoming increase in ground rent, just in time for the next local elections. William's band eased into a Rolling Stones number.

"You know how it is in life," I said. "You don't always get what you want. But sometimes what you get is what you deserve."

END

Afterword

The real events around the 'Oakwood Mutiny' in 2003 and the 'Manila Peninsula Siege' in 2007 are more fascinating and somewhat less believable than the fictional events portrayed in this book. This novel shifts timings and conflates events from 2003 and earlier to create more enjoyable fiction.

Charlie Santos is a fictional President of the Philippines whose involvement in saving Jedburgh's life can be found in 'Reliable in Hong Kong' – the third novel in the Reliable Man series.

To paraphrase Eliot: humankind can't bear too much reality.

The Reliable Man will be back in:

RELIABLE IN ZURICH

Printed by Amazon Italia Logistica S.r.l.
Torrazza Piemonte (TO), Italy